# Tides of Change

# Tides of Change

JOAN DUNNETT

Matador
9 Priory Business Park,
Wistow Road, Kibworth Beauchamp,
Leicestershire. LE8 0RX
Tel: 0116 279 2299
Email: books@troubador.co.uk
Web: www.troubador.co.uk/matador
Twitter: @matadorbooks

ISBN 978 1838590 598

British Library Cataloguing in Publication Data.
A catalogue record for this book is available from the British Library.

Printed and bound in Great Britain by 4edge Limited
Typeset in 11pt Adobe Casion Pro by Troubador Publishing Ltd, Leicester, UK

Matador is an imprint of Troubador Publishing Ltd

# 1

## M A Y  1 7 0 4

J ames Lightfoot didn't want to be put ashore at Figgate Whins. It was a dangerous place. He might be robbed of his remaining few possessions. He waited on the deck of the merchantman while the crew loaded bundles onto the boat: probably luxury goods to be smuggled into England. The ship's legitimate cargo was bound for Leith. A thin strip of light began to appear to the east. The sea was calm, the light breeze cool and fresh. The captain was on deck. He lit his pipe with a steady hand. He must know the risks. The navy would be patrolling the east coast, ready to challenge any vessel in these waters, not just French privateers.

'You're going ashore here instead of Leith,' the captain said. 'That way you'll avoid the press gangs. They're desperate to seize young men like you for the Scots Navy.' He moved closer to James and slipped a paper into his hand. 'I am relying on you to deliver this letter.' He nodded. His breath smelt of wine and stale tobacco. 'A matter of some urgency – and delicacy.'

'I'll see that it's delivered,' James said.

'You must give this to your friend yourself. No one else.'

'Of course.'

'And take care.'

'I will see to it. You have my word.' James secured the letter inside his coat.

The captain was a dour man. Drank too much. But he was an experienced mariner. James could have done worse. He had known it might be tricky making his way back home in a time of war. His sea chest containing surgical instruments and some medicines had disappeared. He carried only a bag with some clothes, along with notebooks and his journal. Anyway, he had been lucky to escape from being pressed into the English East India Company. He knew not to ask the captain awkward questions. He had the offer of a berth on condition that he did the captain a favour by carrying a special message to his friend, Andrew Lawson. He hadn't heard from Andrew since leaving Scotland four years ago. 'Andrew Lawson lives somewhere on the High Street in Edinburgh,' the captain had said. 'He's a burgess now.'

James stepped into the boat, placing himself between an old man and a large box that smelt of vinegar and stale fish. As the boat headed for shore, all was quiet except for the gentle splash of the oars. James watched the emerging thin streaks of light expand on the horizon. He could see the familiar outline of Arthur's Seat. It was good to be back in Scotland.

He was distracted by the man on his right. He was fidgeting and scratching himself. His hands, wrinkled and brown, shook. James wondered how many years this man had spent at sea away from his family. Or maybe, like himself, he had no family. He remembered kind ladies who took it in turns to look after him, and being visited now and then by a tall gentleman. Then at the age of six, he was taken to live with Andrew's family.

The boat landed on the beach near a small wooden hut, the only building to be seen in the emerging daylight. James took off his boots, tied them to his bag and jumped into the shallow, ice-cold water. It was a relief to stretch his legs. Sand dunes and whin bushes lined the shore, giving some cover for the smugglers' activities. He heard the sounds of cattle in the coarse pasture beyond. The road south to England passed through this rough country. It was used by many travellers, and well known for robbers and highwaymen. He sat down in the sand and dried his feet.

A small party of local men had appeared, and speedily unloaded the cargo onto the beach. They took no notice of him, so he slowly edged away towards the whin bushes. Two men were whispering, their voices urgent. James took a position crouched behind a low sand dune, stretched his neck and peered into the dim light. A carthorse moved its head up and down restlessly. Eventually the heavily loaded cart moved off. James stood up – just as the boat was leaving.

Suddenly there was a great to-do. James heard men shouting. A couple of pistol shots disturbed the air, and the cart came to a halt. He dived behind the sand dune. Keeping low, he slowly backed off towards the beach, sneaked beside long grass and crouched behind a whin bush. The spikes scratched the side of his face as he lay still. This was not his fight. Shouts and the clash of steel on steel gave way to grunts and cries of pain. The conflict ceased suddenly. James heard the movement of the wheels of the cart as the thieves drove off with their prize. Low murmurs and rustling came from the grass near the scene of the ambush. He was tempted to stay in the whin bushes. This was the safe and sensible thing to do. The way to stay alive was to keep your own counsel. But the thought of at least one person in pain or discomfort helped him make up his mind.

He groped about the scene of the skirmish to see if there were any wounded. He stopped to listen. The cries of pain had gone. The smugglers must have fled, or been carried off by their companions. Suddenly James heard a soft rustling sound, but couldn't distinguish where it came from. Keeping low, he crawled his way back to the beach. He crouched down behind a dune. A light breeze rose, and sand filled his hair. His eyes felt gritty. He blinked and rubbed his eyes, making them sore.

Then he felt a stab of cold metal pressing hard on the side of his neck. He clenched his fists in the sand.

'Get up – slowly,' a soft voice said, 'and give me your bag.'

James stood up. The figure stepped back, pointing his pistol at James's head. The owner of the pistol was a thin, roughly dressed young man.

With one hand James slowly removed the bag from his shoulder. 'You'll find no money in there. Only some clothes and books.' He dropped the bag on the sand.

With one hand the young man picked up the satchel and emptied out its contents. Books, papers and clothing scattered about. James felt the urge to attack the scoundrel but held himself in check. The thief looked down. He shifted his position a fraction. In an instant James threw a fistful of sand into his eyes. The boy dropped the pistol. James seized the moment. He punched the boy hard. He fell backwards. James grabbed him by the shirt, hauled him to his feet, shook him and jerked him about. He turned his face to the light, to make sure he would recognise him if he saw him again. The boy kicked and broke free. Unable to see, he threw wasted punches, staggered. James knocked him fiercely on the chin. The thief fell and lay still on the sand. James examined him, and set him in a comfortable position. He stuffed the pistol into his belt, gathered his belongings, and ran off.

James needed to distance himself from the lad. Avoiding the road, he made for the burn near the slope of Arthur's Seat, east of the village of Duddingston. Rays of emerging red sunlight shone through the trees. Sliding down the bank, he found a bend in the stream. With cover from bushes, here was a secluded bank to refresh himself. He could not go into the city of Edinburgh looking like he had just been in a fight. His hands were white and sticky with salt. He washed in the cool water, and changed his shirt.

Brushing sand off his coat and bag, he realised he was lucky not to have lost his notebooks and his precious journal. He sat down to study them. Unfolding a paper with a drawing of a bay, he remembered this was where the ship had anchored while the crew made necessary repairs, giving him time to explore, to make observations and drawings of strange animals and plants. He flicked through his journal. Daily recordings on the progress of injured and sick men. Details of remedies and treatments. All useful knowledge for the future. He wanted more than to be a surgeon. He knew what he wanted to do. To study at Leiden, the best medical school in Europe, would be ideal.

Sounds of female voices came from the mill upstream. He repacked his books and clothes, and checked that his money, what little he had, was secure in his belt. Feeling refreshed, he joined the road into the city.

A heavily laden cart trundled along several yards in front of him. Just ahead two fishwives carried creels full of mussels. They glanced back at him. They exchanged words, then looked back again, smiling. He was more conspicuous than he wanted to be. As he neared the small hamlet of Jock's Lodge, a popular crossroads, more travellers appeared. This was a kind of meeting place for vendors going and coming from Edinburgh and Leith. A sickly-looking old man struggled to load bales onto a cart – hard toil weakening the body of a man already suffering from stiff joints. A strong smell of bread wafted through the air from the direction of the inn. James felt hungry, but didn't stop. He would head for Edinburgh, find his friend and deliver the letter which was still secure in his pocket.

James noticed a path leading in a more southerly direction to the park. Another detour would be pleasant before rejoining the road to the Canongate. He stopped for a drink at the well, another popular meeting point of a different kind. Here a group of wives rested on the grass, exchanging local gossip. Children ran around. A couple of old men loitered. No one paid attention to him as he ascended the steep hill to the left of the path. Stopping beside a small ruined chapel, he sat on a stone and took out the letter.

He turned it over to the side bearing the seal. There was a thin crack and a sort of fold in the seal as if it had been broken – someone had attempted to reseal it after reading the contents. It would be easy to open the letter now and reseal it himself. But no. He must have a sense of propriety. A private letter was not his business. His task was to deliver

6

it as instructed. And yet – several months back… It was a hot and steamy day. He had seen the supercargo through an open door. He had a bundle of letters and was reading one. Private mail was often read. Andrew's letter had already been tampered with. What harm could it do if he, a friend, read it?

The letter opened with little effort. The writing was small with the words close together. Some words had numbers between them, and within them. There were words underlined. At the top was a series of numbers. He tried to make sense of the letter. This was some sort of complex code. He noticed, too, that some words had been changed. Was this after the contents had been exposed? Was the letter for Andrew, or was he, too, just a messenger?

## 2

James put the mysterious letter in his pocket, took a deep breath of cool, fresh air, and set off down the hill. He was hungry now. He pressed on, towards the Abbey Hill road; a pleasant, quiet road, past fields and orchards, their trees heavy with pink and white blossoms. He strode on until he reached the intersection with the Eastern Road to Leith. The soft drizzle was now turning into a shower. More carts appeared. He dodged sideways several times to avoid splashes from their wheels.

He entered the residential burgh of the Canongate by the Water Gate. To his left lay the Abbey of the Holy Rood House and the Royal Palace, and ahead was the main street. The shower had eased off. On both sides of the road, large buildings were separated by closes and interspersed with trees bearing young leaves, shining and moist. How was he to ask about Andrew? Did he live here, or in the burgh of Edinburgh, the business heart of the city? He paused outside a door.

'You there, man. Move on.' A smartly dressed gentleman waved his arm as if shooing away a bird.

James marched on. *He must think I'm a servant or a vagrant.* There were no beggars here, though. Well-dressed gentlemen strutted about.

Ahead was the impressive Nether Bow, its huge central tower flanked by two smaller ones. Walls on either side surrounded the Royal Burgh of Edinburgh, and separated it from the smaller residential burgh of the Canongate. A strong smell of freshly baked bread filled James's nostrils. He remembered the bakehouse nearby.

The baxter, a large man as wide as he was tall, was loading oatmeal loaves into the oven. Beside him, a wee boy packed bundles of wheaten rolls into baskets.

'Good day, sir.' The baxter smiled, wiping his hands on a cloth. 'Give the young man two rolls,' he said, waving a floury arm when James attempted to offer payment. 'And fetch him a cup of milk.'

'Thank you. I'm most grateful,' James said, before sinking his teeth into one of the rolls. He slipped a coin to the wee boy. As he looked up he noticed a man dash behind an outer stair. Someone was following him.

Bairns gathered around as he wandered uphill, all eyes on his rolls. He quickly put them into his pocket, watching out for thieves and beggars, and occasionally glancing up at the tall buildings. These stone-built houses rose five or more storeys from the street level, all close together. No trees or spacious gardens here. Children with pale faces and wide eyes crouched in corners. As he passed the entrance to a close, a smell of rotten vegetables hit his nostrils. He moved further into the middle of the road. Tradesmen huddled and chatted in groups beside their shops and market stalls. Two girls chased a pig down the road. He swerved aside to avoid colliding with them. So different from the freshness of the sea air on deck, the wide seas and skies. Would he settle here among this chaos?

A young boy hovered beside him, his bright eyes following James's movements. A tangled mop of fair hair fell about his face. His jacket was threadbare and his shirt grubby, but he had more flesh and muscle covering his bones than some of the other lads roaming the streets. He was much too young to be caddie but might be of service in some way or other. James tried him out.

'Mr Andrew Lawson. He's a burgess,' James said. 'Do you know where he lives?'

The lad held out his hand. James fished out a coin from his purse.

'Aye, he lives up the road.'

'I know that. But where exactly?'

The boy stuck his hand out again. James gripped him by the collar of his jacket, pulled him onto his toes, and lowered himself so that their eyes met. The young lad was shaking and his red eyes held tears ready to flow.

'Dinnae ken.'

James pushed him away. The boy stood and stared. James walked on a bit. He turned round. The lad was following a few paces behind. James stopped and turned to face him. He was a scoundrel, but James couldn't help admiring his persistence. He might make some temporary use of him as a sort of messenger.

'Can you find Mr Lawson for me?'

The boy nodded and ran off.

James spent the morning exploring the streets and closes. At the Cross he mingled with gentlemen, who wandered about or huddled in groups. All were strangers to him. They looked the same in their long wigs and tailored coats. Once again James had a vague sensation he was being followed. He whipped round and his eye took in the gaze of his attacker at Figgate Whins. James was determined to lose him at the crowded luckenbooths where the street narrowed. He lingered there, merging with the shoppers.

A broadside pinned outside an apothecary's shop proclaimed the latest news about the war. Another notice drew his attention. A public dissection: an event held over nine days, each day dealing with different parts of the human anatomy. Presented by senior surgeons. What a stroke of luck! This would be the place to meet with surgeons and apothecaries, and seek employment.

'Sir...'

James felt a tug at his sleeve. His young helper had found him. James turned and followed the boy through Parliament Close. The boy strode on, glancing behind every now and again to see if James was keeping up with him, as he weaved his way between the market stalls. He turned down a close.

'You'll find gentlemen who know Mr Lawson in there, sir,' he said, pointing to steps leading down to a door. He then turned and disappeared before James could ask him further questions.

The aroma of coffee wafted through as James opened the door. Several pairs of eyes turned towards him. Gentlemen in their well-manicured wigs and smart attire were combining business with pleasure. A group, huddled together amid piles of papers, were muttering; and every now and then, cast glances in James's direction, making him feel uncomfortable.

James came straight to the point. 'Gentlemen, I do beg your pardon for the interruption,' he said, addressing a group. 'I'm looking for an acquaintance, a Mr Andrew Lawson.' He scanned their faces.

The gentlemen exchanged glances, and shook their heads.

'I know of him. He comes here sometimes with his lawyer. He could be anywhere.' One man smiled sardonically, waving his arm as if dismissing a servant. He turned his head away.

James thought about ordering coffee and attempting to engage in conversation with anyone who looked willing. But he saw no signs of encouragement, so with some reluctance he left.

He found his messenger at the top of the close. The boy placed a few coins into James's hand.

'I ken you've no much money,' he said.

'And I ken you've stolen this,' James said, handing back the money. He grabbed him roughly by his collar. 'You've a lot to learn, lad. Let me tell you this. The world is a harsh place. I've seen good men go bad in a flash. I've seen boys like you – cheerful and carefree. They find their way into deep trouble and end up dead, floating in a river, for no reason other than being at the wrong end of someone's wrath. Or else they become as corrupt and unscrupulous as the worst of them. I'm warning you. Don't play with mischief.'

The boy was shaking with fear. James smiled. He was overdoing it.

'What's your name?'

'Davie. Davie Bell.'

'Well then, Davie, lead me to a tavern that serves good fare.'

James felt the boy was cunning, but not likely to heed the warning. He wondered if, by now, word had spread of a stranger, a seafaring young man, who was looking for a gentleman by the name of Andrew Lawson.

The tavern was hot and steamy, smelling of fish, ale and boiled vegetables. As James walked into the chamber, one or two faces looked in his direction. Then they resumed their crack, ignoring him. He selected an empty table. A small girl wearing a filthy peenie took his order. She gave him a surly look.

'Herrings and oatmeal bread. And a jug of small ale, if you please,' he said.

She nodded.

James watched her go, and then reappear with his jug. He poured a cup of ale and watched men, women and families as they came in for their midday meal. These newcomers received their food before him. The room gradually filled up. Two men approached him.

'I assume you have no objections to us sharing your table.'

'No – not at all,' James said.

The girl brought his herrings and bread on a pewter plate.

'A jug of wine, Betty, please, and your best fish for us. Francis Atkins,' one of the men said, extending an ink-stained hand towards James. 'My brother, Douglas.'

'James Lightfoot, pleased to make your acquaintance,' James said. He shuffled along to make room for Douglas, catching a strong whiff of cinnamon from his coat. James focused his attention on his herrings, fresh and lightly grilled.

'Are you passing through, or here in Edinburgh on business?' Francis Atkins asked, breaking the silence.

'I've been overseas for a while,' James began tentatively. 'But I've come home to Scotland for good.' He smiled. He noticed Francis Atkins' eyes move around, watching everyone in the room. A man with a curiosity to match his own, James thought. He was plainly dressed and wore a brown jacket that had seen better days, in contrast to his brother who was smartly dressed in an elegant coat and waistcoat, and a cheap-looking wig. James noticed a curious stain on Douglas Atkins' waistcoat.

Francis resumed the conversation. 'I see you're a seafaring man.' He rested his inky hands on the table. 'I hope you don't mind me asking—'

Betty placed the brothers' food on the table. Francis poured more wine into their cups.

'A toast; to the Little Gentleman in Black Velvet,' Douglas said, eying James.

James felt he was being tested. 'And to your good health, gentlemen,' he said, not mentioning the little gentleman in black velvet, whoever he was. 'As I said, I've been abroad. What's the news in these parts?'

'That depends on whether you want to hear good news or bad,' Francis said. 'My trade is providing the news, information and education people ask for. I'm a bookseller, you see. You may have passed my bookshop on the High Street. Books of all kinds. There are books to suit everyone. We have—'

James said, 'I did notice the shop. Right now I don't have the leisure or the money to buy books. It would be nice to catch up on local news, though.' He was pleased that he had managed to get away from the embarrassment regarding the velvet-coated gentleman.

'Well,' said Francis, 'I don't know where to start. We have some new pamphlets. There's—'

'What we'd like to hear is news from you,' Douglas cut in. 'We would like to know more about you.'

'Precisely. Though you put this too bluntly, brother. You see, we're wary of strangers until we get to know them better,' Francis said.

'We're most particular of the company we keep in this tavern,' Douglas added.

'I can assure you I am an honest, worthy gentleman,' James said. 'I declare, though, I'm not in the best of fortune at the moment. You see, after my last voyage, I had heard about the seizure of the *Annandale*, a Company of Scotland merchantman – taken on behalf of the English East India Company. The story goes; customs officers had apparently been looking for stolen money. The crew were badly treated. Feelings against the Scots were running high. I had no wish to be pressed into the English East India Company.'

'So now you are here. I can understand that,' Francis said. The brothers exchanged glances.

James finished his herrings and signalled to Betty. 'A large piece of apple pie, if you please,' he said. He settled into his chair, making himself comfortable. He wasn't going anywhere for now, and it was his turn to ask questions.

'I wonder if either of you gentlemen could tell me where the burgess Mr Andrew Lawson bides. I believe his house is somewhere in the Land Market area,' James asked.

'Lawson? Lawson? You have business with him?' Douglas asked. 'He's a busy man, and doesn't see just anyone. He only deals with the most influential and worthy of clients. And besides, he's maybe abroad just now.'

James felt they weren't taking his request seriously. 'He's a family friend. Andrew was my close companion in my childhood. I haven't seen him for four years.'

'I ken the gentleman,' Francis said. He shuffled along the bench to make way for a man and woman who had just joined them at the table. They all knew one another well, it seemed. General pleasantries were first exchanged before conversation moved to the health of their families and news of acquaintances. James felt he was being excluded. He slowly rose to his feet.

'Oh – the velvet-coated gentleman.' Francis grinned. 'He's a mole. His molehill caused King William's horse to stumble. The poor King was injured, then became unwell and died.' He added, 'Do pop into my bookshop.'

'I will, when I am settled.' James smiled. He liked Francis. He felt sure the brothers knew Andrew well enough but did not trust him, though he couldn't understand why. He had expected people in Edinburgh to be more helpful and welcoming.

As the afternoon wore on he realised that the optimism he had at the beginning of the day had almost gone. He became despondent and weary. It had been a long day. He still had to find lodgings.

A sudden thought occurred to him. He might try the office of the Company of Scotland in Milne Square. He knew that the secretary of the Company, Mr Roderick Mackenzie, had chambers there on the upper storey of the building. He plodded along to the office. The door at the foot of the turnpike stair was open. He was about to go up the stair when he heard a noise. A door opened. He turned to face a startled Mr Mackenzie, holding a bundle of ledgers.

'Ah, Mr James Lightfoot,' he said. His eyes were red with weariness and overwork. He regarded James with a vague expression. 'I remember you. A student of the university.'

James was quite surprised the administrator recalled their brief meeting. Mr Mackenzie was about to go up the stairs with his books.

'Mr Mackenzie, if I might trouble you for a moment,' James said.

'Please be brief. As you can see, I still have some work to do.'

'I have just returned from abroad—' James began.

Mackenzie looked at him fiercely. 'If you're looking for employment, I can't help you. I'm sure you're acquainted of the situation with the Company.'

'No – I'm not asking you for work. I was wondering if you could give me the residence of Mr Andrew Lawson. I believe he lives in Edinburgh.'

'Yes, I do know where he bides. I have the misfortune of being acquainted with him.'

## 3

A loud crash rose above the shouting of a street brawl, disturbing Louise's thoughts. Her mind had been wandering. She stared blankly at the papers on the desk and sighed. The noises came from outside the tavern next door. Once again she added up the figures in front of her, and arrived at a different answer. She was tired, but kept her mind on the work. She needed the money she earned from working on accounts, sewing, and anything that she could do at home while caring for her father. She was grateful to the landlord for tactfully providing extra work. It had been just a few tasks to begin with, but now there was a small pile on the desk. Still, he was a kind young gentleman and there was no pressure to finish the tasks.

Louise rose slowly, and peeped into her father's chamber. He was in bed. These last few days he had been poorly with a chill. She was becoming increasingly anxious about him. The daylight was fading and his room was dim. He appeared to be sound asleep. She closed the door quietly.

Over the years, since her mother's death and his loss of fortune in the Darien Venture, her father had changed.

He was bitter and lazy, and sometimes bad-tempered. She gathered her papers. How would they manage in the future? Mary was not much help. Father was right about her wealthy lawyer husband. Self-serving and ambitious. She could have married a gentleman with a kinder nature.

A loud chapping at the door interrupted Louise's thoughts. She wasn't expecting anyone. There was knocking again, harder, more urgent.

She moved close to the door and shouted, 'Who is it?'

'James Lightfoot. I'm a friend of Mr Lawson.'

Louise opened the door a little. Immediately, the stranger stuck his foot in the door.

'Mr Lawson is abroad. Come back in the morning. His apprentice, Tom, will attend to your business,' she said, pushing the door hard against his foot.

The man shoved the door open wide and strode into the room. He smiled. 'Do you know when he'll be back?'

Louise's heart thumped. She faced him steadily, hoping that her hands wouldn't tremble. 'I... don't know. Tom will know. Ask him tomorrow. You'll find him in the shop.'

Louise took in the man's appearance. His clothes were worn and ragged at the edges. He smelt strongly of the sea and ale. She met his eyes. The smile had gone, and was replaced by an expression she couldn't quite make out. She blushed, and felt a little weak. When she recovered, he was still watching her with what appeared like amused curiosity.

'I don't suppose you can oblige me with a room for the night?' he asked, leaning against the wall, his bag at his side. 'Ah well, you don't know me. Don't trust me. I can understand that.' He moved slowly away from the wall, and staggered a little. He looked as though he was about to say more.

This was difficult. He appeared to be drunk. Or maybe tired. If he was Andrew's friend, she would be obliged to at least offer him a room. Since buying the tenement building from her father, Andrew Lawson had allowed them to stay in this flat for a modest rent.

'As you are a friend of Mr Lawson, you may stay – for one or two nights.' She closed the door, leading him into the parlour. 'I'm Louise Morton. There's a wee chamber downstairs. It's a bit cold and damp just now.' She would have to explain to her father in the morning. No need to disturb him just now. She fetched some linen bedclothes from the press, took a bunch of keys from a hook, and led Mr Lightfoot down the stairs to a small chamber.

The woollen blanket felt damp as Louise spread it across fresh linen sheets. She patted the pillow, turned and took stock of the stranger leaning against the wall, his eyes almost closed.

'My housemaid, Jean, will attend to your breakfast in the morning,' she said before leaving the chamber.

James awoke to a cold dampness. He was not at sea. It took him a few minutes to realise where he was. Murmuring voices came from the close. People were up and about their daily business. He had overslept, and had more than usual to drink. The small window let in a stream of light. The air was chilly, damp, and smelt of soot, sweat and a foul, sickly odour that he couldn't identify. He looked around the chamber. Yesterday he had been too tired to examine his surroundings. There was a small chest, a table and chair, all covered with a thin layer of dust. He tried the door at the far side. It was locked. He fumbled about for coal and kindling to light a fire but there was none. The room obviously wasn't used much. Maybe he could ask if he could stay for more than two nights.

For once he had managed to catch up on lost sleep, and now had a little privacy. He examined his money belt – enough money for food, but not enough for rent. He laid the contents of his bag on the bed; a canvas bag with a change of linen, shirt, notebooks, journal, eye-piece and a box containing small items including thread and buttons. Nothing he could sell.

This was only his second day in Edinburgh. He must not lose heart easily. He had not thought about what he might do if Andrew was not at home. He would think of something.

Someone was chapping at the door. James hurriedly put the money inside the belt, before lifting the sneck. His eyes met steely grey ones. The woman held a bowl of water and some linen cloths. He would rather have seen Miss Morton.

'Good morning. Mr Morton expects you to join him for breakfast, as soon as you're ready,' she said, handing James the bowl and towels.

James hurriedly washed and arranged his attire as best he could. In his present discommodious state, he was not looking forward to meeting the girl's father.

The door to the parlour was ajar. James knocked lightly, and entered a surprisingly large but gloomy chamber. Mr Morton sat at the head of the table in the centre of the room. He rose and indicated a chair. James's eyes took in the furnishings of the chamber, which also functioned as a kitchen by having a press and table with cooking utensils, plates and pots in a recess near the fireside. At the other end stood a large, finely decorated oak cabinet. A spice cabinet stood on top of a small chest. Two small windows faced the close.

Mr Morton looked thin and frail, and his eyes held a weary expression. He was probably about fifty years of age. At one time maybe of strong build, his body now appeared shrunken and weakened.

Jean served porridge. They ate in silence for a minute or two before Mr Morton came to the point. Resting his horn spoon on his bowl, he asked, 'You'll be looking for somewhere more permanent to stay?'

'Yes, of course. Miss Morton said I could bide here for two nights. That is, until I'm fixed with lodgings.'

Mr Morton frowned.

'I'm most grateful to you, sir,' James added.

'My daughter seemed prepared to trust you.' Mr Morton produced a kerchief, and coughed into it. 'She offered you the room because you're a friend of Andrew Lawson. I wouldn't. I would do no favours for the man or his friends. This whole building used to be mine. Five upper storeys, these rooms and the basement. Lawson bought it from me when my business was failing. Took advantage of my situation.' He paused to sup small beer, and coughed again violently. 'He's doing all right now, and I'm ruined.' He took a deep breath.

James studied his bowl of porridge, as if expecting to find a response there. He finished eating and glanced up. Jean was at his side. She took the bowl and refilled it with more steaming hot porridge. Mr Morton gave her a severe look. She retreated to the corner of the room.

After what seemed an age Mr Morton said, 'Before she left the house this morning, my daughter told me you've just finished working as a ship's surgeon.'

'Yes, I was.' He had to explain. 'On a merchant ship, there's always the risk of being captured by pirates. If that happens, they force you to work for them. They value a surgeon, you see – to treat severe wounds inflicted on their crew during fierce battles.' James paused. 'So, I've finished with that life. I have a good education. I want to qualify as a physician.' He hoped Mr Morton would consider his circumstances and regard him favourably as a man of intelligence and dignity.

Mr Morton made no reply.

James continued. 'As I have no family of my own, I thought maybe—'

'That your friend Andrew Lawson would provide a home for you here with him.' Mr Morton moved uneasily in his chair, opened his mouth and closed it again, as if not sure how to select his words. 'Louise was concerned, not to mention a little suspicious, that you have few belongings.'

'The last ship I was on was seized by pirates. During the skirmish I managed to escape on a ship that wasn't taken, but had to flee from that vessel as some of the crew were unfriendly and were conspiring to mutiny. I lost my sea chest.'

'And now you have no money.'

'I wasn't paid for my last voyage.'

'I see.' Mr Morton frowned. 'If it were just your present unfortunate situation to think about, then I could let you stay until Lawson returns. But what really troubles me is that you are just the sort of man my daughter could become fond of. You understand my position?'

'Oh yes – I understand.'

'And you're now looking for employment. You could have gone as a soldier, but you would want to avoid that, I suspect.'

James was silent. He couldn't deny that going into the army was the last thing he wanted.

'My daughter may have been keen for you to stay for a day or two, but I have to disagree.' Mr Morton stood up and left the table. 'I expect you to be gone before my daughter returns later this morning.'

# 4

James waited in the arcade outside the merchant's shop. Inside, the apprentice was unfolding a bale of woollen cloth, showing it to a well-dressed customer. James felt a soft, warm body push against his leg. A large pig. An old woman stared at him, her open mouth showing a few remaining yellow teeth. James watched as the boy proceeded to measure out the cloth, taking his time. The old woman fidgeted and scratched herself. James backed off to avoid the smell of her body.

The apprentice finished his business with his customer, and addressed him. 'May I be of assistance, sir?' he asked while fixing his eyes on James's worn sleeves. 'I have some fine wool for a coat.' He reached for a bale of brown woollen cloth, and brought it to the half-opened door. 'Feel this. Very warm. Hard-wearing too.' He extended his arm.

James stepped forward.

'I see you are a man of the world. This material will suit any type of climate.' He gave James a slightly sardonic look.

James felt the cloth. Not coarse. Thick and warm. 'It's fine wool,' he said. He didn't like the boy's attitude, but he knew that a smart appearance and fine tailored clothes were essential requirements here in the city. How you looked was all-important.

'I'm looking for Mr Andrew Lawson, on a matter of some immediate importance,' James said. He hadn't forgotten the secret letter.

'He's abroad on business,' the boy said, pulling down another bale of cloth.

'Can you tell me when he's likely to return?'

'Can't say when exactly. This wool may suit your purse, sir.'

James felt the cloth. It was rough to the touch. No, that would not do.

'Depends on what deals Mr Lawson has managed to negotiate — and, well, trade is difficult just now, with there being a war,' the apprentice added.

'I know that.' James tried to keep his voice calm. This boy was annoying.

'I may be able to help,' the lad continued. 'I'm apprenticed to Mr Lawson, and may assist on his behalf.'

'My business with him is a personal matter. He's a family friend.'

The boy still held the inferior quality woollen cloth. James shook his head. He glanced at the selection of woollens on offer on the shelves.

'As you're a friend of Mr Lawson, I can offer you a special price on your choice. I can recommend an excellent tailor, too. He lives nearby. On the top flat of the next tenement.'

'Thank you. Yes, I'd like that indeed. But not at the moment.' James smiled. He would buy some linen shirts and a coat later. He was going to ask about lodgings, but hesitated. The apprentice turned his attention to another customer.

James left the shop, and wandered down the High Street. He adjusted his neckcloth tightly round his neck. It was a dreich day, and dampness still hung about. The cool air was heavy with smoke and soot. Its dry taste filled his mouth and the back of his throat. The foul smell of human waste still lingered. Edinburgh had changed in the last four years. There was a kind of restlessness. Lots of people lingering about, not fully engaged. He would go to the public dissection and introduce himself to the surgeons there. Finding work would not be easy, but meeting the right people was crucial.

A caddie wheeling a small cart loaded with a chest glanced in his direction and continued walking down the street. James had a vague sensation of invisible eyes watching him.

The surgeons' anatomical theatre was nearly full when James arrived. Scanning the assembly, he spotted a smartly dressed Douglas Atkins near the front. Atkins waved, inviting James to join him. He climbed up the steps. Holding on to the rail, he squeezed past to join Atkins in the middle of the row.

'Good day to you, sir. I didn't expect to see you here. Do you have a particular interest in anatomy?' Atkins said, regarding James closely. 'I took you for a mariner.'

'I thought you took me for a spy,' James said. 'You and your brother seemed suspicious, and not particularly helpful. Oh, and I did find out the residence of Andrew Lawson. Though my guess is that you knew he owned the tenement just across the road from the tavern.'

He watched Atkins' reaction, but his face was impassive, his eyes focused on the centre of the theatre.

Atkins turned to face James. 'I had a quarrel with Andrew Lawson. He has done wrong by me,' he said.

Another man who felt unjustly treated by Andrew. This was not the friend James knew. Andrew was fair-minded, strong and purposeful. They both had that much in common. However, James felt he must try to gain this man's trust. He might have the means to introduce him to influential people.

'I've worked as assistant ship's surgeon for the last four years,' James said. 'I've also had the privilege of an education at the University of Edinburgh.'

'Oh, a scholar, eh?' Atkins said. 'We had no advantages of university in our family, but we've had good education for all that. I took over my father's apothecary shop. Francis chose to be apprenticed to a printer. His shop is next to mine.' He smiled. 'I'm pleased to see you here.'

'I saw an advertisement for these demonstrations taking place over nine days. I wanted to attend at least one. This must be day five,' James said.

'Aye, it is. The topics today are the thorax, respiration and circulation of the blood. Robert Swinton is the demonstrator.'

James felt a little shove from behind, as a man squeezed past. Students and apprentices jostled for space, filling every corner of the dissection hall. Some chose to stay well back, maybe wary of their reactions to the sights and smells. Others nudged to the front. The strong smell of sweat reminded James of seamen squashed together below deck.

'So, is this the first public dissection?'

'No – the first was November 1702. David Myles. Hanged for killing a baby. His sister's. He was the father. The demonstrations were like this one. Each day presented by a different lecturer, over the period of a week, with a summary by Archibald Pitcairne at the end.'

'Pitcairne?'

'Yes – Archibald Pitcairne. Greatly revered by many, and rightly so.'

James watched as the demonstration table was set by attendants, under supervision by the Masters.

Douglas Atkins continued, 'For teaching of apprentices, Masters of the Incorporation were granted the right by the Town Council to dissect bodies of unfortunate victims. The council requires them to present annual public dissections. This is the second of these.'

'When was this building completed?'

'Oh, a few years back. Built as a theatre and meeting house,' Atkins said. 'If you wish, I'll show you the laboratories and the new public baths, after the lecture.'

The noise of the hall ceased suddenly. Robert Swinton was making ready to begin his discourse.

'He's wearing a clean peenie especially for the occasion,' Atkins whispered.


'Will you be coming to the lecture tomorrow?' Atkins asked as they left the Surgeons' Hall and meandered down to the Cowgate.

'I would like to,' James said. 'There is no substitute for seeing a cadaver. And up close as well.'

'We can do the same tomorrow. Same row. Same position.'

James nodded. 'And thank you for showing me the laboratory and Turkish baths. Who uses these laboratory facilities? The surgeons only?'

'No – physicians and apothecaries as well. It's also used to conduct trials, and for the teaching of chemistry. I'm a weel-kent face there.'

James hesitated. 'I had hoped to meet Archibald Pitcairne. Are you acquainted with him?'

Atkins smiled. 'Unfortunately not. Though, as I said, he's much respected for his scholarship. I've heard he's a kind and likeable person. Treats both rich and poor. So, why not seek him out? He may give you a good hearing.' He turned to face James. 'He has enemies as well, mind.'

'He has?'

'He's been in a few scrapes with the authorities.'

'Is he a Jacobite?'

'He could be, or maybe no.'

James changed the subject. 'I have heard about his scholarship from surgeons I've met on my travels.'

Atkins nodded. 'I fancy you would get on well with my brother Francis. He's more a scholar than I am.'

'Aye, I rather like your brother. I will visit his bookshop sometime.'

Atkins glanced at James and smiled. 'You'll need a lot of spare time, I think. Francis will want to hold your attention. Anyway, you did ask for local news. If you wish political writings, there's plenty to read. Francis will be pleased to supply his own opinions, of course.'

'Of course. I'm a good listener.'

James followed Atkins through the Cowgate and up the steep Niddry Wynd. He wasn't going anywhere in particular, so it was as well to enjoy conversation with his new companion. He walked behind Atkins up the narrow road, picking his way carefully around the filth in the gutters.

Some geese had gathered around vegetable waste, scattering fragments across the road. He stood on something and slipped. Atkins was ahead by a few yards, and almost out of sight. He hurried along to catch up with him, not wishing to lose him.

'Did you find your friend eventually?' Atkins asked.

'He wasn't at home.' James had to find lodgings. He took the plunge. He stopped, and turned to face Atkins. 'I didn't find my friend. Now I've no money for rent. I lost my sea chest. I've nowhere to stay.' He took a deep breath and continued. 'I don't like to impose, but if you could point my way to suitable lodgings, I'd be most grateful. I—'

'My dear fellow, you must stay with us. I'm sure Elizabeth won't mind. There's not much space, though. We have seven bairns now, and another on the way. Very busy, my wife is – she enjoys being busy. Good for body and soul, don't you think?'

James did not feel inclined to disagree or agree on that point. 'I'd be most obliged, but don't want to put you out.'

'Not at all – you'll be most welcome.'

They strode on towards the apothecary's house on the High Street. James was not so sure Douglas's wife would welcome an unexpected visitor. Maybe he would be more comfortable staying with Francis Atkins.

'Does your brother live nearby?'

'He bides in a garret in the next tenement. He's a bachelor.'

James slowed down as they passed the tavern they were in yesterday. 'That tavern. Is it a meeting place for dissenters?'

'Whatever gave you that idea?' Atkins asked. 'No. It's not.'

'I've seen different types of inns and public houses. Each one has its own distinctive features.'

Atkins turned sharply to glance at James, and almost slipped on rotten cabbage.

'A tavern has its own particular folk,' James added.

'I'm not sure how to respond to that remark...'

'I don't mean to offend. I often watched seamen in taverns.' James smiled. 'Not all were heavily intoxicated. They form groups. I heard talk of conspiracies and suchlike arrangements.'

Atkins opened his mouth as if to speak, then closed it.

'As a ship's surgeon I felt I needed to understand people. So that I could spot those faking illness, for instance.' James was simply curious about people.

'This is my shop,' Atkins said with a casual wave, leading the way through a gate in the close, and to a wee enclosed garden. He stopped and said, 'You may stay with us as long as you wish. Don't worry about rent just now.' He added, 'In return, perhaps we may benefit from your skills and experience.'

'Certainly. In what way?'

'Assisting with preparation of treatments – and other duties in the shop.'

'Agreed,' said James. For now, any way for board and lodgings would do.

Atkins showed James into a small chamber. Clothes lay heaped on the top of a small box bed. There was no fire in the grate. A pile of books topped with broadsides sat on an oak armchair. Beside the door was a large bundle of dirty linen, smelling of camphor.

'You may share this room with my two sons. The elder, George, is my apprentice. I'll ask him to set up some bedding for you,' he said, as they made their way through the house.

'Your wife must be overworked,' James said, regretting his quick agreement to terms for lodgings.

Atkins gave him a fierce look. A young girl tugged at her father's sleeve, dragging him away. Atkins pointed to a stair. 'The shop is on the floor above,' he said.

Sounds of angry voices broke out, gradually fading as James climbed the stair. He cast his eyes around. The apprentice was attending to a frail old woman. Shelves with rows of bottles and jars were clearly labelled: antimony, camphor, borax, opium. On the benches were scales, mortar and pestle, and small packages of prepared medicines. Some white powder spilled over the bench and onto the floor. At the back of the shop, dirty bottles lay huddled in the corner. Pungent odours hung there. James peeped into a small room where a row of dried plants hung from the ceiling. Assorted glassware lay scattered around.

'Ah – there you are, James. I'll leave you in the capable hands of my son. Elizabeth tells me there's an old man I have to see urgently. He has pains in the stomach. I'll give him more of the cordial I prepared specially for him. That should do. He's quite prosperous. Prefers to see me rather than a physician, though.' Atkins smiled, and was gone.

James glanced at the list of treatments he had to prepare. He had the remains of the day to finish the task. There was no rush. This suited him as he had the chance to take notes of some recipes for his own information and future reference. He had been working in the apothecary shop for a week now, and still no word about Andrew. James had seen Tom again at the cloth shop in Andrew's tenement. Tom assured him he would let him know when Andrew returned.

He liked being on his own in the shop. Douglas Atkins was often out. James felt he was being put upon, but he had no choice but to stay with the Atkins family. Anyway, Douglas had invited him to the remaining public dissection lectures, and he'd enjoyed the opportunity to hear the celebrated Archibald Pitcairne present his conclusion to the event on the last day.

The front door slammed. James looked up. A tall, well-built man, dressed in a grey coat and wearing a short wig, stood at the bench.

'I have been requested to examine some of your preparations,' he said, his eyes sweeping round the shop. He strode across to James and picked up a small bottle labelled *Treatment for Fevers*. 'There have been some complaints,' he added.

'I'm not the proprietor,' James said. 'Douglas Atkins is not available just now. If you would care to return early tomorrow, that would be the best time.' He turned his attention to a powder for the treatment of kidney stones which he had started preparing. He transferred the weighed ingredients to mortar and pestle.

The man pulled out a paper and deposited it firmly on the bench. 'This is authority to examine these premises and remove selected samples for close inspection.'

James glanced at the paper, his right hand working vigorously with the pestle. 'Whose authority?'

'The Town Council.' The man pointed to the paper.

'I've not heard anything about complaints,' James said, pounding hard. 'I mean—'

'And who are you? An apothecary?' The man wandered round the shop. He picked up a bottle, opened it, sniffed the contents and put it back. He picked up another, and another.

'Well, no – I'm assisting Mr Atkins with some duties,' James said. 'He's out on a call for help – an old lady who suddenly became unwell —'

'He has an apprentice?'

'Yes – he's delivering some medicines.'

'I see. And you've been left in charge?'

James pushed aside the mortar and pestle and wiped the front of the bench with a cloth. 'If you would kindly wait, I'm sure Mr Atkins won't be too long,' he said.

'Very well,' the visitor said. He shuffled around and stopped to study the little packages of preparations. He selected four and put them into his satchel. He took a piece of paper, scribbled a short note and handed it to James. 'Here is a list of the items I've selected—'

The door opened and Douglas barged in. 'What's this?' he said, regarding the paper on the bench.

'I take it you're the proprietor,' the visitor said, stabbing his finger on the paper. 'This is a notice to examine your shop. There have been complaints about the service you provide.' He picked up his hat, turned and walked out.

Douglas looked pale. He walked through to the fire and sat down on a stool, still clutching his satchel. James watched him as he held the paper, as if in disbelief. He found another stool and sat opposite Douglas. The last thing he wanted was to be involved with someone supplying poor preparations, or overcharging. But if Douglas had accumulated wealth from his services, it didn't show. He had only one servant, and a large family in an apartment with four small chambers, his wife heavily pregnant and overburdened.

'He has taken packets containing standard treatments for common ailments, that's all,' Douglas eventually said. He leaned back against the wall.

'Then there isn't anything to worry about,' James said, more cheerfully than he felt. 'But there must be a reason why they have chosen to examine your premises. What do you know of the complaints?'

'I know nothing about complaints,' Douglas snapped.

'Your accounts and details of preparations. Are they complete?' James asked.

'They are.' Douglas stood up and wandered over to the bench. He turned sharply. 'What right have you to question my methods?'

Because he needed lodgings, and happened to find himself here. Good enough reasons to be concerned.

'The Incorporation have the right, I suppose. To… to make checks on prescribing. I mean, standards must be maintained,' Douglas explained. 'Physicians, too, have for some time been critical of some of the practices of apothecaries. They think we charge too much. They think we're too wealthy.'

'Are apothecaries wealthy?'

'No – not the ones I know.'

James wasn't satisfied. As far as he knew Douglas kept records and accounts in the secretaire in his parlour. He never took them into the shop or left papers lying around. He locked his desk each time as soon as he left it. For his tasks James had been using only a notebook of standard recipes and the *Pharmacopoeia*. He would like to find out the fees Douglas was charging. And why was Douglas Atkins being targeted?

# 5

'James – great news from Leith,' Francis shouted from the front shop. 'A French privateer has been seized by the Scots Navy. I'm on my way to Leith now.'

It was early morning, and James was about to start washing glass bottles. He rushed forward, just in time to see Francis' back disappear from the shop door. He would have liked to have gone with him to Leith to find out more. It would have been an opportunity to get to know Francis better.

A short break from the oppressive atmosphere in the household would be pleasant too. A stroll to Leith and a taste of fresh air from the sea. James looked at the large heap of contaminated bottles. If he could bring himself to wash a few that would be a good start. But no. James put the bottles back into the corner beside other assorted glassware.

He found Douglas at his desk in the parlour. Douglas flinched at the interruption. He closed his account books before James could get a chance to peer over his shoulder.

'James. Is anything the matter?'

'No. Just a message from your brother.'

But Douglas showed little interest when James mentioned the French ship. He had been in a foul mood after their unwanted visitor yesterday.

'Would you mind if I took the day off?' James asked.

Douglas gave him a blank stare. 'What? But there's… Oh, very well. I suppose it's all right.'

James was out the door before Douglas could change his mind. He would miss breakfast, but no matter. He strode through the town, past the Nether Bow, and out on the road to Leith. The sun lit up the fields, and there was a cool breeze from the east.

He was not happy working at the apothecary's. The complaints from customers. The crowded living space. The constant arguments between Douglas and his wife. He had been grateful at first, because the work brought some relief to his purse. The sooner he found permanent lodgings, the better. Preferably in Andrew's tenement.

He was frustrated with Douglas. At family mealtimes he asked about Andrew. How well do they know him? How wealthy is he? Where does he trade? What does he export and import? But, as soon as he asked, Douglas changed the subject. James knew little more than he had on his first day in Edinburgh. He knew Andrew was now a burgess, owned a tenement, and had shares in ships. So where was he now? He could be in Scotland somewhere, or abroad investigating possible trade routes. James knew Andrew well enough to know that he would be looking to his own business, even though the war was restricting trade. Andrew had the cunning and fortitude to come out on top, no matter the challenge.

James passed carts on their way to Leith, noticing that none were travelling in the other direction. The reason soon became obvious. He spotted the red coats of guards marching towards him. He moved to the side, to let them pass. Behind the guards, columns of French prisoners of war shuffled along; about twenty of them, roped together. More guards brought up the rear, along with the shouts and jeers of foot travellers.

James headed straight to Leith harbour. There was a buzz of excitement. Groups of curious onlookers hovered around The Shore, mingling with traders loading carts, and the street clutter of barrels and boxes. Some idle men were involved in a heated argument. Others were laughing. James felt the eyes of an old man following him. He turned to face him. The man halted and stepped back.

'I passed some prisoners going to Edinburgh…' James began, facing up to his follower.

'Aye,' the man said, screwing up his eyes. 'From the French ship, that'll be. Captain Gordon's prize. Bound for the Tolbooth.'

James thought about asking further questions about the seizure. The man seemed to be well enough informed. But instead he chose to quiz him about Andrew.

The old man scratched his chin before answering. 'Andrew Lawson. I ken who you mean. Bides in Edinburgh. Young fellow. High and mighty, nose in the air.'

'Have you seen him recently?'

'Here in Leith?'

'Here. Or anywhere?'

'No.' The man hesitated. 'If I do see him…'

'You could mention a friend is seeking him.'

The man gave him a sideways glance, turned and walked away. James wandered on. There was a tavern nearby and he was hungry.

The room was bare, apart from two old seamen in the corner. A young woman carried a jug of ale to their table. James chose a position where he could observe the door and look out the window at the same time. Some caution was required. Press gangs were always about, though they would most likely operate late at night, catching drunken souls as they left the taverns.

The girl came over to James's table and hovered, her large breasts almost completely open to view, and positioned strategically close to his eye level.

'Is it normally so quiet here?' he said, edging slightly away from her.

'Most folks are down by the quay.'

Despite there being no other customers, the girl took her time preparing his breakfast. James stretched his legs out, feeling more at ease here than at the apothecary's. He was determined to settle down in Edinburgh, study hard, and save enough money to see him through his studies at Leiden.

The serving maid returned with haddock, cheese and bread. She smiled. 'Fresh bread, just in.'

Tearing off a piece of bread, James looked past her at four young men who had just come in. He recognised one of them. It was a face he wouldn't forget. The boy who attacked him at Figgate Whins. The four men chose a table at the other side of the room. They were talking in low voices, every now and then glancing in his direction.

He wanted to leave and avoid trouble, but the fish was tasty. The young villain stood up and sauntered over to his table.

'I want my pistol back,' he said.

'Ah – I remember the occasion. You dropped it.' James smiled. 'Did you have a sore head after our encounter?'

The boy didn't move. The others came over and stood behind him. Suddenly, hands pulled James off his seat, cowping the chair. He pushed the men off. The young boy swept his meal onto the floor. James kicked him in the shins, knocking him back. He was grabbed from behind. He broke free. He grasped the man closest to him and threw him across the room. He turned and punched another. A blow knocked him against a table, upsetting two chairs. Ale spilled over the floor. The two old men in the corner ran outside. James tripped over a chair, staggered and fell. The men kicked him on both sides, and James covered his head with his hands. He was hauled to his feet, and felt he was going to faint.

'What's going on here?' a voice cried.

The four men let him go. James fumbled around. They had seized his pistol and dirk. The men headed for the door, and found their way blocked. A small party had just stepped in. James felt sore. He must sit down carefully somewhere. Two men grabbed him from behind and pushed him forwards. James found himself staring into the eyes of an immaculately dressed man with a powdered wig and a mischievous smile – his friend Andrew Lawson.

Andrew moved aside and whispered something to one of his companions. He nodded and the two men slackened their grip on James. Andrew approached James's attackers.

The young reprobates stood still, heads slightly bent. The boy stepped forward.

'This villain attacked me, sir,' he said, pointing to James. 'Two weeks ago, at Figgate Whins. I still have a sore head.'

'Is that so?' Andrew grinned. He screwed up his eyes. 'Well, never mind – we'll deal with him. I'll take his pistol and dirk.' He held out his hand.

'The pistol's mine,' the lad said, handing over the dirk, and tightening his grip on the pistol.

'It's mine now – for the moment.' Andrew held out his hand.

The rascal slowly passed it.

Andrew addressed the two men holding James. 'Take him through the back.'

The two men led James through to a small chamber, told him to wait, and left him, closing the door behind them. He heard raised voices, then eventually all was quiet.

It wasn't long before Andrew entered. He placed the pistol and dirk on the table and rushed forward, gripping James round the shoulders. James flinched.

'Sorry. James – good to see you.' Andrew smiled. 'I had heard you were looking for me.'

'I've been trying to find you for the past two weeks,' James said.

'And causing trouble too, I see. I'm pleased your period overseas has toughened you up. You had too much book-reading while you were at university.' He grinned. 'What happened at Figgate Whins?'

James sat down and related his encounter with the thief.

'Well, the lad won't be bothering you now,' Andrew said.

'And what about you? Have you stayed out of trouble?'

'We'll talk about that later,' Andrew said, helping James to his feet and opening the door. 'I noticed you hadn't finished your breakfast. So, come with me. I know where we can eat more comfortably.'

'That would be grand,' James said. 'Thank you.'


He shuffled along the street, leaning on Andrew for support.

'We have a lot to catch up on,' Andrew said. 'By the way, Captain Gordon sends his compliments.'

'Captain Gordon, who seized the French ship?'

'Yes. He's heard of you.'

'Oh.' James felt dizzy, and couldn't think clearly. He couldn't quite see how Gordon knew about him.

'I see you're puzzled,' Andrew said. 'Captain Gordon is in command of the Scots Navy frigate, *Royal Mary*. The frigate's duties are to guard the east coast, and convoy shipping along the coast.'

'And seize enemy ships?'

'If possible, aye. Apparently, Gordon had information of a young man slipping into the country, unofficially,' continued Andrew. 'It's his duty to be informed of incomers. Francis Atkins has just told me about you, and I wondered...'

'Ah, I see.'

Andrew guided him along, as they turned into the Kirk Gate. They stopped outside a large house. Andrew thumped the huge door knocker.

A servant showed them into a tiny office, poorly lit by a small window in the corner. James heard a female voice in the hall. The door opened.

'How lovely to see you.' A tall, elegant lady in a fine silk gown rushed forward and embraced Andrew. She eventually took notice of James.

'My friend, James Lightfoot. James – Mrs Eleanor Scarlett,' Andrew said.

James bowed and blushed, as she lowered her gaze, and then glanced up.

Andrew wasted no time in getting to the point. 'James's breakfast has been spoiled…'

'So you have been in a scrape… Flora!' she called.

The maid entered, too quickly.

'Been listening at the keyhole again?' Mrs Scarlett shook her head. 'Would you be so kind and set a small table for our guests? Some cold meats perhaps…'

The servant left.

Amid all the small talk, Mrs Scarlett and Andrew exchanged glances. James sensed that there was some intimacy between them. The lady took them up a narrow stair to a small dining parlour. A shuttered window had been partially opened, allowing ample light to fall onto the table. The maid laid platters of cold meats on the sideboard. James helped himself eagerly, filling a silver plate with mutton pie, bread and cheese. He eased himself carefully onto a chair at the table. Mrs Scarlett handed him a cup of small ale. Despite feeling sore, he had not lost his appetite. The meal revived him. He was content, though, just to listen to the friendly banter at the table.

'So how long have you been away from Scotland?' Mrs Scarlett asked. 'I love to hear gentlemen's tales of bravery and adventure.'

James did not reply. She glanced at him briefly, and looked back at Andrew. She took a piece of cheese and dabbed her lips with her kerchief. James felt embarrassed. He was in the way. He cast a brief look round the room. His eye was drawn to the painting above the sideboard: a portrait of a gentleman with dark eyes. He wore a full, curly wig, black velvet jacket, waistcoat and white cravat. The face was vaguely familiar.

'My husband. It was painted after we married – a year ago.'

The left side of his face was in shadow. Of course. James remembered. He returned to the sideboard for more cold meat, taking a closer look at the portrait.

'You have met John – my husband?'

'No – he just reminds me of someone.' James remembered. The scar on the left side of his face. How could he forget? It was four years ago. The man was captain of a pirate ship. Mean Jack, they called him. Fortunately James's acquaintance with him had been short. He had been seized by the pirates to attend the wounded, and soon afterwards he managed to escape. So how did Jack avoid being captured and brought to trial for piracy? By bribery? By covering his tracks and operating as a privateer? How did he come to enter this country and take up residence here in Leith? A fine change of identity. James would have to avoid him. They must never meet. He shivered.

'Are you all right?' Andrew asked.

'Aye – I think so. Just feeling a wee bit sore.'

'So tell me about your adventures…' Mrs Scarlett said.

## 6

'There's a garret, six storeys up, which is not much used,' Andrew said, as he led the way along the close and into the turnpike stair. 'The other adjacent chamber is used by my apprentice, Tom.'

Andrew unlocked the door at the top of the turnpike, and led James up another stair to the garret. The room was furnished well enough – a small bed, a table and chair at the window, a kist, and an armchair by the fireside.

'I use this corner for additional storage,' Andrew said, indicating the chest. Beside it were iron pots and girdles, and an assorted collection of silverware. 'You may stay here as long as you wish.'

'Thank you.' James smiled with relief and settled into the armchair, feeling very much at home already. 'This is grand. You've no idea how much of an improvement this is on my recent abode.'

'Oh yes, I do know. Douglas Atkins may not want to lose you though – a willing pair of hands.'

'I'd rather not work there. I'm not sure that I trust him. There are problems.' James hesitated. 'He doesn't seem to like you.'

'Ah, well. I don't suppose he does. You'll find a better situation, I'm sure. Though I can't understand why you want to be a physician. They don't do anything.' Andrew sat on the edge of the bed. 'When my father was poorly, the physicians hardly looked at him. They withdrew to the library and sat round the table, arguing about vomiting and coughing and suchlike. They spoke in Latin sometimes. When I approached, they stopped talking. It was as if what they were doing concerned them alone, not my father. Surgeons on the other hand...'

'Physicians apply their knowledge to treat the person. They understand, or endeavour to understand, the workings of the body.' James added, 'The skills of both physicians and surgeons are essential and complementary.'

'Oh, I suppose you know what you want. Just as I do.'

'You must have bought this tenement not long after I left.'

Andrew rose and sauntered over to the window. 'I bought it in 1702. Morton was desperate to sell. I needed a house. I had done well, but knew that good fortune was not always in my grasp. So, the income from rents will see me through difficult times. This tenement has chambers to suit tenants from different ranks of society. The house on the first storey fetches the best rent. It has five rooms, high ceilings and ample windows.'

'You've certainly made your mark quickly enough,' James said. 'So it seems has John Scarlett.'

'You know of him?'

'Aye I do. I recognised him from the portrait in the dining room. I had the unfortunate privilege of meeting him, four years ago. He was known then as Mean Jack.' James stood up and joined Andrew at the small window. The coast of Fife was clearly visible beyond the blue estuary of the Forth. 'I must be at the top of his list of enemies.'

'Ah. I can't imagine you having any enemies, James.'

'We all have enemies. I must tell you what I know about him. He's not—'

'Later, perhaps. First we'll see about better clothes,' Andrew said, examining a patch on James's coat. 'So that you look like the splendid gentleman that you are. Tom will organise a tailor for you. In the meantime I'll see Hodges about some temporary clothes. Then, later, there is someone I would like you to meet,' he added, moving to the door.

While Andrew was away, James took out his glass. He scanned beyond the tops of the buildings, to the blue estuary of the Forth dotted with ships. Andrew's opinions on physicians were disappointing; not so different from Douglas's attitude. Were these generally held opinions? But no matter. He knew roughly what he wanted to do. But how to find a way? Where to begin? How was he going to get appropriate experience to set him on the road to an established practice?

A soft knock interrupted his thoughts.

'Some spare clothes that may fit you, sir,' Hodges said, placing a large, neat bundle on the bed.

'Thank you,' James said, examining the collection. Shirts, nightclothes, breeches, waistcoat, silk cravats, and a coat with a touch of embroidery down the sides. He tried on the coat. 'These will do nicely, Hodges.'

Hodges nodded. 'If I may mend your old coat, sir?' he offered, picking it up.

James remembered suddenly that he had put the letter for Andrew in an inner pocket. 'Thank you, perhaps later,' he said, snatching the coat back. How could he have forgotten about the coded letter? He must have been distracted with thoughts about Jack Scarlett.

After the servant left, he removed the letter and tucked it inside his belt.


Andrew's apartment was on the middle storey of the tenement. James chapped at the door. Hodges opened it, and showed him into a large chamber with a painted ceiling and wood panelling on the walls. Andrew's wealth was visible in his possessions. Detailed carving and marquetry on the cabinet and sideboard. Sunlight from two open windows shone on an oak dining table. A woman attended to a big pot at the fire. Two children, playing in the corner, looked up at James, ran over, grabbed her skirt and hid their faces. The woman stood up and straightened her apron.

'My wife and our two sons,' Hodges said.

Mrs Hodges smiled shyly, then turned and bent her head to the fire. The children huddled into the corner.

'Mr Lawson is in his parlour, sir.' Hodges knocked and opened the door.

James strode in. The small chamber was furnished with two faded green velvet armchairs, a cheap cabinet, a pine table and chair. A curtain surrounded the bed in the corner. The shutter was partly open, yet the room had a slight sweaty smell. Andrew was sitting at the table, writing. He put down his quill and looked up. Hodges withdrew and closed the door.

'I was asked to give you this,' James said, pulling out the letter and extending his arm. 'I have kept it safely, and this is the first chance I've had to hand it over.' He stepped forward.

'What's this?' Andrew turned the letter over, running his fingers over the surface and edges. 'The seal has been broken, then resealed, I think.'

'Yes – but not by me.'

'It was given to you like this?'

'Yes.'

'There was no outer cover?'

'No. It is as you see it.'

'Did you study the contents?'

'No.'

Andrew stood up and faced James. He gripped the back of his armchair. 'Come, James. I've never known a man so bound by curiosity. A flower, a beetle – you must have noticed the seal had been broken. I ask you again. Did you read the letter?' He relaxed his grip and began to pace up and down.

'I… thought that as the seal was broken… the contents were no longer private anyway.'

'So you read it?'

'Well, yes. Sort of.'

'Ah, I thought so.'

'Well, no matter. It's in code anyway. You have your letter. I did my job in delivering it, in return for my passage here. I was running short of funds, having not been paid for my last voyage.'

Andrew sat down and studied the letter closely, then folded it and put it in his pocket. He stood up, walked back and forth in the room, and eventually turned to face James. 'Why didn't you give this to me sooner?'

'I told you. I've been trying to find you since arriving here in Edinburgh.'

'But you've not been trying hard enough, it seems. This communication has been compromised. I need to know if the delay in delivery was deliberate as well.'

'Just what are you accusing me of? The letter is no concern of mine.' James felt hot. He turned and reached for the door handle.

But Andrew was too quick for him. He stepped in front and leaned against the door. 'Sit down,' he said.

James sat down in a cosy armchair, and waited for Andrew to say something. He studied the complex design on the carpet, wishing his body could relax. He didn't want conflict. He'd had enough of that. He longed to hear of Andrew's adventures, and news of his family. He wished to be part of his family again. Andrew was the older brother he'd never had. He had taught him to hunt, fish and handle a sword. He was a regular companion until he was sent to finish his education at Edinburgh University. James had seen little of Andrew afterwards. And now – well, this was not what he expected.

He looked up. Andrew was bent over his desk, his pen quivering as he wrote. He stopped, his quill poised above the inkwell. He dipped the pen, added more to the page, then dusted it.

'You're not an easy man to find,' James said. 'Your apprentice told me you were abroad. People here are suspicious of me, a mariner asking questions. You remarked yourself on my appearance.' James turned and looked at the fire, then faced Andrew again. 'As for the letter, I know nothing more. But I would appreciate some idea of your involvement in this.'

'Do you think I would tell you?' Andrew looked hard at James. He leaned forward, one elbow on the table. Then he stood up, opened the cabinet, and took out a decanter and two glasses. He set them on the table.

'In truth, like you, I am simply a messenger,' Andrew said. 'I have just written a covering letter. This note, along with the document you have given me, will be bound in a sealed package.'

Andrew handed James a glass of claret. James tried to feel more at ease. Maybe now he could mention Scarlett.

'There's something else.' James took a long sip of the warm claret. He watched Andrew secure the package.

'Well? Out with it, man.'

'John Scarlett.'

'Ah, yes. It seems you're not fond of him.'

'How well do you know him? His background?' James asked.

'We're joint owners of a merchant vessel. I first met him in Leith in 1702. A year later he married. Eleanor was a young widow and owner of the mansion you just visited. Their marriage is, I think, a business arrangement. They have separate bedchambers. And, before you ask, she is not my mistress. Not that it's any of your concern anyway. You can choose to keep well away from Scarlett if you don't like him.'

'Oh, believe me I shall,' James said. 'Back in 1700, I met him. Pirate or privateer; I didn't know his real name, or much about him.' He wasn't going to disclose details of his confrontation with Scarlett. That was a private quarrel. 'What I don't understand is how the villain managed to slip into the country without facing charges of piracy. In fact, I'm surprised he's still alive. He must have lots of enemies.'

'Including you. I do examine lists of those wanted for apprehension but, as you say, he has changed his name, and must have hidden the trail of his past. Made the transition from pirate to privateer. That's often the way. I've worked with many seafaring men with dubious past experiences. I don't enquire too closely about a sea captain's previous activities. Accusations of piracy fly about, and some men were forced.' Andrew paused. 'I needed a man to work with who was willing to spend more time at sea than I was able to do. Scarlett suits my purpose.'

James nodded. 'But he's not to be trusted. You don't know what he might be doing…'

'Let me warn you, James, to mind your own business while you live here.'

James did not feel at ease. This was not good. Where was Scarlett now? Was he in Leith? Andrew refreshed their drinks, and settled into his armchair. Like James, he seemed deep in thought.

Andrew regarded the wall clock. 'I have to attend to this,' he said, taking his coat from a peg. He picked up the small package and stuffed it into his coat pocket. 'I'll call on you later, and take you to meet Archibald Pitcairne.'

Douglas was not at home when James returned to the apothecary's shop. He collected his notebooks, clothes and bag containing medicines, taking a last look round the dingy bedchamber. He sneaked into the parlour and left a note on Douglas's desk, thanking him for the temporary lodgings. He added that he had a chamber at Andrew's tenement now, and that he was grateful for the opportunity to visit the new Surgeons' Hall. He did not mention the possibility of a meeting with Archibald Pitcairne. This, he thought, was a cunning move by Andrew; to give him the introduction he so desired, in return for his cooperation and compliance regarding the matter of the mysterious letter, and his association with Jack Scarlett. Andrew, as ever, was the quick thinker; always several steps ahead of him.

James had just returned to his new lodgings when there was a knock on his door. It was Andrew with a brown shoulder-length periwig in his hands.

'No. I'll not wear a wig. I'm just getting used to not having a beard,' James said.

Andrew strode into the chamber and wandered around. 'Take it anyway. You never know. You may suddenly find yourself in need of a disguise. You've already annoyed the Atkins family, I expect. Not that you're the only one.'

James took the soft, curly wig. An expensive piece.

'I heard you coming up the stair,' Andrew said. 'I've arranged for you to meet Archibald Pitcairne.' Andrew sat James down in the armchair, pulled over a stool and perched on it, resting his hands on his knees. 'Pitcairne requires assistants to help at Paul's Work, and in the parish giving treatments for the poor. If he likes you, you won't be short of employment.'

James turned the wig over in his hands. It was clean and free from nits. 'Thank you,' he said.

'I knew you would be pleased.' Andrew added quickly, 'So how do you like your chamber?'

'It's good. I like the view of the Firth of Forth.'

'I thought the outlook might suit.'

'Douglas Atkins said that as well as having a great reputation, Pitcairne is much admired among local people. Do you know him well?' James asked.

'Not all that well. As a merchant I have many acquaintances. The good physician's social circle is among those of his colleagues in his profession, as I suppose you realise. Pitcairne's acquaintances often seek supplies of good wine, a difficult task in these times. I am pleased to say I have successfully managed to procure sources to Pitcairne's satisfaction.'

'Is he a Jacobite?'

'One thing you don't do here, James, is ask direct questions.'

'Well, Douglas said—'

'Douglas Atkins says a lot without foundation,' Andrew said. 'Some say that Pitcairne has sometimes been indiscreet. It is well known that he was imprisoned in the Tolbooth a few years back. He was released on his word of honour that he would not communicate with rebels.'

'And now?'

'And now, we will be having supper with him.'

So that was that. James would avoid mentioning anything to do with politics from now on. These matters were not his concern anyway.

It was still mild outside. Streaks of sunlight between gaps in the houses cast a warm glow onto the street.

'The city has changed much in four years. It's crowded. More filth in the closes and wynds,' James said.

'Ah, yes. There are many idlers seeking employment.' Andrew stopped. 'Pitcairne told me we would find him here,' he said, leading James down the steps and through to Willie Bell's tavern. 'He's a gentleman who enjoys good company.'

James peered into the smoke-filled darkness. The smell of beer and sweat filled the air. He let Andrew guide him to the back and down a few steps to a small room. Four gentlemen sat at a round table, engaged in an earnest discussion. One of them stood up and extended his hand.

'So is this the young adventurer back from far-off countries. Here to entertain us with his traveller's tales, I wonder. Archibald Pitcairne. Pleased to make your acquaintance.'

He indicated empty chairs. James and Andrew settled round the table. Pitcairne poured generous amounts of wine into two cups.

'The best claret from Bordeaux. Wine is good for you,' the physician said, giving Andrew a wink. 'To your good health, gentlemen.'

James sipped the fine wine.

'You have a toast to propose, sir,' someone asked.

All eyes were on James. Other gentlemen had entered the room, and stood around, eager to catch the conversation. He remembered the Little Gentleman in Black Velvet.

'I...' James began.

'I'm very desirous to hear about your work as a ship's surgeon,' Pitcairne said.

'It must have been a rough life among seamen. Pirates or merchants. Privateers or buccaneers. Depends which flag is displayed. Am I correct?' a young man leaning against the wall said.

'Quite so. Perfectly correct, sir,' James replied, trying to hide his irritation. He took a sip of wine. He felt he was being baited by the young men, possibly students. He looked sideways to see if Andrew was smiling. He wasn't. James looked down. There was an uncomfortable silence. The conversation resumed, and James was content just to listen in.

'More wine, young lad.' Pitcairne refilled James's cup.

'Thank you, sir,' James said. 'Excellent wine.'

'I keep an admirable wine cellar. My merchant sends bottles to my friends in England. Difficult for them to purchase braw wine, these days.'

James was relieved and delighted when the supper arrived on the table. Chicken with carrot and turnip, followed by bread-and-milk pudding. He was aware of the others watching him. He couldn't eat and speak at the same time. The food was there to be enjoyed. The conversation came round to the topic of the public dissections.

'I was fortunate to arrive here in time to attend days five to nine of the public dissections. I missed the first four,' James said.

'And how did you find them?' Pitcairne asked.

'I learned a lot,' James said. 'It was enlightening. A wonderful opportunity.'

'Good. I will test you on your knowledge of the circulation of the blood and respiration.' Pitcairne grinned. 'Please help yourself to more bread pudding.'

'Thank you, sir.' James filled his plate.

'Knowledge of mathematics is useful, don't you think?' Pitcairne asked.

'It is,' James said. He wasn't sure where this was leading. 'I have read your dissertation on geometry and its use in medicine, sir.' It was fortunate that he'd had some free time to read the dissertation Tuesday last, when the shop was quiet.

Pitcairne fixed his gaze on James. 'Take note of your observations. Compare them with those of other learned men. Evaluate the evidence. And, most importantly, do not be quick to make assumptions.' He patted James on the shoulder.

The chimes of ten and the drum roll of the Town Guard startled James. He had been enjoying the physician's company and hadn't noticed the passing of time. He stood up, pleasantly surprised to feel his legs were reasonably steady.

'If you value good education you may wish to sit in attendance at one of my clinics.'

'I would be delighted. Thank you, sir,' James said. He watched as Archibald Pitcairne bid his friends goodnight, and strode along the street accompanied by the three young men.

# 7

L ouise pushed her way past the stalls in the market, anxious to be at home. There was news that Andrew had returned from his venture. She must speak with him about his friend, James Lightfoot. She was furious that her father had refused to accept him as a lodger. He would have provided useful rent once he found regular work. She turned into the close.

'Good day to you, Miss Morton,' said a loud voice in her ear. It was the laird who lived on the first storey. His huge, grotesque body blocked her way. She tried to step aside to squeeze past him. He was too quick. He gripped her arm and dragged her to the foot of the turnpike stair.

'Let's have a feel,' he said, pushing her against the wall with one hand, and reaching up under her petticoat with the other. The full weight of his body was pressing against her. She could hardly breathe.

She dropped her basket and tried to push him off. Then she heard footsteps. Someone was coming down the turnpike stair. He let her go.

'Another time, my dear,' he said, breathing heavily.

'There'll be no other time,' she shouted.

'You should be taught good manners and deference, girl.'

'My manners are better than yours.'

She shoved past him, and almost bumped into a smartly dressed gentleman who had just reached the foot of the stair. He picked up her basket, and held it out to her.

'Are you all right?' he asked.

Louise adjusted her skirt, and took her basket. 'I think so. Thank you kindly, sir.' She turned towards her house door. The gentleman followed. She didn't want to speak to him. She wished only to go inside.

'You look upset,' he said, placing his hand gently on her elbow to steady her.

'I'm all right.' She stopped and leaned against the wall, realising her legs were shaking. 'I am much obliged for your help,' she added.

'My name's Henry Brand. I'm staying here at Mrs Grant's lodging house.'

'I'm Louise Morton.'

So he was the new lodger everyone was talking about. A handsome Englishman, and rich too, someone had said. He was well turned out; blue velvet coat and a matching waistcoat trimmed with silver.

'I'm so pleased to make your acquaintance,' he said. His bright eyes lingered on hers just a little too long. 'My business has brought me to Edinburgh. I may be staying here for some time.' He hesitated. 'As we are neighbours I expect we will see each other often. I do hope so,' he added.

Louise thanked him again. Her legs were still trembling as she opened the door of her house. Mr Brand seemed kind enough, but it was all upsetting. The laird's behaviour was despicable. She was glad to step inside.

'The visitor from overseas is staying in the garret now,' Jean said. 'Mrs Hodges told me today.'

Father was seated at his desk. He turned towards them. 'Well, I'm thankful he's not lodging with us,' he said.

'But—'

'If we are going to use the lower chamber we need to make sure the tenant can pay the rent regularly. Surely you know that, lass?'

Louise bit her lip. 'We could have had him in the wee room. It's not being used.'

'The garret is bigger and brighter for the young man,' Jean added.

'Our chamber has a fire and a window. It's adequate,' Louise said.

Father shook his head. 'Don't you realise? We know little about him.' He stood up. 'Anyway, now he has lodgings he won't be back here.'

'You seem to forget; Andrew treats us kindly. We must at least be agreeable to his friends. It's Andrew Lawson's house, not yours.'

'Aye, that's what I told that young man the day he came here, and I told him—'

'Yes, I know what you keep telling people. Sit down. You'll make yourself ill.'

'I'll tell you what makes me ill. It's the likes of Andrew Lawson making himself rich, while we suffer.' He took a deep breath and started to cough.

Louise averted her eyes to avoid further talk. Father sat down at his desk, picked up a quill, fiddled with it, and put it down again.

'I wonder that you've taken a liking to this stranger. Well, if so – forget about him.'

Louise needed to clear her mind. She sat by the fire, and picked up a shirt she was mending. Her father wandered over and settled into his usual chair. He lit his pipe. He always did this when collecting his thoughts. Louise wondered what was coming next. He took a draw on his pipe, and gazed into the fire. She sighed as she noticed another tiny hole in the shirt. Selecting a remnant of linen, she cut a patch. The clock ticked away the time. In the kitchen recess, Jean was chopping vegetables.

Father shifted in his chair; looked up as if he was about to say something. He rested his arms and put his hands together. 'You're sixteen now,' he began. 'Old enough to be thinking of your future. Of marriage.'

The sound of chopping vegetables stopped, then started again.

'I don't want to be married. Not now. Maybe not all.' She pricked her finger on the needle. Laying down the shirt, she began fumbling about in her work basket.

'You should. As the daughter of a burgess you should have no problem attracting suitable gentlemen.'

Louise sighed. She would never be as desirable to men as Mary.

'There is someone I'd like you to meet. He's coming here today.' He continued, 'He's older than you. He's wealthy, and commands considerable respect and influence.'

Louise made no reply. She looked at the far side of the wall. The thought of sharing her life with an old man did not appeal.


Louise examined the rose-patterned embroidery, feeling quite satisfied with it. She looked up to find Bella's eyes on her.

'You're very contemplative,' Bella said.

Louise was dreading being introduced to Mr Lancelot Turnbull, savouring every moment of her time at the sisters' chambers. Mr Turnbull was forty years old, a lawyer and a merchant – a worthy gentleman. He was probably with Father just now, both of them waiting for her to return. She would let them wait.

'Oh, it's nothing. Just thinking. Father is poorly sometimes. Foul-tempered.'

She watched Rose and Bella, both spinsters, happy at their work. It was comfortable sewing with the two sisters in their workroom. They sat round a large table by the window. Boxes of threads, beads, needles and pearls lay scattered on the surface. Silks and half-finished garments covered the bed and an armchair. Curiously though, there was a hint of masculinity; possibly the odour of tobacco, or was it her imagination? She scanned the room for men's clothes but there were none.

She would be happy to stay here all day. Their chambers being in the same tenement meant she often had the opportunity to work with the sisters. If she did not marry, what then? What did she really want? Her own employment like Bella and Rose? She had hoped Father would let her wait a few years. On the other hand, if a fine young gentleman came along…

Bella looked at her again over the top of her spectacles and frowned. 'I thought you said your father's health had improved. That he had got over that chill.'

Louise frowned. 'I fear his chest is bad.'

There was a loud knock at the door. Andrew Lawson entered. 'Good afternoon ladies; I do beg your pardon, and apologise for the intrusion.'

'You're welcome at any time, sir,' Bella said.

'Miss Isabella…' he said, using her full name, not Bella as he usually did. It must be business, not a social visit. 'Miss Isabella, I wonder if I may speak with you on a private matter.' He looked at Louise. 'About a letter from a mutual friend. Louise – you will excuse us please.'

'Of course,' Louise said. She rose and gathered her embroidery into her bag, reluctant to leave.

'We'll see you tomorrow,' Rose said.

Louise nodded and slipped down the stairs. She listened at her house door, hearing voices. As soon as she stepped inside a huge man stood up, showing a body with a large spread around the middle. Louise backed towards the door.

'Louise.' Her father smiled. 'Let me introduce you to Mr Lancelot Turnbull.'

'Delighted to meet you,' Mr Turnbull said, leaning forward. His breath smelt foul.

She instinctively pulled back.

'Your father has told me much about you, Miss Louise.'

Louise gave her father a stern look. So this was the man her father thought was an eligible suitor. What could he be thinking of? Surely he wasn't serious. Unattractive, and probably in poor health. She realised she was staring at Mr Turnbull, and he was smiling. She turned her head away.

It was an effort to maintain polite, intelligent conversation, as she knew she must. After exchanging a few pleasant remarks, Mr Turnbull and Father moved on to discuss matters of finance, ignoring her completely. She felt anger rising from somewhere deep within. Her cheeks were burning. She resisted the temptation to jump up and shout.

She said, 'Perhaps I should leave if you wish to go over matters of business. I have Mr Lawson's accounts to attend to.' She rose and strode towards her chamber.

'No, please,' Mr Turnbull said. 'I thought to mention to your father – but of course, it's just that I'm not used to talking about… things of interest to ladies. My late wife, she and her companions compared opinions about domestic matters, and—'

'Mr Turnbull, Louise will stay. She is a bright, intelligent young girl. With experience, she will, I'm sure, become more at ease in conversation,' Mr Morton said.

Louise sank into her chair. Any confidence she might have mustered had now gone. She thought hard about what might make for intelligent talk, but couldn't come up with anything. The longcase clock was staring at her, as if refusing to move its hands. Eventually the large gentleman heaved himself from his chair.

'I look forward to seeing you again,' Mr Turnbull said. 'We have much to discuss and arrange.' He leered at her.

She imagined confronting him in the close, like the encounter with the laird. She watched him pick up his hat and coat, and leave without a smile or backward glance.

Louise was in no mood for a confrontation with her father. She slipped away to her own chamber and sat down, resting her elbows on her desk. She took out her handkerchief and dabbed her moist eyes. Opening the account book, she took a deep breath and began checking the sums.

## 8

S ix o'clock in the morning at the Greping Office, Pitcairne
had said. James was in good fettle as he strode down the
High Street in the cool air. His lodgings were comfortable,
and Hodges had provided him with an adequate early
breakfast. Best of all though, was being introduced to
Archibald Pitcairne, a remarkable gentleman. The church
clock chimed. James took his timepiece out of his waistcoat
pocket. A present from Andrew, and keeping good time.

It was not difficult to find his way to the Greping Office
where Pitcairne held his consultations. Below the Pillars
past St Giles, he had said. James followed a woman carrying
a sickly child, and dragging another. He overtook them.
A man with a limp entered a passage. James followed him
down a stair, groping his way in the dark. This was why they
called it the Greping Office. He eased his way through a
small gathering in the lobby at the bottom.

'Miss Morton?' A thin strip of light from a small window
shone on her face. 'Are you unwell?'

'I'm well, thank you. It's Jean's bairn who's sick.'

James smiled. He studied the face of the child before she buried it within the folds of Louise's skirt.

'I'm looking for the physician, Archibald Pitcairne,' he said.

Louise pointed to a closed door. James knocked and popped his head into the chamber. It was a wee room with one window. A lamp and the soft glow of the fire added extra light. The patient, a frail old man, sat in an armchair. Pitcairne and two gentlemen were in discussion around the table.

'Ah, good to see you again, lad.' Pitcairne rose, extended his hand, and indicated an empty chair. He took a sheet of paper and scribbled a note, then handed it to the old man. 'This mixture should settle your stomach. Take as often as you need, when you feel discomfort.'

James led the old man out.

The physician introduced him to the two other students. 'Observe and learn, gentlemen,' he said.

James watched Pitcairne treat each patient with dignity and good humour. The physician at times turned his attention from the patient to fire questions at his students. James attempted to answer some, but the other two responded before him, as he thought they might. They were obviously familiar with these ailments and their symptoms. A different pattern of health and sickness here from what he noticed at the apothecary's shop. There it was often self-help and a reliance on Douglas's recipes. And he had doubts about some of those.

At the end of the clinic the students rearranged the table and chairs, and put the curfew over the fire. James followed them to John's Coffee House. The warm smell of coffee was the same, but this time there were no hostile glances from the patrons as there had been on his first visit here two weeks ago. Now he was clean-shaven, wearing a waistcoat with touches of silver embroidery, and in the company of Pitcairne and friends.

James sipped the warm coffee and leaned back.

'I suggest you start a daily journal for your own information,' Pitcairne said. 'If you don't already have one.'

'I kept a notebook with me at all times when I was at sea,' James said. 'I have records of plants and their curative properties. We often had time ashore for exploration. I have notes of tropical illnesses and their remedies. I have—'

'Excellent. I see you are a gentleman with great curiosity. Record your observations carefully. Phthisis, flux, fever and smallpox are the most common illnesses here. Stomach problems in poor folk are the result of poor diet or bad preparation of food. We try to correct the faults in the habits of patients if we can. You will notice that sometimes complaints have their origin in a man's trade. I don't need to mention the conditions affecting mariners. These you know. Oh, and in whore houses in Edinburgh and Leith, some of the women aren't clean.'

Pitcairne took some books from his satchel, and passed them to James. 'As physicians we are aiming to understand the workings of the body. This morning the practice of medicine. Now the study.'

James felt Pitcairne's eyes on him as he browsed through the books. The physician poured more coffee into his cup, took a sip, then launched into a discourse on how the application of mathematics aids understanding of the circulation of the blood. James listened closely. Much was new and refreshing.

The learned physician stopped abruptly and took out his timepiece. 'I have an appointment shortly. So I will bid you good day, gentlemen,' he said.

James strode back to his lodgings, delighted with the encouragement given by Pitcairne. He proceeded into the close, and chapped on the Morton's door. Louise greeted him.

'I'm grateful to you,' she said. 'It was what I expected. A healthy diet is what the girl needs. Jean's struggling, though, with a family of six at home. She's a widow. Her husband died at sea.'

'That must be difficult for her.' James hesitated. 'I'm here to enquire after your father's health.'

'My father—'

'There's nothing wrong with my health. I'm perfectly well,' Mr Morton shouted as he shuffled towards the door. 'I don't need any physic.'

'My father has recovered from the chill he had two weeks ago. Thank you for asking.' Louise stepped back. 'Now if you'll excuse us, we have much to do,' she said, closing the door.

James felt frustrated. He only asked, and had expected Mr Morton's attitude to have mellowed a bit. He was concerned the gentleman could have phthisis. He headed up the turnpike stair to his chamber, clutching his books. Today he had learned a lot. And he would be assisting Pitcairne with treating the poor. It was a start. His afternoon was free for studying, and later a visit to Douglas Atkins would be appropriate.

He unlocked the door of his chamber, and stopped. Jack Scarlett was sitting comfortably in his armchair, and had put the remaining lump of coal on to revive the fire.

'How did you get in?'

'Spare key.' Jack took out the key and dangled it.

James studied Scarlett's face: the scar on the left side, partially hidden by his curly wig; his cold grey eyes. He gripped his books, aware of the sweat in his palms.

'I used this room once. Like you, when I came here to start anew,' Scarlett said.

'How did you get the key?' James persisted. Perhaps from Hodges, he thought.

Scarlett offered no reply.

James walked over to the window, and placed his books on the table. His legs felt weak and were trembling. He gazed out over the rooftops. The haar on the Forth had cleared. How calm it all looked. James turned round. The soft curls on the top of Scarlett's wig were just visible above the high-backed chair. James clenched his fists. The door of his chamber was still open. Without much difficulty he could pull Scarlett from the chair, drag him to the door, and push him out. He would tumble down the stairs.

James stepped round the armchair to face Scarlett. 'What do you want?' he asked.

'I was just passing by, to present my compliments. To extend my good wishes,' Scarlett sneered. 'I thought you might have been more welcoming. Offered me some wine, perhaps.'

James walked to and fro, regarding Scarlett sideways. He turned to face him. 'Ha! You may think you have bought your way into worthy society,' he said. 'But I can tell you, you'll never succeed.' He fixed his eyes on Scarlett's. 'No one will accept you here. No one will trust you.'

'Ah, but that's where you're wrong.' Scarlett shifted in the chair and looked away. 'I have my friends. I have—'

'Ha! Friends, eh?' James walked round, positioning himself in front of the fire. 'You've a lot to learn.'

'So have you. Do you know what people are saying about you in the taverns? And whispering in polite places? Laughing…'

'No. No. You're just trying to unsettle me.' James shook his head. He gripped the side of the chimney piece.

'There are rumours – the medicines you prepare…'

'What do you want, Jack?'

Scarlett made no response. He stretched out his legs. James felt an enormous urge to kick them. Apart from the scar, Scarlett's polished appearance was that of a city gentleman and prosperous merchant.

'How did it happen that you weren't brought to justice? For the seizure of—'

'We had a letter of marque.'

'That's a lie.'

Scarlett sat upright.

'Do burgesses and lawyers know your background?' James asked. 'I think not.'

Scarlett jumped up. 'And what do your friends know about you? What if I told folk how I came to have this?' Scarlett shoved his face in front of him and touched the scar.

'But you won't,' James said, easing away from him. 'I was at your house. I noticed your portrait; the left side of your face in the shade to hide the blemish. A fancy picture on your wall doesn't make you a gentleman.'

Scarlett lunged forward and gripped James's neckcloth,

pulling it tight. He let go. James stepped back. His body began to shake.

'You're not welcome here,' James said.

'Well, I come here quite often. I expect you know that Lawson and I are partners. We—'

'Your business is with him then, not me.'

'I was meaning that you're likely to see me now and again. In passing, so to speak.'

'As little as possible, I hope,' James said, shuffling towards the door. He held it open.

'It would be nice if we could be – well, at least attempt to be agreeable. I'll see you again,' Scarlett said, hesitating at the door. 'Good day to you.'

'The key, if you please.' James held out his hand.

Scarlett took the key from his pocket and handed it back. James closed the door, and leaned against it. He was still trembling. His palms were wet and he felt a little cold. He listened carefully at the door for a few moments. He heard other footsteps, softer ones, and then a knock. It was Hodges.

'Mr Lawson is expecting you to dine, sir.'

'Aye. Of course.' James stepped to his table and rearranged his books. 'I was involved with my studies. Does he have any guests with him?'

'Aye, a gentleman of your acquaintance, sir.'

*9*

J ames followed Hodges down to Andrew's chambers on the third storey.

'Who is the dinner guest, Hodges?'

'Mr Atkins, sir.'

'Anyone else?'

'No others. You seem a little troubled, sir?'

'Not at all. Just had a busy morning,' he said. So Scarlett hadn't been invited to dine. That was a relief. Scarlett had called solely to annoy him. His wife must have informed the rogue of their meeting yesterday, and Scarlett had remembered him from their previous unfortunate encounter, an incident he had wanted to forget.

James was relieved to notice the guest was Francis Atkins, not his brother. Tom, Andrew's apprentice, was also at the table.

'James, my friend. Good of you to join us at last,' Andrew said. 'We were wondering if something had happened to you. James has a large appetite, and is not inclined to miss a meal.'

'My apologies for lateness,' James said. Hodges held out a chair. He quickly took his seat at the table.

'Pleased to see you again, James.' Francis Atkins smiled.

'And you,' James said. 'So, that day I first met you in the tavern, you knew the residence of my friend.'

Francis coloured deeply, and Andrew shot James a warning look. He regretted his comment immediately. It was rude. It was obvious that Andrew and Francis were acquaintances or friends of long standing. He sensed that Andrew was on more favourable terms with Francis than with his brother. From what he knew of Douglas, that came as no surprise.

Mrs Hodges brought in steaming hot mutton and cabbage on silver platters. Her husband served James with a generous glass of claret. James helped himself to a large chunk of bread. His eyes took in the silver dishes on the sideboard.

'Gentlemen, I suggest we propose a toast,' Andrew said. 'To the health of my good friend, James Lightfoot.' He raised his glass. 'We wish him well here in our great city, now that he has returned, and intends to make Edinburgh his home.'

'Thank you,' James replied.

'You are a little on edge James?' Andrew whispered.

'I've had an interesting morning,' James said. He sipped the warm claret. 'Most stimulating. I had the privilege of attending Archibald Pitcairne's clinic. I can tell you, my experience with him has exceeded all my expectations. And he has kindly given me a loan of some of his books. He has—'

'Excellent, James.' Andrew grinned and thumped him on the back.

'You must come to my shop. We have a wide stock of learned publications,' Francis said. 'As well as books and pamphlets on items of topical interest.'

'Thank you. I will.' James put down his glass, warming to the bookseller's suggestion. He poked at the mutton with a silver fork. 'I apologise for my ill-chosen comment. You were right to be wary of my intentions – a stranger in town. I must have looked, well, a little odd in the tavern, the day I arrived in Edinburgh.'

Francis smiled and inclined his head in acceptance.

'Francis will try to lead you into political discourse,' said Andrew. 'Beware of party alignment, James. As for myself, I firmly believe a man of commerce should have no party allegiance. Trade is his priority. For success he must foster good relations with all clients.'

'Quite so,' Francis said. 'But no one is entirely neutral. We all have ideas and opinions. Is that not so? It's my business to publish them and encourage readership.'

'Radical pamphlets, James. To distract you from your studies,' Andrew replied. He was still acting like an elder brother. But what was the secret letter, if not political intrigue? But then he said he was the postmaster. Another way of making money. Ambition and profit always uppermost in Andrew's mind perhaps.

'My reading for now will be on physic and mathematics. I have no time for political pamphlets. I will study—' James said.

'More claret, James?' Andrew reached over the table to fill his glass.

A loud pounding at the door interrupted the conversation. George, the young apothecary's apprentice, rushed in.

'There's a crowd at the shop,' George said. He stood still, looking ill at ease, casting his eyes around the table. The company had stopped eating. All eyes were on the lad. 'Beg pardon, Mr Lawson, sir, for the intrusion. They say that my father has been charging too much for treatments. They say... They say his preparations are bad; his methods dishonourable.' The boy stood erect.

Francis stood up. 'If you would excuse me. I thank you for your hospitality.'

'Please stay. Your brother brings misfortune on himself. His gaming habits; his fondness of the bottle – who knows what underhand dealings he pursues?' Andrew said. 'Let the magistrates deal with him.'

George strode across to the table. 'I will not hear such utterances about my father.'

'Your father is a wastrel. It is a wonder that he still has the apothecary shop,' Andrew retorted.

The boy looked as though he was about to reply. But he turned and strode out, his footsteps clattering down the stairs.

Andrew leaned back and rubbed his chin. 'Francis, may I suggest you see my lawyer, Walter Duff. He'll know the best course of action. His wife and children deserve some consideration. They suffer for the deeds of the unfortunate man.'

'Thank you, I will,' Francis said.

James watched Francis leave, feeling some regret. He had anticipated some interesting conversation. From what he could gather, Francis was an avid reader, and must have a fund of knowledge. He would know about recent publications. He wondered if any adventurers had recently published accounts of their discoveries. If so, he would like to read about their journeys.

Andrew had risen and brought a bottle to the table. Tom shook his head, declining the offer of more wine. The apprentice rose and took his leave. Hodges cleared the table and withdrew. James stretched his legs under the table, feeling cosy. The wine soothed and comforted his mind.

'This is a most unfortunate affair, James,' Andrew said. 'Not a good start for you.'

'It's not my problem,' James said. 'As you said, Douglas Atkins is the creator of his own misfortunes.'

'Hmm… Though I fear it affects you. I would advise you to develop a good relationship with Archibald Pitcairne. He's a fine gentleman to have on your side.'

'Yes. I agree.' James paused. 'Do you really have no political leanings?'

'I have none. None at all,' Andrew said. 'These are dangerous times, James. There are those who may seek to influence you, for their own ends. Political will is often combined with fierce personal ambition. You must be on your guard at all times.'

'I am not as naive as you may think.'

'Perhaps not. But you must establish your reputation, and develop acquaintances with worthy gentlemen.'

James nodded. 'I mean to. With hard work and diligence.'

'Excellent.'

For the rest of the afternoon, Andrew related accounts of his recent ventures, and descriptions of some of the honourable gentlemen he had traded with, smiling all the while at his own successes. He spoke little of his family. His father had died two years ago, and his elder brother had inherited and now managed the estate.

Eventually Andrew glanced at the clock, and rose from the table. 'I have an appointment in a few minutes.' He guided James to the door. 'We must meet sometime to have a fencing bout.'

'That would be grand. Though you will find me a poor match in a scrap.'

'I could arrange some tuition for you. I know a fencing master who comes highly commended,' Andrew said.

James shook his head. 'Not at the moment. Later, perhaps. When I have the means to pay.' He didn't know when that would be.


James took a piece of paper and drew a diagram to represent the circulation of the blood. Then he drew a line through his work, and crumpled the paper into a ball. He pushed his chair back, stood up and stretched. He gazed out the window at the Forth. The hills beyond were clear and sharp. In the past week since Pitcairne had loaned him the books on physic, he had been busy reading at any opportunity. He closed the books and put them aside. It was time for a break. A brisk walk, to clear his head.

He heard footsteps, and then a loud chap at his door. Hodges walked in.

'Mr Duff here to see you, sir,' Hodges said. He moved forward and whispered in his ear, 'I expect it's about the unfortunate Mr Atkins.'

James frowned. He had put all thoughts of complaints about medicines from his head. These troubles were not his.

'Come away in, Mr Duff,' he said. 'It's a pleasure to make your acquaintance.'

'Good to see you at last, sir. I am sorry to trouble you.'

'It's no trouble, sir. Please be seated.'

James indicated the fireside chair. He pulled across a stool and sat facing the lawyer. Mr Duff was a man of middle age with a permanent frown on his forehead as if he had grave news to tell. He seemed uncertain how to start. His fingers moved across the document case on his lap. He took out some papers, and placed them on top of the case.

'As you know I am Andrew Lawson's family lawyer,' Mr Duff said. 'I do know a little about you. You attended the University of Edinburgh, and then found employment as an assistant to a ship's surgeon, and have been overseas. Am I right?'

'Yes.'

'And now you wish to take examinations to practise as a physician.' Mr Duff removed his spectacles from his pocket and polished them with a cloth before putting them on. He glanced over his papers. 'When you returned, you started work with Mr Atkins.' Mr Duff took his spectacles off again and peered at James, as if waiting for a response.

'That's correct.' James wished he would come straight to the point. He was impatient to resume his work.

Mr Duff put his spectacles on again and shuffled the papers on his lap. 'You will be pleased to hear that the dispute over the medicines has been resolved, for now anyway. The matter concerned some of the apothecary's own preparations. It appeared that some customers complained the mixtures have been too complex and too expensive. Your name had been mentioned on two of the letters of complaint.'

James took the two letters and studied them. 'These only refer to me being in attendance at the shop. I did not arrange dispensing of the medicines.'

The lawyer's large brown eyes held his gaze.

'Are you suggesting that I'm to blame?' James asked.

'You were working there, assisting the apothecary.'

'I followed instructions on preparation. I have no knowledge of costs.'

'Indeed. But as someone studying to be a qualified physician you do have a responsibility for fairness and good practice.'

James did not like his attitude, especially his emphasis on the word 'qualified'.

'Young man. I'm not trying to make things difficult. Pitcairne appears to think highly of you on first slight acquaintance. This is just as well, because gossip about you is not good. It has been said that you have been on a pirate ship, that you arrived here suddenly and have taken to wandering around undesirable areas of Leith. These rumours are more serious than the business of Atkins' medicines, which are the responsibility of the apothecary.'

'These accusations are unfair. Though I cannot think why there are some persons who think badly of me. I've been here such a short time.'

'You may have upset someone of influence and power.'

'But I haven't met anyone of influence and power.' James stood up and wandered around the room.

Mr Duff put his papers in his bag, and leaned back. 'There is a proposal which may make life more comfortable for you, and might improve your reputation – at least in some areas. With your permission, the Incorporation of Surgeons would like you to consider working with them on, let's say, observing the practices of apothecaries.'

'Me?'

'Aye. You're the ideal person to look into the practices of prescribing. You're not a Master of the Incorporation, nor a member of the College of Physicians, nor an apothecary. You have the advantage of not being attached to a particular faction. And you have some knowledge of physic.'

'I won't agree to anything unless I know exactly what's involved.'

'I'll explain.' Mr Duff took out his snuffbox and took a pinch. 'For some time, Pitcairne has been concerned about complexity of prescriptions. And about apothecaries selling their own preparations, often at exaggerated prices, and made with dubious ingredients. He would appreciate some help in making observations discreetly, you understand; taking notes, as a student.' Mr Duff sneezed into a large kerchief, and mopped his brow.

James was finding this hard to take in. Any more involvement might make his position worse.

'Keep a diary and send regular reports. I'll do my best to see that you're not implicated in any dispute. This is an offer I urge you to accept.'

# 10

No one was in attendance when James arrived at Atkins' shop. A frail old man leaned against the bench. His red, watery eyes gazed at James.

James called, 'George!'

The young apprentice rushed forward from somewhere at the back of the shop. James frowned.

'Not my fault, sir,' the boy said. 'My uncle, he detained me... he...'

'Please attend to the gentleman,' James said.

James glanced at the dispensing bench and shook his head. Spillages of white powder, used bottles, loose papers. This would not do. He had been managing the shop since Douglas had disappeared, but he couldn't be present all the time. Andrew had coaxed him into taking care of the shop, as a further way to enhance his reputation. Thinking it would be for a short interlude, he had agreed. It had been eight weeks now since the allegations of overcharging, and there had been no sign of Douglas. No one knew where he was. His brother had said vaguely that Douglas often disappeared without notice. No one was concerned, as if running away from trouble was a normal course of action for the apothecary.

James heard muffled voices in conversation from the back of the shop. It had been a productive morning assisting Pitcairne with his consultations, but he felt instinctively that things were about to change for the worse. He found Francis and two men he didn't know perched on the bench in the small chamber at the back, amid rows of upturned dried flowers hanging from the ceiling, and bundles of parcels, recently delivered, under the bench.

'Ah, James – we've just been discussing the seizure of the *Worcester*,' Francis said.

'You should not distract George, and allow him to leave the shop unattended,' James said.

The two men leaped from the bench and made a quick exit. Francis followed James into the dispensary.

'James, you haven't heard?' His eyes peered into James's. 'No, I don't suppose you have.'

'I've been busy.' James took a cloth and wiped the bench, carefully removing the spillages. 'I've work to do, even if you haven't.' He moved aside empty bottles, making a clear space.

'I have been working too. Let me explain. This will interest you. A small trader, the *Worcester*, has been seized—'

'I was saying, I've been busy, with many duties as well as this shop,' James said. He studied a recipe that George was working on. He rummaged around the papers looking for receipt of payments. The boy was obviously still not giving consideration to the importance of keeping accurate records. 'I've taken on additional work treating the poor at

Paul's Work.' James was careful not to mention his work on compiling reports on medicines. He was still under obligation to continue with covert investigations. 'Where's your brother hiding anyway? You must have some idea.'

'I've already told you, I don't know,' Francis said. 'He'll be back. He was quite upset. The complaints about his preparations, amongst other problems. Anyway, about the ship—'

'I don't think much of people who run off leaving others to—'

'Aye, James.' Francis took a deep breath. 'I was going to tell you about this English vessel that has been taken.'

'English vessel? I thought the navy were supposed to be protecting shipping from the French, not seizing English ships,' James said. He looked down the list of medicines to be dispensed.

'It was captured by the navy on behalf of the Company of Scotland,' Francis said.

'Oh.'

'This vessel, the *Worcester*, has been sailing down the east coast on its own. It's now anchored off Burntisland. That's about as much as I know.'

'When did you find out?'

'This morning. One of the pleasures of having a garret is watching shipping activity on the Forth. I sent one of my lads to Leith to find out more. He's just come back,' Francis said. He edged towards the door of the shop.

'Has this anything to do with the taking of the *Annandale*?' James said, following him.

'I'm going to Leith myself. I'll try to find out, if I can, if this ship has been seized in retaliation. There's been much anger against the English East India Company. This is bad politically, you must realise. You would expect traders to show restraint. Politicians are trying to secure more freedom of trade for us.'

'Do you have any idea how the crew of the *Annandale* were treated in March?' James asked. He turned to face Francis. The pamphleteer's eyes were wide open, and his face blank. 'They were abused as if they were robbers and pirates. Pressed into the English Navy.'

'Aye, and I heard the dispute about the *Annandale* still rumbles on. I'll pack a bag to take with me, in case I stay over in Burntisland,' Francis said. 'Shall we take a lookout?'

James followed him into the next close, and into the turnpike stair. At the top, Francis unlocked a door, then proceeded up a further stair to the garret. James watched him open a cabinet and stuff some personal items into a satchel. He crossed to the window and drew back the shutters. From over the rooftops of the tenements, James gazed at the estuary of the Forth. He took out his glass and scanned the view.

'This is an unfortunate affair,' Francis said. 'There is some hatred of the English. That shouldn't be. They are our neighbours.'

'I must make haste to the shop,' James said, remembering his responsibilities. He wanted to put thoughts about his experiences on board ship behind him. He was beginning to see that there must be more to anti-English feelings than disputes among merchant companies.

At the shop Louise was being served by George. She wore a pretty, light green dress and carried a shopping basket.

'Ah, Miss Morton, a pleasure to see you again.' James smiled.

'I've come for the jelly for my father,' she said. 'He doesn't want to admit it, but I think he finds your recipe helps ease his discomfort.' She sighed. 'I wish he would give you credit for your care and attention.'

'I regret I can do little. His condition is very advanced. Phthisis is such a terrible illness.'

'I know,' Louise said. 'As you recommended, I have been giving him more milk, and trying to encourage him to eat what he can.'

James took the jar of jelly from George and handed it over. His hand and Louise's touched briefly. Louise looked up, and their eyes met. He noticed a faint blush on her cheeks. She appeared reluctant to go.

'Andrew said you were pleased with the coat and waistcoat, and that you chose the woollen cloth he recommended. It's warm and soft, yet hard-wearing. Good for winter. He said, too,' Louise paused, 'that you may wish for some shirts. I could make them for you; and do some alterations if you like. I mean...' She stopped suddenly, and shuffled towards the door.

'That would be grand.' He could hardly afford to pay her, but knew she needed the work. Anyway, the more smartly dressed he was, the more confident he would feel, without being showy of course. He added, 'I will come and see you about it, but not now.'

'Yes, please do, any time. My father doesn't mind me doing extra work.'

*I'll bet he doesn't,* James thought. He watched as she left the shop. *She needs a husband to look after her, and take her away from drudgery.* He sighed.

Louise meandered through the busy market, carefully avoiding begging bairns and aggressive vendors, as more people emerged to enjoy the warm day. The prospect of mending clothes for James was a delight, and a welcome change from ladies' dresses. James looked like quite the handsome gentleman now, an improvement on the rough seaman who'd arrived at her doorstep three months ago. It was pleasant to spend time wandering about the stalls, eyeing up linen table covers with crewel embroidery, lace cuffs and collars, ribbons in many colours – different patterns and textures.

'How nice to see your lovely smile.' A voice came from behind as she turned into the darkness of the close.

'Good day, Mr Brand,' Louise said.

'Call me Henry, please.'

'Good day, Henry.'

'That's better.' His eyes wandered all over her body. 'You're looking radiant today. You are well?'

Louise felt the heat rising in her cheeks. 'Thank you – I'm very well.' His gaze unsettled her.

'I called earlier and your father said you were out,' he said as he pulled out a small package from his pocket. 'This is for you.'

She hesitated before holding out her hand to take it. She had already sent back gifts from Mr Turnbull, and eventually he had stopped pursuing her, much to her father's frustration. And now here was another gentleman with gifts.

'Please open it.'

Louise removed the paper to find a beautiful silver brooch. She looked up. 'I can't accept this. It's too grand.' She handed it back. Before he could say anything, she turned, opened her house door, and closed it behind her without a backward glance.

She was not long inside before she heard a knock. Jean opened the door. Henry Brand pushed past Jean, and strode straight into the middle of the parlour.

'I'm sorry if I offended you,' he said.

Jean walked over to attend to the fire. Louise faced Mr Brand. His expression was serious.

'Please, Mr Brand—'

'Henry.'

'Please – let me explain. I do not wish to give the wrong impression. I mean...'

'I understand, I think.' He stood, and looked down at the gift in his hand. He wandered round the room avoiding her eyes, appearing to consider what to do next.

There was a gentle chapping at the door.

'James Lightfoot is here to see you,' Jean said, showing James into the parlour.

James met with the cold stare of a tall, handsome gentleman as he stepped into the parlour. Dark brown hair with thick eyebrows and brown eyes. The man slipped a small packet into his pocket, as if wanting to hide it.

'I believe we haven't met – Henry Brand.'

'James Lightfoot.'

'You must excuse us, sir,' Brand said, moving forward towards Louise and gently directing her to an armchair. 'Miss Morton is tired.'

Louise sat down.

'I've come to see Miss Morton regarding some business,' James said. He was prepared to stand his ground. His eyes sought Louise's and he calmly waited to gain her attention.

'I am a little weary, gentlemen,' Louise said without looking at either of them. 'I will see you tomorrow, James, and Mr Brand – Henry – thank you for your kindness.'

James hesitated. 'Your father?'

'My father has slipped out with a friend, for some fresh air,' Louise said. She gave James a sideways glance.

Jean moved to the door and held it open.

'After you, Mr Brand,' James said. He gave Jean a broad smile.

Mr Brand strode towards the turnpike stair, and pushed the door. It held firm. He fumbled for his keys.

'Allow me, please,' James said, pushing the stair door open. It was stiff. The back door was not locked. He found this was sometimes the custom during the day, though not always. He stepped inside first. 'Is your stay here a short one, Mr Brand?'

'I took up lodgings with Mrs Grant three months ago. Very pleasant here indeed, once a visitor becomes accustomed to the crowded streets and the smells.'

'Ah, yes. The smells.' James climbed to the second storey, and turned round to face Brand in front of the door to Mrs Grant's. 'I am surprised our paths haven't crossed. Like you I took up residence here three months ago.'

Brand was examining his keys. He shuffled from one foot to the other, anxious to pass, but James gave him a few more seconds of discomfort before stepping aside.

Then James made his way to Andrew's apartment on the third storey. He was ready to dine with Andrew. This had become a habit – the cost was included in the rent for his room, Andrew had said. Success seemed to come Andrew's way. For all his friendliness, though, Andrew did not discuss details of his business deals with him. The talk was general and polite. He supposed Andrew's weakness for gambling seemed not to get the better of him. He made friends easily, and obviously had the wit and intelligence to manage his affairs.

James remembered that Andrew had promised to give him some fencing practice − not that either of them had much free time.

The table setting for one occupied an insignificant corner of the enormous table. Mrs Hodges' back could be seen as she worked in the kitchen. She turned round.

'The master is not at home. Please help yourself.'

James was disappointed. He would have liked Andrew's company, and his thoughts on Henry Brand. He viewed the selection of cold meats, cheese and bread on the sideboard. He filled a glass from a flagon of wine, and took a seat.

He was well looked after here at mealtimes. James leaned back, feeling full once again. A satisfying meal was a great pleasure. He glanced at the clock. Andrew probably knew about everyone in the neighbourhood. His servants, too, would be amply supplied with local gossip. He decided to ask Mrs Hodges about Brand, while she was removing plates from the table.

'I've never met Mr Brand.' She stopped, a platter of bread in one hand and an empty dish in the other. 'My husband doesn't know him either. He's some sort of travelling merchant, I think. Though what he sells, I know not. He's been staying at Mrs Grant's lodgings. She told me he stays here for a few days trading and then goes away.' She put the plates on the corner table, and went to answer a knock on the door.

She showed Francis Atkins into the parlour.

'Please excuse me, Mr Atkins. I have to collect the children soon. Help yourself to cold meats and wine.'

Francis ignored the meats, poured a glass of wine, sat down and leaned back in the chair. He was slightly out of breath, and sat for a few minutes without saying anything. 'I was hoping to see Andrew,' he said eventually.

'I didn't think you'd be back so soon,' James said. 'Anyway, I have a question…'

'About the *Worcester*?'

'Well – no.'

Mrs Hodges hesitated at the door. 'I think Mr Brand writes history as well. He was asking about the opinions of people, so that he can write a book.'

'Who are we talking about?' Francis said after Mrs Hodges left.

'One of Mrs Grant's lodgers, Henry Brand. A handsome gentleman who is actively pursuing Miss Morton, at this very instant.'

'Oh!'

'I don't like him. Don't like the way he is befriending Louise Morton.'

'Not jealous are you?'

'No. Of course not.'

'So he's a writer?' Francis frowned, and studied his glass of wine. He looked up and smiled. 'Anyway, where is Andrew? I came to tell him the latest gossip, though he might know already. The captain and first mate of the *Worcester* have taken lodgings in Edinburgh.'

'And what about the *Worcester*?'

'To be demobilised at Burntisland, so that she can't be

taken by the English East India Company.' Francis took a sip of wine. 'This won't help. Politicians are seeking royal assent on the resolution that nomination of a successor will not proceed until there is an agreement on commerce. Formally seizing the *Worcester* won't help.'

'Neither did legal action against the *Annandale*.'

'Anyway, I'm sure the Queen will be favourable.'

'You think so?'

'Well, she needs the men for the army.'

James stood up. 'I have more important matters to attend to. I should go back to the shop.'

## 11

DECEMBER 1704

James would rather have eaten in the tavern, but it was Francis' idea to invite Henry Brand to dine with them. They chose a hostelry where gentlemen displayed their prosperity in their dress and polite manners. The rich smell of coffee and the warm glow of the crackling fire set a cosy atmosphere. There was no slackening of activity here. Over the winter months there were always business deals of one sort or another, Francis had told him.

Brand entered, nodding to several gentlemen in the room. He appeared comfortable and relaxed in the company of these worthy merchants and lawyers, so much so that James was beginning to doubt his early suspicions of the man. Brand removed his long, dark blue woollen coat, revealing a tailored matching waistcoat and breeches. He smiled as he took his seat. He did indeed show the ability to charm anyone.

A servant brought huge bowls of steaming chicken broth. James warmed his hands on his bowl, then slowly supped the tasty soup. Brand took the lead in the conversation. His business prospered. He was happy to tell them so. He had met many intelligent gentlemen here in Scotland.

'I hadn't realised the country was so civilised,' Brand remarked.

James choked. 'The broth is hot. Indeed, we have advanced a long way from barbarism. Learning and refinements of art flourish here.'

'And throughout the whole of Scotland—' Francis began.

'The current situation of national poverty is most unfortunate,' Brand said.

Francis frowned and James's attention was beginning to wander as the man blethered on and on.

Then Brand turned to James. 'I believe you visit Mr Morton regularly, as his physician,' he said.

'I am not his physician, though I wish to take examinations someday,' James said, delighted to have a chance to speak. 'I fear Morton is very poorly. His weakness and shortness of breath cause great alarm.'

'There is no cure?'

'Sadly, there is none. I prescribe black spleenwort jelly, but I'm not sure how effective it is. Rest and eating well, plenty of milk are recommended. I give Mr Morton chest massage as well.'

Brand nodded. 'Miss Louise is most attentive to her father's needs. A very accomplished lady. She must have many admirers. I am pleased, though, that she has chosen me as her companion. I would dearly love to escort her, should she wish, and see her place in society fulfilled. But that is not to be. She is most diligent in her care for William.'

'I'm sure Miss Louise finds comfort as a loving and dutiful daughter,' Francis said. 'I have heard it reported that you are a writer, Mr Brand. As a publisher, I would be most interested to know more. Do you write books or pamphlets?'

Brand shifted in his seat. 'As with trading, I often work on different writing ventures at the same time.'

'Such as?' Francis asked.

Brand blinked. 'Mainly essays on travel.' He began to fidget.

'Travel journals are always popular,' Francis said.

The servant cleared the bowls away, and presented platters of salted beef, vegetables and bread.

James eyed the selection of dishes. 'I have some jottings and sketches of the various plant varieties I encountered on my travels—'

Brand stabbed a portion of beef and cut it into small pieces. 'I, too, have written about life in other countries. I will show you.'

Francis smiled. 'Excellent. We would be happy to view your work after dinner.'

'I have an appointment, but, yes, I would be delighted to show you my publications. Some other time that suits.'

'How about two days hence?' Francis asked.

Brand nodded. James smiled inwardly at Francis's persistence. It was a quality he admired in the printer. It was his way of finding interesting and contentious stories to publish, and of exposing charlatans as well.

'So, you see, your fears about Brand have little foundation,' Francis said after Brand had left.

'I suppose so. But Mrs Hodges thinks he's writing about us.'

'And not favourably, it would seem. Though he knows now we're not barbarians.' Francis grinned.

'He's English and—'

'And might be seeking feelings and opinions of Scots.'

'So he's not charmed you?'

'Of course not. But enough of Brand. I've heard news from friends in Leith about the *Worcester*. The captain, first mate and some of the crewmen have been arrested.'

'The charges?'

'Piracy, robbery and murder. Crewmen were seized in Burntisland. Others were taken in Leith. Key witnesses have been detained at Edinburgh Castle. All this in response to the news from England of the sanctioning of the seizure of the *Annandale* by the Lord High Admiral of England.'

'On what grounds?'

'Scottish vessels trading in breach of English monopolies. So relations between Scotland and England are worsening.'

A biting wind from the north greeted them as they emerged from the coffee house. James watched Francis head off to pursue news of the crew of the *Worcester*, or to write up another pamphlet of great importance, in his eyes anyway. He was always full of restless energy, and it was contagious. James felt edgy, too; unsettled.

James turned into the courtyard at the back of Andrew's tenement. Andrew had invited a large party of merchants to dine. He saw some of the gentlemen emerging from the building, merry with drink, but still sensible enough. Andrew was among them deep in discussion with Jack Scarlett. James hadn't seen Scarlett in the last seven months, thankfully. Now his enemy was glaring at him. Andrew waved James over.

'A final meeting, James, before we all depart in separate directions,' Andrew said, stepping between James and Scarlett.

'Not much trade over the winter then?'

'There will be some business,' Andrew replied. 'But with the state of the nation so impoverished, so little money around, trade will be slow.'

James noticed that Scarlett had retreated, but continued to stare at him. Andrew wandered around, shook hands and bid farewell to his guests.

Andrew turned to James. 'I'm free for the rest of the day,' he said. 'Shall we engage in some fencing practice?' Andrew gently gripped James by the elbow and eased him away from Scarlett. 'I will fetch two small swords from the closet. I suggest Calton Hill. We have to make haste. There's only an hour of daylight left.'

Heavy clouds gathered as they strode down Leith Wynd. The wind had lessened. It was almost dusk by the time they stumbled up the hill. James concentrated on his footing. He was less familiar than Andrew with the paths. They reached a grassy spot.

'You never mention your family,' James began. 'Do you correspond regularly with your brother?'

'We rarely write.' Andrew exercised his wrist and arm. 'I can't even recall my last visit.'

'There are rumours he has substantial debts.'

'As have many lairds. Those without debts are a rare breed.'

'Like yourself.' A sudden gust of wind caused James to sway slightly to the right, giving Andrew an advantage.

'My business is moneylending. A more comfortable situation when others owe you.'

'And Jack Scarlett?

'I don't enquire into his affairs other than what concerns our partnership.'

Andrew gave an unexpected thrust. James parried, stumbled and almost lost his balance. Andrew stood poised, waiting for him to recover.

'Speaking of the affairs of others, does Francis Atkins have any news of his brother?' Andrew asked.

'No,' James said. 'Francis never mentions him.' He held his hand up, and shook his head. He needed a rest from play.

'Does it not strike you as odd that Francis doesn't appear concerned at his absence?'

'Hmm… He said that Douglas sometimes travels about the country selling medicines.'

'He'll return soon then, now that winter is upon us.' Andrew paced up and down, eager for James to resume play.

'The sooner the better.'

After a few practice bouts James's confidence grew, but he knew he was no match for Andrew.

'Have you had any dealings with Henry Brand?' James asked. He was tired, and his legs began to wobble.

'No. I am not on familiar terms with him. I suggest just one more turn. We should finish soon. I shouldn't like to be on this hill after dark,' Andrew said.


A week had passed and Brand appeared to have forgotten about showing James and Francis his writings. James sought him out at his lodgings and nearby taverns, and was vaguely disappointed that Brand was not to be seen. He had a free afternoon. A proposed visit to a house at Fountain Close had been cancelled. That, too, was disappointing. The College of Physicians had recently purchased the property. It would have been interesting to know what plans they had for it.

The bitter wind stung his hands and face. The dark, unsettled skies suggested heavy rain or a snowstorm was imminent. He was glad of his new winter clothing. He hadn't forgotten the unpredictable and sometimes harsh Scottish weather.

James called to see Mr Morton. He was pleased they were on friendly terms at last. He enjoyed the pleasant companionship of Louise and her father. But sadly the invalid's health was deteriorating rapidly. Mr Morton's bed had been moved to the parlour; near the fire, with his armchair placed nearby. The fire had gone down. James poked life into the coals and put on another lump. He rubbed his hands to warm them.

'I'm poorly the day. Feeling the cold,' Mr Morton said. 'Having a restful day in bed.'

'How's your appetite?'

'Not good, laddie. Not good.'

'Is Miss Louise here?'

'She's gone with Henry Brand to have tea with one of his partners, somewhere on Castlehill.'

'So you've been on your own?'

'Jean's gone for messages. She'll be back soon.' He glanced at the clock.

'I could stay with you until she's back. That is, if you wish for company.'

Mr Morton nodded. James adjusted the cushions and bedcovers. The frail body had little flesh. In the seven months since James had met him, it seemed that Morton's body had aged several years.

'That's grand,' Mr Morton said, and leaned back with a soft sigh.

James drew a chair closer to the bed. Morton's eyes were seeking his.

'I have been thinking about Louise. About who will look after her when I'm gone.' He coughed. 'My thoughts are turning to Henry Brand. He's right for her. What do you say?'

'I have no opinion,' James said, not meeting his eyes.

'A most agreeable gentleman.' Mr Morton was waiting for James's response.

'He is pleasant, I suppose,' James said.

'He's a man of considerable means. His business prospers. Full of enthusiasm and good cheer. What more could a young lady wish for? I have heard he has an estate—'

James heard a key being inserted into the lock, and a rustle as the door opened.

'Ah, that'll be Jean,' Mr Morton said.

Louise stepped in. James rose, and rushed forward to take her basket and parcel. She removed her cloak. James stared at her russet woollen dress with lace cuffs. How mature she looked.

'I thank you.' She blushed as their eyes met. She frowned. 'Is there…'

'There is no cause for concern, Miss Louise,' James said. 'Your father and I were enjoying good crack.'

His eyes followed her as she hung her cloak over a chair, and set the basket on the table.

'I didn't mean to be out for long,' Louise began. 'It would have been impolite to excuse myself.'

'I understand,' Mr Morton said.

'Henry has many acquaintances and partners now. He has made his name in society here in such a short time.'

'My dear, I am so pleased.' Mr Morton closed his eyes.

'I was most impressed by the way he conversed and entertained the company with his stories. His sense of humour. He held everyone entranced.'

James moved towards the door.

'No, please stay and take a dish of tea with us, James.' Her soft brown eyes held his gaze. She took his arm, and guided him back to a chair.

'That would be grand,' James said, unable to resist, despite a sinking feeling.

'I will see to my purchases. Henry bought me green silk and matching ribbons. Look.' She opened a parcel. 'And this.' She unwrapped a small paper to reveal a pearl necklace.

'He must have a long purse,' James said. He was struggling to control a growing anger.

'I must have a gown made with the silk,' she said, holding it up.

'The colour suits you,' James said.

She smiled.

'Perhaps I won't stay for tea,' James said, edging towards the door. He strode out and through the close, bounding up the turnpike to his own chamber.

## 12

J ames looked at the grubby scrap of paper George had shoved into his hand. *Come at once, bad foot injury*, the note said. It would soon be dark. James still had to visit others as well before the end of the day. He made haste, almost knocking over an old lady as he left the shop. He had only a vague idea where to find his patient, a dour man claiming to be not fit enough for employment, living with his sister. The clouds had thickened and there was a chill in the air. He stepped into the unnamed close, pausing briefly to let his eyes adjust to the dimness. The stench made him retch. A dog growled from behind a closed door. He skidded on something greasy. If he lost his balance here his clothes would stink from the muck lying around.

The back gate at the bottom of the close was locked. A cellar door stood partially open. He keeked inside. The smell of wine hit his nostrils. There was a faint murmur of voices from within. He edged his way inside. In the distance he glimpsed a faint light. He picked his way along, past boxes containing bottles stacked in orderly fashion. He crept round a corner.

He froze, taking in the scene. Four men were huddled over a board, intent on a card game. In the feeble light, he noticed empty bottles lying around. The men stopped playing and stared at him. James moved closer. He recognised Douglas; half fou, dirty neckcloth loose, his brown checked waistcoat soiled. James circled the players, examining the cards in each pair of hands. The apothecary was losing. The others each had a pile of coin.

'I insist you explain this intrusion, sir,' one of them said. He wore a fine coat with lace cuffs and cravat. The silver trimming of his waistcoat sparkled faintly in the dim light.

'My humble apologies…' The words were sticking in James's throat. All these months, while he'd been working in the apothecary's shop, Douglas had been hiding here. He felt hot with anger. 'I was looking for the residence of—'

'James, allow me to introduce… to introduce… my good friend…' Douglas began.

James set down his bag. He leaned forward, grabbed Douglas by the collar, and pulled him up. 'You're coming home, now.' How could Douglas do this? His wife and children were at home, unaware he was here in Edinburgh, gaming with reprobates.

The men stood up, and one drew his dirk. James lunged towards him and sent the weapon flying. It disappeared behind a box. He found he was being tossed between two strong men. He staggered, steadied himself, and raised his head. Someone had come to his aid. James found his strength returning. He was grabbed from behind. He twisted round and dealt a firm blow to his opponent, sending him back against the wall. He turned and came face to face with Jack Scarlett.

'I thank you,' James said.

'My pleasure.' Scarlett smirked. 'You give a hard punch.'

James shivered. He recalled a scene from long ago. The two of them. He knew what incident Scarlett was referring to; when he had given Scarlett a hard blow. But now, in a turn of fortune, his old foe was on his side. James rubbed his arms, and looked around. The well-dressed gentleman had disappeared. The other two slowly picked themselves up from the floor and reached out for their money. James let them slip away. Douglas had sat down, his head bent. James attempted to pull the apothecary to his feet. Scarlett stepped forward to assist.

Douglas struggled. 'You're not taking me home. Elizabeth and the children – they mustn't know.'

'You're coming with us,' James said, pushing him forward. He picked up his bag.

'Where—'

'To your brother's first. Then I have a patient to see.' He shuffled Douglas along the passage.

At the doorway, Scarlett edged out and looked up the close. There was no one around. He took out a key. James steadied Douglas against the wall. How did Scarlett happen to be on the scene? Was he acquainted with the others?

'It was fortunate you were nearby,' James said.

'I came here to inspect my goods. The cellar door was open. I heard voices.' Scarlett fiddled with the stiff lock. They dragged Douglas along the close. A door opened and a woman peered out.

'Are you the apothecary?' she asked.

'I'm his assistant.'

'You took your time.' She scowled.

James left Douglas with Scarlett, and followed her into a cold, damp chamber lit by a single lamp and a faint glow from the fire. The draught from a tiny window did little to disperse the foul human smells.

'I don't need a physic.' The voice came from the man lying in bed. 'Leave me be. I've no money to pay.'

James lit a lamp and asked the woman to hold it. The bedcover and clothes were filthy, and felt damp and greasy. There was no indication of bleeding or broken bones. The man's foot was swollen.

'You're right. You don't need a physician.'

'I told you to leave me be,' the man said to his sister.

James rubbed on some ointment. A trial preparation, part of George's apprenticeship. He passed the jar to the woman.

'Is that it?' she said.

James nodded. 'Rest, then up and about. You will be fit for work in a few weeks. No charge for the jar. A new recipe.' James picked up his bag and left.

'Do you hear that?' he heard the woman shout. 'Fit for work soon.'


The heavy clouds had disappeared when James emerged into the close. Though it was approaching dusk, there was still sufficient daylight to grope about. James hoped that Scarlett had taken Douglas to his brother's chambers. He knocked on the door of the workshop first.

The new apprentice regarded him suspiciously. 'The master's no here. He suddenly felt unwell, and has gone to bed. He's not to be disturbed.'

'I'm his brother's assistant.'

The boy opened his mouth, then closed it.

James dragged himself up to the top storey. His legs ached. He could have used some of the ointment he gave to that ungrateful man.

'How was your patient?' Francis asked, leading James into his wee chamber.

'He'll survive. A minor injury. His main affliction is a dislike of honest toil.'

'Ah. A common malady,' Francis said.

James found Douglas snoozing in Francis's armchair. Andrew was there, standing in the far corner by the window. Douglas's head jerked. He raised his eyes, fixing James with a scowl. James set down his bag and took out some powder. He spooned some into a cup, and poured in some warm water from the kettle.

'Drink this.' He shoved the cup into Douglas's hands. 'I won't tell your wife if you stay off the bottle. Francis will keep you here.'

Douglas frowned. 'I need to go—'

'You will stay here until you're cured,' James said.

'Of gaming or drink?' Andrew asked, moving forward.

'Of both, if possible,' Francis said.

'Tastes foul. What is it?' Douglas asked.

'A special preparation I used to give to seamen. Makes them vomit. Sobers them up. Subdues violent tempers.'

'Let's go, James,' Andrew said. He guided James to the door. 'Don't provoke him.'

James stooped to lift his bag. He handed Francis the jar of powder. 'Keep him here.'

Francis shrugged.

James stepped onto the landing. 'I don't know what Scarlett told you of the affray. I can tell you, though, the players were cheating.'

'Scarlett? It was my apprentice who brought him here,' Francis said.

So Scarlett was being elusive. James knew he was trouble, and would ruin all he dealt with.

'Did you know your brother was still here in Edinburgh?' James asked. 'Gaming in cellars?'

Francis lowered his eyes.

'Yes, you knew.'

'James, we must make haste,' Andrew said, pulling him to the top of the stair. 'I'm leaving tomorrow on the tide – for the far north, a part of a convoy,' Andrew said as they descended. 'There is a delicate matter I must discuss with you.'

They strode up the High Street in silence. Andrew was obviously not in good fettle. Whatever Andrew had to say, James knew his work at the dispensary must come to an end. He would be firm. He would not toil away while the apothecary wasted his life.

'Here's Miss Louise with Henry Brand,' Andrew said as they approached his house. 'She should be attending her father, not imposing a further burden on her housemaid.'

Brand paused at the entrance to the close, waiting for them. Louise pulled her faded brown cloak tightly round her shoulders. James caught her eye. She lowered her head to avoid his gaze.

'Good afternoon, gentlemen,' Brand said, eyeing the stains on James's coat. 'Well sir, I see you have been brawling. Not able to control your drink, or your temper perhaps?'

'Good afternoon,' Andrew said. 'I trust you've had a pleasant day, Miss Louise.'

'Yes, indeed we have,' Brand answered, turning towards Louise. He faced James. 'I had promised to show you my illustrations and writing of plants of the world. Unfortunately, I mistook you for a gentleman.'

'Poor sense of judgement,' Andrew said. 'But then you lack the maturity and refinement.' Andrew tugged at James's sleeve, and he felt himself being dragged into the close. He had time for a brief glance behind. Louise had turned her head towards him.

'Leave him be, James,' Andrew said. 'Let's go to my chambers.'

They ascended by the back stair. Andrew unlocked the door which led directly into his office.

'You tell me not to provoke Douglas or Henry Brand. Yet that's what you do,' James said. He winced as he eased himself into a chair. 'I had no intention of annoying Brand. I haven't the strength right now. Neither in mind nor body.'

Andrew disappeared into the main chamber, and returned with a small parcel. 'You would be doing me a service if you could give this parcel to Pitcairne tomorrow.'

James took the bundle. It was wrapped in clean linen and tied with ribbon.

'Papers for his perusal,' Andrew said. 'And some letters for his friends in Tweeddale. He is travelling south the day after tomorrow.'

James remembered the letter he was asked to deliver on his arrival in Edinburgh. He turned the package over in his hands.

'I see you are thoughtful,' Andrew said. 'Pitcairne, so I am told, corresponds with clients and friends, dispensing advice and remedies for ills. Such is his reputation far and wide, as indeed you know.'

James nodded.

'But I must ask for your discretion. You will see to it that no one else has sight of this parcel.'

## 13

Louise awoke suddenly. She opened the tiny shutter. Excited voices came from the courtyard. She remembered. This was to be the day of the executions of the three condemned men of the *Worcester*. Crowds would be gathering in Edinburgh and Leith. The trial had aroused widespread curiosity and controversy. She pulled on her dress, and hurried to her father's bedside. He was still asleep and appeared comfortable, helped by the laudanum he had taken. There had been an overnight frost, and the room was cold. She poked the fire. The parlour would soon warm up. Someone was banging at the door, at this early hour. The door creaked as she opened it and peeped into the gloom. It was Tom.

'You should avoid going out today, Miss Morton,' he said, pacing to and fro in the parlour. 'I'm just going to open the shop, but if there is trouble I'll close it.' He stopped, and regarded Louise with the hint of a smile. 'Miss Morton, I have to tell you the good news. The master is going to allow me to make a voyage on my own soon. With my own cargo. He thinks I'm ready.'

'That's grand, Tom. Oh, I'm expecting my sister to arrive here sometime. Maybe today. Can you please look out for her?'

'Aye, of course, Miss Morton.' He hesitated. 'Maybe next week, I'll be leaving. More wool has to be purchased for the venture.'

'That's good. Your mother must be pleased.' She was a widow and had hopes for his future.

'Oh yes, Miss Morton. She's pleased.'

As Tom went out, a tall, fresh-faced young man with long fair hair hovered at the doorway. 'I'm here to tell you that my mistress has sent us ahead with her accoutrements. We're just taking them to her chambers,' he said.

'Has Mary arrived then? Where is she? How is she?' Louise asked.

'She's here, and is well, Miss Morton. At the inn, having breakfast,' the boy said.

'I'll give you a hand,' Tom said.

Jean had not yet arrived, so Louise began preparing breakfast. Mary would likely be consuming a generous meal in style at the inn. It was just like Mary, to arrive with more than she needed. Despite their differences, Louise longed to see her again. Would she still be frosty? Mary had wasted no time in replying to her urgent letter. She would be staying at Mrs Grant's lodgings. The children were staying at home with the nurse.

'Miss Morton! Miss Morton!' Tom shouted from outside the open parlour window. Louise dashed into the street, but

Tom had vanished. He had shut up his shop. From the edge of the arcade her eyes scanned the market area, searching for him.

Bundles of cloth lay scattered in the street, and were being kicked about by excited bairns. A woman carrying a squawking goose shouted abuse at anyone in her way. Angry men chanted, 'No reprieve! No reprieve!' Louise spotted a sedan chair stuck in the middle of the street beside the shouting rabble. Mary was standing beside it, unable to move.

Louise hurried back to the house, grabbed pattens and edged her way into the crowd. An upturned stall had spilled linen and hosiery in front of the sedan chair. Several pairs of hands were trying to shift the mess and clear a path for Mary. A huge man with a protruding stomach bumped into Louise. She stumbled, dropped the overshoes, and fell to her knees. She scrambled around, picked up the pattens, pulling her hand away to avoid it being crushed by a heavy boot. Back on her feet again, Louise held up the overshoes in outstretched hands.

'What's happening here?' Mary shouted above the noise, as she grabbed the overshoes. A porter managed to clear a space so that Mary could sit on some bales of linen cloth to put on the pattens.

'Public executions today, my lady. People are waiting around to see if the condemned men will be given a reprieve or pardon,' Tom said, as he appeared at her side. 'The sooner it's all over one way or another, the sooner the street will be cleared and things will be back as normal.' He offered an arm to Mary, and guided her to the close. 'I don't care if the reprobates are hanged or not.'

Louise noticed that Mary's cloak was soiled, and there was a tear at the bottom. Mary asked, 'How is Father? I had to see that the children had clean linen before I left. And there was so much to do...'

Louise stopped at the entrance to the close. She turned to face Mary. Strands of hair had broken loose from her pins, and partially covered Mary's eyes. Louise tucked them under her bonnet.

'James said he has not long. Maybe only a few weeks,' Louise said.

Mary blinked and took a deep breath. 'I feared so. I wish I could have come last week. Who is James?'

'The apothecary's assistant. A kind young man. He has been most attentive. Come, Father has been longing to see you. Let's see if he's awake now.'

Louise guided Mary inside. Jean had arrived and Father was propped up in bed. Mary rushed to his bedside.

'So good to see you lass,' he said, his eyes moist.

Louise set a chair by the bed for Mary, and left them together for a while. She had to attend a meeting with Andrew about his accounts: there would be time later to hear Mary's news. Her letters had been full of details of the children; their lessons, their play, and how they grew out of their clothes. But beneath the surface Louise knew Mary was troubled.

Later in the morning Louise found Mary in her lodgings. Mrs Grant had given her the best bedchamber: three windows overlooking the street, a four-post bed, armchair, table and oak press.

'He's so thin,' Mary said, as she carefully placed a green silk dress in the press. 'His face is pale. I hardly recognised him. And so weak. He used to have lots of energy.' She turned her head away from Louise, took a handkerchief from her reticule, and dabbed her eyes. She sighed, and picked up a small bundle.

Louise watched as she carefully folded silk hose and put them in a drawer. Perched on the edge of the bed, she waited for Mary to speak. She looked older than her twenty-two years. More mature. And so like Mother. Louise supposed that caring for her own children had brought about these changes. Not so cold-hearted as the person she had been in the early years after their mother's death, when the role of mother was forced on her.

Mary sat down in an armchair at the corner of her bedchamber. 'It was a shock to see him so poorly,' she said. 'And hard for you. I had no time to come here before. I had the bairns to see to.'

'I know, but you're here now.'

'You mentioned the young man, James.'

'Yes, he's been at his bedside nearly every day,' Louise said, dragging her hand across to smooth the bedcover.

'Is he knowledgeable?'

'I believe so. He's worked as an assistant ship's surgeon.'

Mary shrugged. She stood up, opened the shutter and looked out. "There's still a crowd of people out there,' she said.

'They'll be waiting to see the prisoners brought down from the castle.'

'I had forgotten what life is like here. Riots and filth in the streets.'

'It's not so bad. Most days are quite ordinary.'

'And what about you? I expect you have met lots of eligible young men,' Mary said with the hint of a smile.

'My days are fully occupied attending to our father, and other work of course.' She didn't mean this to sound bitter.

'But you have Jean.'

'Jean is not here all the time,' Louise pointed out.

'You will have to think about your future.'

Louise stood up, aware of Mary's piercing gaze. She wandered to the window. The street was buzzing. 'I'm too busy to think about the future.'

'I do so love the latest styles. Have a close look at what I've brought with me,' Mary said, opening the press. 'You look so dull in these clothes.'

Mary spread out a scarlet satin petticoat trimmed with lace, a brightly coloured matching gown, and a dress of fine reddish-brown silk. 'This colour would suit you,' Mary said, holding up the silk gown. 'Please. It's for you.' Mary draped it over Louise's shoulders.

Louise gently ran her hands over the russet silk. 'Thank you,' she murmured. She carefully folded the gown and laid it on the table. She turned round. Mary was sitting on the bed, partly obscured by the curtain. Her hands covered her face, and her body was shaking as she sobbed. She fumbled for a handkerchief, dried her eyes and straightened her body.

'My husband has a mistress,' Mary said. 'Apparently, I'm not enough for him.'

'How do you know?'

'He told me.'

Louise watched Mary carefully fold the petticoat and gown. So marriage was not so wonderful after all.

'I have my children and they need a father.'

'Do you still love him?'

'Ah, love… It doesn't last, you know,' Mary sighed.

Suddenly there were shouts in the street. Louise opened the shutters wide and put her head out. The noise came from Castlehill. The landlady rushed into the room, followed by Henry Brand.

'That'll be the condemned men being escorted from the castle,' Mrs Grant said. 'Let me see.' She pushed forward and leaned out. 'Here they come.'

They hung out the windows, watching as the Town Guard forced the crowds back, clearing the centre of the street. A cart bearing the three condemned men passed the house. One of them looked all around him – puzzled, bewildered, as if wondering why he was being led to his execution. The other two hung their heads.

'This is barbaric,' Henry Brand shouted. 'These men are innocent. This is the Scots method of retribution—'

'Henry, allow me to introduce you to my sister, Mary,' Louise said, dragging him from the window.

Henry greeted Mary, and Louise could see clearly that he was admiring the curves of her bosom, loosely covered with lace and silk.

'A pleasure, madam,' he said.

James soaked the linen, and gently dabbed the girl's face. He patted the skin with a dry pad and smiled.

'There now. You'll be fine soon,' he said. 'The wound will be sore for a bit. These stitches will help your body to heal. Come and see me next week.'

He gathered up his instruments, and glanced round the tavern. Several pairs of eyes had been watching him working.

James blinked as he emerged into the sunlight outside. The crowds had now dispersed and street business was as normal. It was the young and innocent who were injured the most in these public demonstrations and riots. The girl had a bad cut to her face. It was fortunate he had noticed, and taken her to the tavern to clean and treat the wound. His shirt was spotted with the girl's blood. There was a lecture he must attend on the hour. He would have just enough time to change his shirt and clean his instruments first.

James ran into the close and almost bumped into an elegant lady emerging from the entrance to the turnpike stair.

'Get out of my way, you scoundrel,' the lady said, pushing past.

'I apologise, madam.' James leaned back against the wall.

'Your behaviour is a disgrace. Causing an affray in the street. Upsetting the good and worthy people of this city. All of us gentle folk suffer from those such as you.'

Henry Brand grinned and stepped forward. 'Allow me to introduce James Lightfoot.'

Mary stared at him for a moment, then caught Louise's arm. 'Louise, what do you mean by this? Is this the kind young man who has been attending our father?'

'You misunderstand—' James began.

'Come.' Mary took Louise's arm.

'I went to aid an injured girl…'

They weren't listening. Louise, Mary and Henry entered Mr Morton's house and closed the door behind them, leaving James standing in the close. He dashed upstairs, dumped his instruments in a pan of water, and put it on the fire to boil. He poured some water in a basin, took off his shirt and washed the street dirt from his body.

There was a soft knock on the door. It was Louise. She was staring at his chest. She blushed.

'I am sorry, James. You… you must forgive my sister. She… she has not seen Father for a while you see. And has troubles of her own.'

James gestured, and stepped back to allow Louise to enter. He strode to the press and pulled out a clean shirt. 'I was attending a little girl who was hurt in the mob. No doubt Henry Brand has put ideas into your sister's head. The man has no regard for me.'

'You misjudge Henry. He's a good man.'

'Hmm… I have a lecture soon. I will see your father this evening.'

'Yes, of course.'

Louise left. He heard the sound of her soft footsteps grow fainter on the stair.

## 14

### JULY 1705

'Miss Rose was here an hour ago, sir,' Hodges said. 'And two seamen's wives were asking for payment, and—'

'I know, I know.' Andrew waved his arm. The pay would have to wait.

'The women say they are desperate, sir.'

'They'll be back.'

'And there was a man here earlier about some Norwegian pine. He's waiting below in the tavern.'

Andrew walked through to his office, sat down, and rested his elbows on his desk. It was still early afternoon on a day going badly. A bundle of correspondence awaited his attention. He pushed it aside to be dealt with later. He loosened his neckcloth and mopped the perspiration on his brow. He opened the shutters, feeling the cool breeze. A patch of sunlight lit up a corner of the carpet. He glanced at Hodges. His servant inclined his head, and quietly closed the door behind him.

Ten minutes later the door opened.

'Miss Rose Hunter here to see you, sir,' Hodges said.

Rose Hunter strode into the chamber without waiting to be asked. Hodges drew up a chair. She shook her head and waited until Hodges left the office. 'We have a gentleman visitor who has an urgent matter to discuss with you,' she said.

The papers on his desk rustled in the breeze, and two flew off. He picked them up and closed the shutters. 'There is a merchant waiting to see me,' he said. 'After that, I may have some time to see your gentleman.'

Rose straightened her shoulders. 'Our guest has been waiting several hours to have a word with you. He would like a private discussion, now if you please. He's in our parlour.' Andrew noticed her hands were trembling.

'Very well.'

He stood up, and followed Rose to the sisters' chambers on the floor above. Bella and their guest were taking tea in the parlour. The visitor rose quickly to greet Andrew.

'Mr Robert Charles,' Rose said.

'Delighted to make your acquaintance, Mr Lawson,' the visitor said.

'I'm pleased you grant me the honour to be of service, sir,' Andrew said. 'I can only spare a few moments. I have a pressing engagement.'

He noticed what seemed like a flash of irritation across the visitor's face. 'A few moments then,' the guest said.

Bella stood up. 'Please be seated, gentlemen,' she said.

Andrew settled into Bella's favourite crimson velvet armchair. Bella poured tea, then withdrew with her sister.

Robert Charles sipped his tea, pulled his chair close to Andrew, and leaned forward. Lowering his voice, he said, 'I have a letter for you from the Countess of Errol at Slains in Aberdeenshire. She requests your services there on a matter of some urgency.'

Andrew took the letter. He glanced at Charles but his face was blank. 'She asks for me?'

'She requires someone who she can trust. And who has an intimate knowledge of the east coast, by sea and land. Please read the letter.'

Andrew looked down at the letter, broke the seal and read it, aware that he was keenly watched by Robert Charles. The letter stated that he had been requested to undertake a special assignment. He must tell no one about his destination.

'The letter doesn't state how long this mission will take.'

Charles waved his arm. 'I cannot say. Maybe days. Maybe weeks. Maybe months.'

'Mr Charles, I am in the middle of arranging cargo for one of my ships which is due back soon. I am engaged with a major purchase. My apprentice is currently undertaking a venture on his own, and I will soon be anticipating his successful return. This is the first of three voyages he must undertake as part of his apprenticeship.' Andrew stood up and made for the door. 'I cannot undertake this commission without knowing how long I will be engaged.'

'We must serve in our cause. Your conscience will be your guide. Please be seated,' Mr Charles said.

Andrew felt heat rising in his cheeks. He returned to the crimson velvet chair.

'You have been chosen,' Robert Charles continued. 'A young gentleman like you has the wits to cope with difficult situations that may arise. We know you are trustworthy. You have the right skills and, shall I say, a certain courage.'

Andrew felt a warm glow. This was praise indeed. But he needed to see to his own affairs. He must decline, of course. He knew nothing of the proposed enterprise.

'Mr Lawson, perhaps this may help to settle your mind. Some compensation.' Charles withdrew a bundle of coins from his satchel, and placed them on the small table. 'I was told you would be difficult,' he added. 'You will leave tomorrow at first light.'

Mr Charles stood up and opened the door. Rose emerged from a side door and saw him out. He shook hands with Andrew.

'My best wishes. Good luck.'

Andrew left Edinburgh at dawn. Heavy clouds and a steady drizzle darkened the streets, making it easier for him to slip away. Hopefully no one of his acquaintance would notice his departure and follow him. To be sure he wore an old shirt, breeches and waistcoat, a grease-stained bonnet, and carried an old cloak dampened with stale wine to add authenticity to his disguise. From now on he would assume the character of a servant, seaman, guide, vagrant, merchant – whatever the situation required. He walked to Newhaven, passing some women outside their houses packing baskets with oysters. They ignored him. At the busy harbour he picked his way along the quayside, surrounded by the screech of gulls and shouts of fishermen. A dour boatman glanced in his direction. Andrew waved. The man seemed uninterested, but Andrew jumped aboard. He sat down and pulled out his bulging purse.

'Burntisland,' Andrew said.

The man nodded, eyeing the purse.

The crossing of the Forth was slow. Clouds hung over the estuary. Andrew pulled his damp, foul-smelling cloak around him. He carried few belongings in his bag, and had only a dirk for defence. As well as the cloak, Rose and Bella had supplied him with wigs, false moustaches and beards, and other accessories to aid his concealment and subterfuge. He disliked being dirty, untidy, and having to present the subservient attitudes of a person of lower rank. Worst of all was the feeling of being wrenched away from his business. He had not been introduced to his employer, the Countess of Errol, but he must have earned her trust. He had in the past, with some risk, undertaken delivery of some letters to Slains.

At Burntisland he acquired a horse. No questions were asked. Drizzle persisted for most of the day. He kept off the main routes, avoiding towns and villages, riding as hard as he was able to through the muddy tracks. He would have preferred to spend the night in the open, but as the day progressed he knew it would be too wet.

On the Gowrie road he stopped at a small inn for a meal and a bed for the night. He stood waiting for someone to take his horse, then realised he would have to attend to his mount himself. The inn was full to bursting. He sniffed the air: body sweat and ale. The floor was wet, and scattered about were bits of food. A dog was sleeping, ignoring a piece of meat beside it. He bought a mutton pie and some ale, and sat at a bench near the door listening to his neighbours. Strange voices of farm workers from all parts mingled with those of the locals. He finished his meal and sought the sleeping accommodation. This was in a large barn nearby. It smelt of damp bodies. It was quiet, apart from the heavy snoring of those who had already found their pitch. He found a dark corner where he could guard his possessions. His foot touched a soft body. The man stirred but didn't wake up. Andrew slept under his damp cloak, its chill penetrating his tired body.

He rose early while the farm workers still slept, and wandered into the yard. A man stood nearby with horses and cart, ready to offer rides to the first labourers on the road. He must leave, before being mistaken for a field worker. At the stables, he was just in time to see a boy leading his horse out.

'Got you, you young rascal.'

'I was bringing your mount out for you,' the lad said.

'Stealing it more like. You didn't expect me this early.' He grabbed the reins and pushed the boy aside. 'Away with you!'

The boy fled. He heard shouts from the barn, as men were being roused for farm work. Time for him to be off. He rode through the Mearns, keeping near the foothills. The skies had cleared and the day was warming up. A rider, several yards behind, followed at the same pace, making no attempt to come alongside or to overtake him. Andrew had been cautious at the inn. The innkeeper was curt, and no one else spoke to him or asked his business. The best way would be to confront this stranger. Andrew stopped to rest his horse.

The man drew up. 'Good day to you. A fine, pleasant morning.'

'Good morning, sir,' Andrew said.

'Where are you bound?'

'North.'

'In that case I would be glad of your company.'

The stranger dismounted, and sat on a stone. He pulled out a parcel, opened it and offered Andrew some bread and cheese. Andrew hadn't eaten, and besides it would have been discourteous to refuse. He accepted and sat down beside the man.

'I've known these parts since childhood. I can tell you're not quite familiar with this region,' the man said.

'I know well enough where I'm heading. I prefer the hills. The freshness of the air.' The man was ill-mannered. He had no right to question him.

It was a mistake. He had forgotten his disguise. He was supposed to show deference, though he guessed this man's station in life was probably that of a servant. He appeared arrogant and confident; a little older than Andrew, well built, muscular. They continued eating in silence. The man gave occasional glances, watching Andrew.

'So what brings you to these parts? Family? Looking for employment?' he asked.

'I have been given a situation in Buchan.' Andrew eased himself up and wiped his hands.

'Well – it's a fine day to be travelling.' The man patted his horse and mounted. 'I'm going to Fetteresso. You may have supper with us if you wish. My father is a groom there.'

The stranger rode on. Andrew followed on the narrow track. This was not good. Fetteresso was the property of the Earl Marischal, William Keith, one of the most powerful barons on the east coast.

It was but a short ride. At the stables Andrew was shown to a house with a cosy parlour, and was left in the care of an enormous middle-aged woman with a beaming smile. Two young men were seated at the table. They nodded to Andrew as he squeezed into a place and was served with a large bowl of broth.

After the meal his travelling companion took him to a small parlour in another house, and left him alone. This chamber was more like an office than a parlour. Bookshelves were stacked with ledgers and piled high with documents. The desk at the window was covered with papers. There was just enough light to take a peek.

As he was examining the contents of a letter on the desk, Andrew heard a creak of the door opening. He turned abruptly. A man of about twenty years studied him. He twisted his hands, and advanced slowly. This was going to be easy. Andrew was used to deceiving older men with more cunning, and this boy looked naive and ill at ease.

'I am the personal servant of My Lord's secretary,' he said. He stood perfectly still.

Andrew moved forward and inclined his head. 'Thank you for your hospitality, sir,' Andrew said.

'We are obliged to enquire of your business in these parts,' the clerk said.

'I am travelling north to take up a position of manservant with a family acquaintance,' Andrew said.

'Your name?'

'Brock. Andrew Brock.'

The boy placed a sheet of paper on the desk. 'Please write down the particulars of your destination,' he said. 'For security purposes, you understand.'

'No sir.' Andrew fidgeted. 'It's difficult… I can't… I can't write properly. I mean, I've never had any need for writing.'

'I don't believe you. My man reports that your personal etiquette and table manners are excellent. "Too refined for a mere manservant," was his observation. Now write.'

The door opened and the large woman came in. 'Sir, the laird is asking for you.'

'I will be back,' the clerk said. He turned and strode out.

No time to waste. Andrew picked up his bag and ran across the quadrangle to the stables. Glancing along the stalls, at the far end his travelling companion held a young girl in a tight embrace. He didn't see Andrew. Edging along, he retrieved his bridle and saddle. His horse was tired and nervous. He chose another mount. Andrew noticed that his amorous companion was making progress with the girl, and not going to be distracted. He had enough time to escape unnoticed.

He rode towards the coast, hoping anyone following him would ride directly north. He spotted Dunnottar Castle – on a promontory, surrounded by steep cliffs on all sides, almost an island. Only a narrow ridge connected the rock to the mainland. The castle, once the Earl Marischal's residence, was now used as a garrison. Andrew took out his glass. A keep on one side and a tall lodge on the other, both buildings probably well guarded. He remembered the view of the castle from the sea. He recalled also one stormy day when his boat was driven against the rocks. He had scaled the cliff, climbed through an open window in the most easterly building, and had lain exhausted in what turned out to be the cellars next to the bakery. But to reach there without being spotted by guards would be impossible. Anyway, he would have to leave his horse somewhere, and climb the steep cliff on the north side. He did not want to risk losing his horse.

He dismounted, looking for a gentle slope to the beach. The light was fading. In the dimness he could just make out two figures heading towards him.

## 15

Andrew regretted choosing to travel unarmed. He scrutinised the two men who approached him. One was tall and broad with a firm stride, the other short and more cautious.

'It is late to be on the road,' the tall man said.

'My horse can go no further,' Andrew said. 'I was seeking shelter.' He regarded the men. They both stared, so he continued. 'I was heading north and wandered off. I would be obliged for a bed for the night.'

The men exchanged glances, withdrew a few paces and mumbled. Andrew made out a few words – vagrant, horse thief. His brain was muddled; his whole body weary. He needed a story, and a strategy. He took out his purse.

It had the desired effect. The men stepped forward.

'You can bide with us,' the tall man said. 'There's a wee corner ben the room.'

'Thank you,' Andrew said.

He followed them to a cottage by the river, and was left to see to his horse, while his host held discussions with his wife. They re-emerged and led him through the house, past four gaping bairns. The wife pointed to a filthy mattress. He took his boots off, and lay down for the night.

He had been asleep for what seemed like just a few minutes, when a loud banging on the door disturbed him. Despite the late hour, it was not quite dark. He heard mutterings, and then soft voices in conversation. The door closed and all was quiet. A figure approached him and knelt down.

'That was two of the guards from the castle,' his host whispered. 'They said the laird's men are searching for a stranger.' The man's face was in shadow. He was close enough for Andrew to smell his foul breath. 'They were looking for you, I suppose,' he continued.

Andrew did not reply.

'I could call them back and have you arrested.'

He was waiting for Andrew's response. Andrew retrieved his purse from under his pillow, and handed over some silver. The man shook his head. Andrew counted out three more shillings and added them to the pile. The man closed his fist around the coins.

He nodded and grinned. 'They won't find you.'

In the morning a hearty breakfast of porridge, herrings and bread awaited him on the board. All eyes were on him as he ate. He wondered if any of his money would go towards providing for the four skinny bairns. Probably not. When he finished he stood up to go. The tall man of the house followed him out.

'Thank you for your hospitality,' Andrew said. It had been expensive bed and board, and there was no guarantee he was safe. By now inhabitants of the entire east coast of Scotland must know that a stranger fitting his description was at large.

The weather had changed. Wind from the north east had picked up. Gusts laden with sea mist stung Andrew's face and penetrated his clothes. Heavy rain showers slowed his progress. Fortunately no one challenged him. Daylight was fading when he glimpsed the rooftops of Slains, just north of Port Errol. Andrew rode towards the main entrance at the west-facing side of the house. The rest of the building, he remembered, was on the edge of high cliffs, with two deep, steep-sided gullies, one on either side. As with Dunnottar Castle, the view of Slains from the land appeared less imposing than from the sea. As he moved closer he heard the rumble of waves pounding the rocks below.

At the stables, he dismounted, and handed the reins to the groom. He stretched his aching body.

The Countess of Errol welcomed him at the front door. 'I see you have ridden hard,' she said. The Countess, a lady of about fifty years, ushered him into a small anteroom, and withdrew. A manservant brought some borrowed clothes. He removed his damp cloak, and shivered as he dressed.

Lady Errol reappeared. 'How was your journey?'

'A clerk and another in the employ of the Earl Marischal were curious about me, but I managed to slip away. Otherwise uneventful.'

The Countess frowned. 'Your mission requires the utmost secrecy,' she said, ushering Andrew through a door into a long passage, and then straight into the dining room. 'I shall write to my niece at Fetteresso, so hopefully you may rest easy on that incident. We'll see that whatever occurred is forgotten.'

A housemaid was setting the large oak table for a late supper. She brought a dish of beef with carrots and turnips.

The Countess opened a bottle of wine, and handed him a glass. 'The best claret. How is your trade faring in these difficult times?' she asked.

'Well enough, my lady,' Andrew said. Questions were running round his head, but his brain was becoming too tired to focus. He was anxious to talk about the real purpose of his visit, but this was not the time and place.

The Countess spoke of her family and friends, those nearby and at large. The beef was delicious. The maid produced strawberry cakes to follow.

'I fear for our country,' Lady Errol explained. 'My son is at present in Edinburgh, as the Parliament is in session. I'm proud of him. If he were here, I'm sure you would find him an excellent companion.'

Andrew nodded. He sliced a portion of strawberry cake, aware of the tick of the longcase clock in the corner of the room. Lady Errol sipped her wine. Andrew could never figure out the complexity of the female mind, working on a different plane to a man's, yet somehow smoothing the way and solving problems. He had observed ladies supporting their menfolk, and often taking the lead, showing exceptional organisational ability. The Countess, he thought, was one of these fine ladies. His questions would have to wait. He was here to be given instructions.

After the meal Lady Errol took a candle and led him to the library. She slid aside a section of a panel next to a bookshelf, exposing a keyhole, inserted a key, and revealed a secret door, whose outward appearance was that of shelves of books.

'My office,' she said, indicating a closet with no fire and a window facing the sea. 'We may speak freely in here.'

The space was tight. Bundles of books and papers lay scattered on chairs and on the floor. Andrew's eyes scanned the documents on the desk. Domestic accounts and bills. He removed some papers from a chair and took a seat.

Lady Errol began. 'When conditions are favourable I receive correspondence from my brother, James, who is at the Court at St Germain-en-Laye. These are batches of letters for me and my friends, written sometimes months ago. You are acquainted with James Carron?'

Andrew nodded. He knew Carron, a Scot now in exile in France.

'Like you he's familiar with the east coast of Scotland.'

'That's right. He served in the Scots Navy as a lieutenant under Captain Edward Burd. I have not seen him in a while.' Andrew wondered where this was leading. Was he being drawn further into Jacobite intrigue? Being the occasional messenger and source of intelligence was within his capabilities, but a deeper commitment…

The Countess was studying him closely. 'Some time ago I wrote to my brother with information of the utmost importance. Since then I have been eagerly awaiting some news from abroad. I feel there has been much delay. Every day I scan the horizon, hoping…' Lady Errol took a deep breath. 'We are expecting letters and messages to be passed to certain gentlemen. I should like you to assist with whatever arrangements are to follow. I need someone I can trust.'

'I am at your service, my lady,' Andrew said. This was indeed an honour, and a great responsibility.

'We must not miss any opportunity. These summer months are passing. We must look to the weather. It has been changeable. I… we are impatient.'

The Countess rose, reached for a decanter and poured two glasses of brandy. He took his glass and gazed into the liquid. He now knew why he had been chosen for this task: his experience as a messenger. Also, he was of insignificant rank in society, and could pass as a servant or merchant. Now he was involved in a conspiracy. He was aware of the growing bitterness between Scotland and England, which was an advantage to the French.

Lady Errol frowned. 'Either we send someone over to France, or they send an emissary to us,' she said. 'If they send someone, and that is a possibility, he may arrive here at Slains.'

'So why, if you'll permit me to ask, my lady, did you ask for me to come at this particular time?'

'A week ago, I received a brief letter, indirectly. I was prompted to expect a package soon. There may even be an emissary from France. But that could be days, weeks or even months. We must be prepared for that event. I will make arrangements for his reception and provide hospitality. Should an agent arrive, you will be my first choice as his guide and companion.'

'I see.'

'In the meantime please become acquainted with the house and its environs.'

'My presence in Edinburgh will be missed,' Andrew said. He hadn't expected to be away for longer than a week. 'I have, I hope, seen to most of my immediate business. More prolonged absence, unexplained, will arouse curiosity.'

'Mr Charles, I'm sure, will attend to your affairs with care and circumspection. He is aware our enemies in Edinburgh have big ears.'

She opened the door and ushered Andrew through the library, down the stairs, along a passage, up a turnpike stair, and to a small chamber at the top of the tower. The room had a bed, two armchairs, a table and a chair. A varied selection of clothing lay on the bed.

'There is a chamber next to this one for another visitor. My servants are loyal. Nevertheless, we must be vigilant. For the moment you are simply my guest – a family friend.' She held her hand on the doorknob, and turned. 'Are you quite sure no one recognised you?' she asked.

'I'm quite sure.'

She bade him goodnight. He listened to her footsteps on the stair until the sound disappeared. The wind howling across the rooftops resembled a gale rather than a stiff breeze.

Andrew awoke to the bright eastern sun shining into the room, dazzling his eyes. He had slept soundly. The chamber had a window on each side, one facing the sea, the other a gully – one of many on the deeply indented coastline. To the south beyond the gully, out of sight, lay the sandy bay of Port Errol. Hefty clouds scudded through the sky. The steady, rhythmic roar of waves crashing through the gully indicated that the wind direction hadn't changed, but was less fierce. Taking out his glass, he scanned the horizon.

He didn't hear the manservant ascending the stair, bearing a jug of warm water and some towels. 'My lady wishes you to join her for breakfast,' he said.

Andrew washed, and dressed in fresh clothes befitting a gentleman of middle rank, and more to his liking. He would prefer to be armed. He noticed Lady Errol was of the same mind. As he entered the dining chamber his eyes fell on a sword, dirk and pistols on a chair by the wall. Excellent.

'For you,' the Countess said. 'I trust your accommodation is satisfactory.'

'Perfect, my lady.'

'You may make use of our library, at your leisure.'

After breakfast, Andrew hovered at the entrance to the library. He was never inclined to reading. Those pursuits were for dull people with little mind for the world, or for those too sickly for life out of doors. Returning to his chamber, he viewed the sea, coastline and clouds. He wandered to the room next to his. It was similar, also equipped for a special guest. The Countess was hopeful, more so than he was, on reflection. He descended to the foot of the stairs, picking his way in the dark. Light shone from the outer door, and the draught tasted of sea salt. This door must be at the edge of the gully. It was locked.

Back up a few steps he noticed a lower passage. Here the air was damp, smelling of wine and vinegar. Creeping along the passage, he reached the kitchens. He retraced his steps so as to not surprise the kitchen maids. A maze of passageways led to several chambers. This was only a preliminary exploration of the interior of the house.

He wandered outside, past the vegetable garden. A servant looked in his direction but didn't approach. He entered the house again, peeked into a small parlour and, as no one was about, climbed out the window. He was on the cliff edge at the back of the house. Here the ground dropped steeply to jagged rocks below. The wind forced his back against the wall. He wobbled, and his foot slipped. He pulled himself inside. It was a mistake; the wind was too strong. A manservant watched him close the shutters.

Andrew returned to the huge library, filled with books from floor to ceiling, except for the false panel leading to Lady Errol's office. If James were here he would lose himself among the volumes. How was he to occupy his days here? He knew the answer to this question. He must become familiar with every detail of the house, the cliffs, the gullies, the bay and Port Errol. He must know the best approaches by sea and land.

## 16

'It's been some time since you've eaten with us,' Mrs Hodges said, ushering James to the dining table. 'You've no taken a dislike to my food by any chance?'

'Not at all, Mrs Hodges. Your meals are excellent,' he said, as the housekeeper placed a large bowl of broth in front of him.

She nodded, flashing a beaming smile.

James hadn't seen Andrew in the last few days. Andrew had promised him some fencing practice, and he had been looking forward to it. He sighed. Andrew was the better swordsman.

'Is your master at home?' James asked.

'No. He left three days ago,' Mrs Hodges said. 'Quite suddenly. He usually mentions where he's bound,' she added, setting a platter of bread on the table. 'I thought you might know.' She frowned, and her hands moved nervously as she smoothed the corner of the tablecloth.

James tore off a piece of bread and watched Mrs Hodges retreat to the kitchen. He had a vague feeling of unease.

Something was not quite right. She looked worried. But then women were often anxious.

The housekeeper re-emerged carrying a platter of mutton, carrots and neeps.

'The broth was delicious, Mrs Hodges.'

She smiled as she took the bowl. 'I have strawberry cake to finish off with,' she said. 'I don't think the master has gone on a voyage. He told my man he had a lot of work to do here. Now he's off.' She shook her head.

'Well, I suppose someone must know where he is.'

'Young Tom's no here. He was sent on a voyage on his own,' she said. 'When Andrew goes off on a venture, he usually arranges for Tom or another to manage things here.'

'He'll be back soon, I'm sure,' James said as he attacked the mutton and vegetables.

'Another thing. There have been people coming here expecting to be paid. The wives of seamen. They're angry.' She clattered dishes on the sideboard. 'I don't blame them. It's not right. Women have to feed the bairns.'

James was puzzled. In the past year he'd had some opportunity to observe Andrew's methods of trading. He was mysterious sometimes. He took risks, but was cool-headed. He always took command of his own world. That meant seeing that men were paid promptly, to keep them happy, and therefore easier to manage.

James sipped his wine and leaned back. The feeling of unease was settling in. Louise would know Andrew's plans. James would have liked to ask her, but she had been avoiding him since the death of her father in May. The story, according to Rose, was that she spent much time with Henry Brand. Matters were becoming serious. Her sister, Mary, was encouraging the relationship. It seemed like the insufferable man was here to stay.

If Mrs Hodges left, he could sneak into Andrew's office and take a peek at the documents on his desk. He must have papers showing his current deals. He made his move after she entered the servants' chamber and closed the door behind her. He tried the door to the office. It was locked.

James had to see a patient in the Canongate, and then go to the hospital. He was satisfied that he had time to visit the poor folk there. On his way back to the High Street he visited Douglas Atkins. He had seen little of the apothecary since rescuing him from the gambling den. That episode had been covered up quickly. Even Francis had had nothing to say when James made enquiries into who might be involved in Douglas's downfall. He knew Douglas was avoiding him. Was it embarrassment? Or was it because he refused to return to working in the shop? Francis had reported that Douglas was drinking as heavily as ever, but as for gambling he knew little of his brother's activities.

'What brings you here?' Douglas asked from the front door of his shop.

James had not expected hostility. He produced a list.

Douglas read over James's requirements. 'I will see that these items are prepared on the morrow.' He raised his head, and fixed his eyes on James. 'I don't often see you in person. Usually you send a messenger. I suspect you have something to say. So, I will tell you I no longer frequent the gaming tables. Must consider the family—'

'Your activities are no concern of mine.'

'Indeed they are not. You think you are more worthy than the rest of us.'

'You misjudge me.'

'I thought differently of you. If you had stayed to work with me, and with your experience as a surgeon, you could have qualified for the Incorporation. I would have seen to it.'

'With your reputation in disarray, I don't think so.'

Douglas placed James's list on the bench, then turned to face him. 'I can't understand why you want to be a physician. They discuss philosophy. They stand aloof. A surgeon uses his skill and knowledge; works with his hands.' Douglas held up his hands. 'Surely that is more satisfying.'

'The skills of physicians and surgeons are both necessary,' James said. He was about to turn and leave the shop. He stopped. 'Have you seen Andrew Lawson?'

'No. Not for several weeks. He's no friend of mine.'

'I don't suppose you have any friends.'

'I am a bit particular. Lawson is too big-headed.'

James clenched his fists, choosing to ignore that comment. 'There are seamen's wives waiting to be paid. Their husbands have gone on a venture with Andrew's apprentice, and the men haven't been paid for their previous voyage.'

'It seems I'm not the only one who needs to look to his reputation.' Douglas grinned. 'Ask Francis.'

'I will. I am concerned he may have had some misfortune.'

Francis was not at his workshop. Back at Lawson's Land, a group of women had gathered at the end of the close. There was much pushing and jostling as he squeezed past, with his head down to avoid them. He ran up the back stair and knocked loudly on the door of Rose and Bella's flat. He heard voices. He waited, shifting from one foot to the other. He knocked again.

The door opened and Rose's head slowly appeared. 'Ah James, you're not usually impatient. Is anything amiss?'

'Well, I hope not. Have you seen Andrew recently?'

Rose looked sideways. She looked a little distracted.

'He seems to have made himself unavailable,' James continued. 'I was wondering when he might be back. Has he said anything to you?'

'I haven't seen him,' Rose said, her head still peeping round the door. 'And anyway why would we know?'

'May I come in?' James asked.

Rose slowly opened the door. Bella was standing behind her.

James entered and stood in the middle of the parlour. 'Anyway,' he said. 'I just thought you might know where he is.'

'Please sit down, James, and have some tea with us.' Bella smiled. 'You do like tea?'

'Yes, of course, I thank you.'

'We have heard good reports about the services you give to the poor and destitute. Maybe you'd like to tell us more,' Bella said. 'You see we are much involved with—'

'I'd be delighted,' James said. 'But I am troubled about Andrew's sudden disappearance. It makes me think... I think he may have had some misfortune.'

'I'm sure he's fine,' Bella said.

'Perhaps. But there's a group of angry seamen's wives in the close out there.'

'Oh. He's usually well organised,' Rose said. 'I thought he would have made arrangements for someone to pay them.'

'Anyway,' Bella said, 'you know we regularly provide clothing to the hospital for those who need it.'

'Yes, Pitcairne has mentioned that, but about Andrew—'

'My dear James, Andrew Lawson is perfectly capable of looking after himself,' Bella said. 'Your work at the hospital now —'

'We take turns, and manage a routine. The number of sick and poorly coming in continues to rise.' James paused. 'We are grateful for the commitment you ladies have to the hospital; not just with providing clothing, but also seeing to the welfare of the children.'

James thought it was odd that the sisters showed little concern for the seamen's wives. Anyway, it was satisfying to spend time talking about his work at the hospital.

The tavern was warm and thick with the smell of ale and body sweat. Willie Bell was taking orders, looking more jovial than usual.

'Ah, Lightfoot – come join these merry gentlemen here,' he said. 'You need to be more cheerful. You're too glum for a man of your age.'

'A word with you, please.' James tugged the man's elbow and manoeuvred him behind the counter. 'I have a job for your boy, Davie,' he said. He was going to say important job, but best not to make too much of the task he had in mind.

'The lad does as he pleases,' Willie said. 'And so do I. Can you no see I'm busy?' He shot off, bearing a flagon of wine.

James followed. 'I'm busy too, and I would be grateful for Davie's services.'

'For what?' Willie turned round and stared at James.

James glanced round. Davie had just come in, followed by half a dozen men. The boy led them to a vacant table. James was quick.

'Davie, come with me,' he said. He pulled the lad outside and down a close, almost as far as the Grassmarket, and out of reach of his father. Their way was blocked by four women coming up the close, each carrying a goose and with bundles on their backs. They squeezed past. Then James noticed that Davie had disappeared. He scanned the Grassmarket, the wide street full of stalls, carts, animals and all kinds of folk. No sign of Davie.

He felt a light touch on his right elbow. He whipped round, and caught Davie's arm in a tight grip. The boy yelled, a woman dropped her basket, and a couple of dogs dived for a cut of beef which had tumbled out.

'That was sair,' Davie said.

'Don't play games with me,' James shouted. Lowering his voice, he continued, 'I wanted you for some work I have in mind. For a good reward.' He took out a bundle of coins, jangled them in his hands, and pretended to count them.

Davie's eyes widened.

'It looks like I'll have to hire someone else. Someone able to conduct himself in a more mature manner.' James pocketed the coins and walked off.

Davie followed. James let him follow to an open stairway. The smell of filth was unbearable. He turned, and lowered his body to face Davie. The boy had his hand over his mouth and nose.

'Now listen. Mr Lawson is not at home. I'd like you to find out if anyone knows where he might be. Also, if you can find out who he has been keeping company with for the past two weeks…' He paused. It would be useful to know the whereabouts of Jack Scarlett, but this was not a task for young Davie.

The boy nodded and vanished.

Now he would have to ask Louise. A small group had gathered round the tenement. The red coats of two officers of the Home Guard stood out amongst the crowd. The luckenbooth was closed. Passing into the close, James saw that two small panes of Louise's window had been broken.

## 17

'Please come in, Mr Duff,' James said. 'Mrs Hodges said you wished to see me.'

Walter Duff sat down, took out a kerchief and mopped his brow. His face was red, and he was out of breath. He removed some papers from his satchel and, after searching through them, placed a sealed parcel on top of the pile.

'Sir, I would be obliged of your assistance with a few matters,' he said.

'Of course. How may I be of service?' James perched on the edge of his chair.

Mr Duff shuffled uneasily. 'Mr Lawson has business in the Northern Isles. He left with a convoy of vessels, escorted by the navy—'

'Did he not think to pay his crew before he left? Last night—'

'The disturbance was regrettable. Mr Brand—'

'I returned just as order was being restored. I wasn't allowed near the house.' James stood up, and paced across the room. 'An officer informed me there were no injuries.'

'Mr Brand took control of the situation. Miss Morton sought his assistance as soon as she suspected trouble.' Mr Duff leaned forward. 'He has been kind and supportive to her. I understand he is arranging repairs to her property at his own expense. Some damage to the door and two broken windowpanes.'

'And Miss Louise, how is she? I have been told she doesn't wish to see anyone. Do you not think Brand is being overprotective?'

'He is caring for her welfare.'

James returned to his seat. 'Regarding the purpose of your visit, how may I help?'

'At Miss Morton's request, I have appointed Henry Brand to organise Lawson's affairs until his return. Brand will personally arrange the payments of wages, and will deal with any other urgent matters. You may rest assured that sufficient coin has been procured for any outstanding moneys, so there won't be any more trouble.'

James heard a faint rustle outside the door. 'May I be excused for one moment?' he said.

Opening the door, he found Davie about to put his ear to the keyhole. He gripped the boy by the elbow and pulled him to the top of the turnpike stair.

'Well?' James said.

'Nothing, sir. Nae news about him,' Davie said. 'I've been asking about Tom as well. He's no back yet.'

James looked straight into Davie's eyes. 'Has anyone been scaring you?' he asked softly.

'No, sir.'

'All right then. Well done. Mr Duff here tells me Mr Lawson has gone abroad.'

Davie grinned and turned to dive down the stairs. James was too quick for him. He dragged the boy back.

'Find out where Captain John Scarlett is trading just now.'

Davie nodded, and clattered down the steps. James returned to his chamber.

'That was Davie Bell. I had asked him to deliver some prescriptions this morning. The lad's all right. Gives me more time to see patients.'

'Hmm. To return to the reason for my visit – to ask you to deliver this wee parcel to Archibald Pitcairne when you next see him. He's never at home when I call. And… and I was wondering if I could trouble you with an advance on your rent, which is due in a few days' time.'

'I thought Miss Louise would be collecting rents. Or her paramour Mr Brand.'

'You don't appear to like Brand,' Mr Duff said.

'Not particularly.'

'Perhaps there is a little jealousy here, am I right?'

'I'm not jealous. I don't trust him.'

'I made several enquiries before agreeing to allow him access to Lawson's accounts. Henry Brand is a man of quality and considerable wealth,' Mr Duff said. He loosened his neckcloth, and mopped his brow again. 'Mrs Grant and her other lodgers find him pleasant enough.'

'He's charming and polite, I suppose.' James took a key from his pocket, opened a drawer and scooped up a bundle of coins. The drawer smelt of cinnamon. He was saving a little now, and had been able to buy this spice cabinet, a bureau, and another chair. Shelves had been fitted to accommodate his growing collection of books. He handed Duff the money.

Mr Duff pocketed the coins, and handed James a receipt. 'I've been told that Brand is taking an interest in our history and our manners. In the past year he seems to have settled in. I think he has a mind to stay.'

'I hope not.'

Mr Duff added, 'Mrs Grant says he's writing a book.'

'Ah, I know about that.' The trouble was, he didn't know. Even Louise was vague about Brand's writing projects.

Mr Duff studied his hands. He looked up. 'All this extra business is vexing. Makes me anxious, and not good for my health.'

'Is there something in particular that ails you?'

'I find the stairs to the garret hard on the joints. I'm a little breathless too.' Mr Duff stood up and buttoned his jacket. 'It's warm enough in here, but the fresh, cool breeze sometimes takes my breath away.'

'I think you know to take more rest,' James said, seeing him out. 'Let others take the load.'

He watched Duff pick his way down the steps, wondering why he hadn't sent one of his clerks with the parcel. He was not pleased that Duff had chosen Brand to manage Andrew's affairs. The infuriating man had wormed his way into the confidence of many with his superficial charm, in just over a year. Was he jealous? No. Definitely not.

He should try not to think about Louise Morton. After the sad death of her father, she had shut him out completely. It was disappointing. He had enjoyed evenings with Louise and her father over the winter months; just the three of them. Mr Morton's frail body nestled in his armchair, listening intently to his tales of places he would never see, and Louise with her sewing, stealing glances at him now and again. Brand had turned her against him.

The parcel for Pitcairne lay on his desk. He picked it up. A walk to clear his head, followed by a stimulating discussion, was what he needed to raise his spirits.

It didn't take Davie long to find out about Scarlett. The next day the boy burst into James's chamber, after running all the way from Leith.

'He left four days ago on the *Lady Margaret*,' Davie reported. 'Fully laden with wool, coal and some books.'

'Bound for?'

'The Baltic.'

'Any news of the apprentice?'

'No, sir.'

'Right. You've done well. Now I will teach you mathematics.'

'Why? What good is mathematics?'

James positioned Davie at the table and set a book in front of him. 'Well, it helps to improve your mind.' He grabbed a chair and sat beside the boy. 'And knowledge of mathematics makes you wealthy.'

'It does?' Davie grinned.

James's eye caught sight of a slip of paper that had been passed under the door. He hadn't noticed it when Davie entered. He stooped to pick up. 'Did you drop this?'

The lad shook his head.

'Did someone slip it under the door? Did you notice anyone on the stairs?'

'No, sir. No one.'

James peeped out, stood at the top of the turnpike and listened carefully, but all he heard were footsteps in the courtyard and distant shouts above the babble and clatter of the city. He opened the note and read:

*Sir,*

*I send this appeal to you as a mutual loyal friend of Andrew Lawson. He is at present undertaking a commission on my behalf. As far as I know he is safe and well. I will not reveal any details, and I hope I can rely on your judgement to keep the matter secret. I ask you therefore to cease making enquiries. The activities of your young servant have been causing much trouble and embarrassment, and indeed may put friends in danger. So please, exercise great caution.*

*Destroy this note.*

There was no signature. With his back to Davie, James put the paper inside his daily journal and replaced the journal on the top shelf, taking his time. Davie was looking at him with wide eyes.

'I've just remembered. I have to see a patient,' James said.

'What's wrong with him?'

'That's what I have to find out,' James said, gently easing Davie towards the door. 'Tomorrow, I'll give you a lesson. So, I'm thinking...' James opened the cabinet. 'Here's the final reckoning.' He placed a bundle of coins in Davie's hand and showed him out. 'You've done enough searching for now. No more. Right?'

The boy nodded.

James retrieved the letter from his journal and examined it closely. The note was freshly written, the paper smooth –

not crumpled by being inserted into a pouch. Could it have been written by someone living nearby? Or even within this tenement? So Andrew had gone north on a venture; a special commission.

*18*

AUGUST 1705

A ndrew took out his glass and scanned the horizon to the east. It was late morning, and his head still ached from too much wine. The sun appeared between light clouds, warming up his lofty chamber. In the past three weeks, he had kept a sharp lookout, observing vessels on their way north, escorted in convoy by the Scots Navy. Local fishing boats passed regularly. He gazed more keenly now that gentle southerly winds brought more settled weather, hoping for a ship from France, eager for some action.

He descended the turnpike to the bottom. The Countess had revealed more than he ever expected, indicating the importance of his assignment. He imagined the possibilities. Would the rightful King come over himself and raise an army? The King, here at Slains? The Countess and her son had expressed their loyalty, but what of others of high rank? Would they come out? Those of property had too much to lose. Yet here he was, a man of a lower rank being pressed. Did he not warn James of the consequences of participating in political discourse? Did he not vow himself to stay neutral?

After all, Scottish merchants traded with Englishmen as well as with the French. Yet it was England that declared war with France. The Scottish Parliament did not. And if there was a French victory, what then? Scotland would be free to trade with France. Whatever the outcome in political affairs, it was the ordinary business of trading that really mattered – to Andrew and others of his kind. But his thoughts were running too far ahead.

He groped through the lower passages in the dark, fairly satisfied with his familiarity with the house. He made his way along the main lobby. Outside Lady Errol's parlour he detected unfamiliar female voices. She had visitors. He would speak with her later to seek permission to write to his apprentice. Tom would have returned from his venture, and would be in need of guidance.

He entered the library. Spotting an inkstand and quills in the corner of the room, he took a seat, selected a sheet of paper and began to write. It was a note with brief orders and instructions. He sealed it and walked across to the window. A solitary vessel had appeared on the horizon. He headed up to the top of the stairs, opened the shutter and leaned out. The ship was approaching. He strained his eyes, watching until the vessel was close enough to see its signals. Yes, there was no doubt.

He gathered his coat, rushed down the stairs and along the passage to Lady Errol's parlour. He waved the housemaid away, knocked and walked in.

The faces of three elderly ladies stared at him.

'Beg pardon, my lady,' he said, catching Lady Errol's eye. He bowed and stepped back to withdraw from the room, leaving the door slightly ajar.

'Please excuse me,' Lady Errol said to the ladies. She rose, and closed the door behind her.

Andrew led the Countess to a quiet corner further along the passage. 'My lady, a frigate approaches,' he whispered. 'It is the one.'

'Take the rowing boat out. I'll escort our guests to their carriage,' the Countess said.

Andrew took the keys and descended to the lower passage. He groped along to the end. Unlocking the outer door to the gully, he picked up a rope from behind the door and tied it to a metal hook in the wall. He stepped out, easing his way down the cliff. He stood on a loose stone. His foot slipped. He grasped the rope to regain his balance. Reaching the bottom, he untied a rowing boat, pushed it out, and jumped in. He manoeuvred beyond the gully, and headed towards the frigate. He rowed vigorously. Glancing up, he saw the larboard side lined with curious faces. As he drew closer, Andrew recognised James Carron. The ship was *L'Audacieuse*. Appropriate name.

Commander Carron lowered himself into the little boat, and nodded to Andrew. Andrew held the boat steady while two parcels and a chest were handed down. Another gentleman came on board. He sat down, doubled over, as if in pain. Andrew couldn't see his face clearly. He rowed in silence towards the gully.

The Countess stood at the open door, and watched as Andrew eased the boat in to rest in the little bay. The visitor scrambled out, climbed up the rocks, and disappeared inside the house with the Countess. Carron followed up the slope, leaving Andrew to secure the boat and haul up the parcels and chest.

'Take this to the bedchamber for Lady Errol's guest,' Carron said, handing Andrew one of the parcels. 'The other one is for the Countess. Then go to the library.' Carron disappeared into the gloom before Andrew could say anything.

Andrew deposited the visitor's parcel in the chamber next to his. The chest had already been placed in the room. In the library he found Carron looking out at *L'Audacieuse*, a glass of wine in his hand. He turned and smiled.

'My young friend, Andrew Lawson. Good to see you again.' He strode forward, clapped Andrew on the shoulder and guided him to an armchair at the bay window. Carron eased himself into his chair, and stretched out his legs. Andrew sat upright, tight as a spring.

'My name is Andrew Brock,' Andrew said.

'Relax, Mr Brock. Please be at ease,' Carron said. 'We await our instructions. Lady Errol wishes that we allow no one else into this library.' He finished his drink and poured another. 'Excellent wine,' he remarked.

Andrew leaned back, willing himself to be less tense. It was the waiting, the doing nothing he disliked. He knew not what tasks were in store for him. He was there to be commanded by others; not easy at all. But Carron seemed to be almost enjoying this.

'So, you keep well I trust?' Andrew asked.

'Good enough. And yourself?'

'Life has its ups and downs, but I keep good health. I don't suppose you're going to tell me how you came to be in command of a French privateer.'

'No.'

'I thought not.'

'Life has its ups and downs for me too. I may have a command, but I am often ill provided.' Carron spoke softly. 'I don't press for more,' he added.

Andrew asked no more questions. He trusted James Carron. They were alike in some ways; accustomed to adapting to any situation and making the best of it.

The Countess emerged from her little office with the visitor. 'Allow me to introduce Andrew Brock – your guide and companion, as and when you require his services. Mr David Colville, our honoured guest.'

Andrew took in the appearance of the visitor. He was about average height and build; pale skin; keen, sharp eyes. He seemed a little out of sorts.

'We will dine shortly. Mr Brock, please. I'd like a quick word with you in my office,' the Countess said.

In the concealed room, she sat down, put on her spectacles and arranged the pile of newly arrived letters which covered the surface of her desk. She selected one and handed it to Andrew.

'It's from my brother, James,' she said. 'You can see from this letter that he holds Mr Colville in high regard, and considers him most worthy to our mission.'

Andrew read. His attention fell on one line, instructing Lady Errol to choose well the person who will act as messenger. He felt a warm flush of pride.

Lady Errol turned her chair round to face Andrew. 'Colville will travel to Edinburgh, under cover as a merchant.

So consider carefully. Use whatever means and reasonable deceptions to keep him safe. You know the manners of the mercantile community. When you are in Edinburgh, Mr Charles and my son will offer some guidance.'

Andrew placed the letter on the desk. He noticed that two others had been opened.

'I have much to discuss with our guest later, but now we'll dine,' the Countess said, leading Andrew through to the library.


There were only four for dinner. The housekeeper set the dishes on the sideboard and withdrew from the dining chamber. Lady Errol began by serving hot beef broth.

'A lot has changed here in the past year,' she said, addressing Colville. 'There is mistrust, and some loss of zeal, I fear. This is causing me some anxiety.'

Andrew exchanged glances with Carron, wondering what he was thinking. Supping his broth slowly, many thoughts rushed through his mind. Colville appeared intense. Andrew noticed the agent finished the broth but barely touched the mutton or duck that followed.

'We have much still to arrange, Mr Colville,' Lady Errol said when they had finished dinner. She stood and pushed back her chair. 'In my office, if you please.'

She turned and smiled. 'Mr Carron. Thank you so much for bringing our visitor safely to Slains. I expect his business will take several weeks. Await at anchor, and you'll hear from me soon. Mr Brock will take you back to your ship.'

Colville rose and followed the Countess.

'I'm in no hurry to be back,' Carron said, reaching for his wine glass.

The housekeeper came in.

'Let's retire to the library,' Andrew said.

He picked up the flagon of wine and led Carron along the passage. He turned the handle of the library door. 'Locked. We'll go to my chamber,' he said, leading his companion along the passage and up the turnpike stair.

'What a rare view,' Carron said, scanning the sea and sky from the window in Andrew's chamber. He turned. 'Did you know about this unease among the gentlemen?'

'No, of course not,' Andrew said, draining his glass of wine in one go. 'I didn't expect the Countess to be so frank in our company.'

'Neither did I. You need to keep a clear head after today, Mr Lawson – I mean Mr Brock. You must take great care.'

'So everyone is advising me,' Andrew said, filling his glass. He sat down on the edge of the chair. 'Mr Colville looks sick.'

'He travels poorly at sea. He had a fever a month ago on our first attempt…'

'What do you mean, first attempt?'

'It's a long story,' Carron said, easing himself comfortably into the armchair. 'I first heard from Colville last May. Then I waited awhile. I got command of *L'Audacieuse* eventually. Good reputation as a fast frigate. Then another delay until money and crew were provided. We lost good weather then – those weeks in June.'

'And what about Colville? His health?'

'He was sick during this time. And he was even worse when we eventually set sail. The weather turned foul. We were making no headway, so we returned to the Dunkirk Roads.' He sipped his wine. 'That was after ten days at sea.

When we did get away on the second attempt, the voyage took us four days.' Carron topped up his glass.

The commander changed the topic of conversation. Andrew was plied with questions about seafaring acquaintances, merchants, traders and fisher folk. He knew little of the local gossip of the east coast ports these days, as he spent less time aboard ship and more time arranging deals ashore in the burghs. He noticed that Carron was becoming too comfortable, yet showing no obvious signs of the effects of drink.

Andrew rose and gazed out the window. This was enough to prompt Carron. He stood up and pulled out his timepiece. 'I must go now.'

Andrew led the commander down to the boat in the gully. The man seemed untroubled by danger and uncertainty, and steady on his feet.

The next day a slight noise awoke Andrew in the early hours. He lay listening to the gulls. Colville rushed into his room.

'A sail on the horizon,' Colville said. 'From the south.'

Andrew leaped out of bed. He grabbed his glass. From his window, he saw *L'Audacieuse* at anchor close to the castle. In the distance, sails were clearly visible on the horizon. He watched as a large vessel drew close enough to be recognised.

'It's the *Royal Mary*, sir, a Scottish frigate,' Andrew said. He glanced at Colville and noticed fear in his eyes.

'Then we are undone,' the gentleman said.

Andrew dressed, and donned a finely embroidered borrowed coat. He grabbed a bundle of coins, happy to be in the role of a merchant of means. He ran down the turnpike, listening to Colville's footsteps behind him. He burst into Lady Errol's parlour.

A housemaid dropped her duster. 'The mistress has not yet arisen.' She rushed out.

Andrew sat on an armchair and waited. Colville paced up and down the parlour, bumping into the table.

Lady Errol appeared wearing a fine silk robe. 'Good morning gentlemen,' she said.

'Good morning, my lady. The *Royal Mary* is passing our way,' Andrew said.

The Countess frowned, then smiled. 'Do not be alarmed, sir. This situation may be resolved,' she said, addressing Colville. She ushered him to an armchair.

Lady Errol sat down at the secretaire, took a sheet of paper and wrote a few lines. She dusted the paper, folded and sealed it. 'Take the cutter, and give this to Captain Gordon with my best wishes,' she said, handing the letter to Andrew.

Andrew ran down the stairs, happy to leave Lady Errol to deal with the agitated Mr Colville. He must reach the *Royal Mary* as quickly as possible. In the steady breeze it wasn't long before the boat picked up speed. He kept the frigate in sight, leaving Slains and *L'Audacieuse* far behind. Thankfully the frigate had not drawn nearer the coast. As he approached the vessel, he remembered when the *Royal Mary* had captured a French privateer and brought it to Leith a year ago. Captain Gordon had captured three French ships in that year. Quite impressive for the small Scottish Navy. Now he observed the ship at close quarters. He sailed the cutter alongside. Several hands secured the boat and welcomed him on board.

'I'm from Slains, sir. I wish to speak with Captain Gordon,' Andrew reported.

He was led to the captain's cabin. The officer knocked, and put his head round the door. 'A gentleman from Slains to see you, captain,' he said. 'Your name, sir?' he asked, turning to Andrew.

'Andrew Brock.'

'Come away in, Mr Brock,' Captain Gordon said, waving his arm. 'And see that I am not disturbed,' he added, addressing the young officer.

Andrew closed the door behind him. 'Captain Gordon, sir, the Countess of Errol sends her best wishes. She regrets she is indisposed.' He handed the Countess's letter to the captain.

'Welcome aboard, Mr Brock.' Captain Gordon indicated a seat at the large oak table. A chart and several documents covered the surface. An unfinished letter lay beside his inkstand.

The captain broke the seal and read the note. 'Ah, the Countess has visitors.' He looked up. His face was grim. He rose, flung the cabin door open and called for his lieutenant. Words of a change of course were all that Andrew heard.

'Please send my deepest regards to Her Ladyship,' Captain Gordon said when he returned. He reached for his quills and ink. 'We'll be sailing south, and won't be returning north for two or three weeks.'

Andrew watched as the captain penned a short note, sealed it and passed it to him.

'This is for the Countess. I'll write to her again as soon as we arrive at Leith.' He took a sheet of paper. 'And now for a series of signals for Carron,' he said softly. He leaned back in his chair and rubbed his chin. He dipped his quill, wrote a few lines, paused, then continued.

Finally he laid down the quill, and smiled. 'When I see Carron's correct signal – that is, a Holland ensign at the main topmast head and a Scots ensign at the mizzen peak – I will respond with the Scots ensign at the main topmast head and the Holland ensign at the mizzen peak. Carron will know then that I will not pursue his vessel.'

Andrew took the letter. He shifted his chair back, and was about to stand up.

'Before you go, let us share a glass of claret,' Captain Gordon said. He rose and opened a cabinet, reached for a bottle and poured two generous measures. 'I heard you claimed I took your crew once,' he said, still keeping a low voice. 'There are no bad feelings, I trust?'

'None at all, sir,' Andrew said brightly. 'I've had worse—'

'I'm sure you have.'

It was bad enough. Andrew had formally engaged his crew, lost them to the navy, and by the time he had got another crew the weather had turned bad and most of his cargo was spoiled.

Captain Gordon was watching him. 'What of your young friend who came back to Scotland, May last year?' Gordon asked.

'James Lightfoot. He's settled in nicely. Working and studying with Archibald Pitcairne.'

'Very nearly landed in trouble, back then. I was informed he had sneaked ashore before reaching Leith. We thought he was a spy.'

'James doesn't know sometimes when he's sailing close to the wind. He lives in a world of his own.'

Captain Gordon spoke of his own family, and the disadvantages of being at sea for unpredictable periods. The pleasant exchanges were short. Andrew must deliver the note to Carron.

'It was a pleasure to meet you, Mr Brock. I wish you well.'

Back in the cutter, Andrew set sail for Slains. He made good speed, feeling some anxiety until spying the French ship. He drew alongside *L'Audacieuse* and climbed on board. Carron was not on deck. The French crew eyed him suspiciously, appearing somewhat reluctant to escort him to the commander. Some mutterings were heard from his cabin. One man gripped his arm. Andrew pushed him off and strode into the cabin.

Carron was slumped in a chair, bottle in one hand, the other arm dangling listlessly over the arm of his chair. He drew himself upright when his eyes met Andrew's.

'From Captain Gordon of the *Royal Mary*.' Andrew held his temper in check as he handed over the letter. He watched the changes in Carron's face.

'How...' Carron began.

'The ship has departed south. He knows the Countess has visitors. I don't think you realise you've had a narrow escape.'

Carron read the letter, and nodded. 'I thank you... Mr Brock.' He stood up. Pushing past his first mate, he staggered up on deck.

The Countess of Errol looked relieved when she read the note from Captain Gordon.

'Our visitor has confined himself to his chamber. He has been unwell, and anxious about his ship. Please ask him to come to the library,' she said.

'*L'Audacieuse* will be safe for about three weeks,' the Countess said to Mr Colville as he entered. 'We have matters to discuss.' She led the French emissary into her private study and closed the door.

For the next two days the Countess held talks with her visitor, leaving Andrew in the library during these long hours. It was a great relief for him when, on a fine August morning, he set off for Edinburgh with his merchant companion. They rode briskly through open countryside, avoiding Aberdeen and other burghs, arriving without incident in Edinburgh in the early morning of the fourth day.

## 19

'Mr Lawson's back, sir.' James heard Davie's voice behind him as he strode down the High Street.

James was on his way to see a new patient, Mrs Alexander. Pitcairne had told him she was with child and had been feeling poorly.

'I've seen him in the tavern with a stranger,' Davie said, as he caught up with James. 'Then they left.'

'Where did they go?'

'Up the hill, to the Duchess of Gordon's big hoose. I saw them go in. Thought you would be interested.' He looked up at James.

James gripped Davie by the shoulders, and looked him in the eye. 'Now listen. Not a word to anyone about Mr Lawson. Do you hear?'

Davie nodded. James hurried on.

'You going to see a rich patient, sir?'

'I'm visiting a patient. All patients are important.'

'Especially rich ones.' Davie grinned.

'I said all are important. Rich and poor. You remember that.' James stopped at the mansion house of Mr Alexander.

'I'll speak to you later,' he said, lowering his voice. 'And stay out of trouble. There are dangerous people about.'

Davie nodded and smiled. James waited until the lad moved off before chapping the door. The boy was right though. He needed wealthy clients, and this family looked reasonably prosperous. He had met Alexander and his wife on several occasions. Their influence in social circles was well known. The gentleman was a lawyer who made it known that he gave generously for the relief of the sickly poor.

The housemaid escorted James into the drawing room, a spacious chamber with a fine oak bureau and cabinet. His eyes focused on a drawer, partially open, showing a collection of rock samples.

He turned as Mr Alexander entered. 'My wife is resting just now,' he said, as he poured generous measures of claret into fine glasses. Alexander led him across to two enormous fireside armchairs. 'I hope you don't mind waiting. Her maid will be down to let us know when she's ready.'

James did mind waiting. Other folk demanded his time.

Mr Alexander leaned back, studying him through narrow eyes. 'I have returned from a meeting with Fellows of the College of Physicians. You may know it is my intention to provide funds towards the furnishing and expansion of their premises in Fountain Close.'

'The college will be grateful of your generosity, sir.' James sipped the claret and placed his glass on a small table.

'You are an ambitious man, I hear,' Alexander said, resting his elbow on his armchair. 'Pitcairne speaks well of you. Though, whether he's sober or intoxicated, I rarely see eye to eye with the learned physician. We are of different political persuasions.'

James made no reply. He examined his wine glass. He had often been with Pitcairne when the physician had launched into heated political discussions, which went on well into the night. James usually placed himself at the end of a table so that he could slip away when he had heard enough. He knew that his mentor was a Jacobite, and that he had been imprisoned in the Tolbooth for a short time. It was common knowledge also that he had been released on condition that he didn't correspond with rebels. His experiences obviously did not stop him voicing his opinions loudly, especially when he was half fou.

'You share Pitcairne's views no doubt?' Mr Alexander asked.

James had not given any thought to anything other than his work, his studies and the patients he cared for. That was enough for now. He was not going to be drawn into a political discussion with Mr Alexander or anyone else. He studied the pattern on the wine glass, then looked up. 'I hold Dr Pitcairne in great esteem as my teacher,' he replied. 'I admire his skilful practices. He is innovative, intelligent, thoughtful, and of course has made a huge contribution to medicine. As a student I have learned so much in the past year—'

'I meant do you share his politics?'

'I have no allegiance to any party, sir,' James said. His neck and hands were perspiring. He put his glass down on the table so that it would not slip out of his hands. 'What I mean to say; I share Pitcairne's views on some controversial topics in physic. But I have my own mind, too.'

Mr Alexander lifted an eyebrow. 'Fair enough,' he said after what seemed like a long pause. 'You're young and inexperienced. You would benefit from lighter social engagements.' He leaned forward. 'How would the occasional evening of music suit? My daughter, Anne, is a wonderful singer.'

'Thank you, sir. I'd like that very much.'

'There's always good conversation. For you there is the opportunity to increase your confidence in polite society.'

'I suppose so, sir.'

'Ah. You have much to learn.'

This was too much. How dare this man attempt to influence how he thinks and feels. He looked away, and his eyes fixed on the collection of rocks in the open drawer.

'Are you interested in fine rock specimens?' Mr Alexander stood up and walked to the cabinet, signalling to James to come across. 'I have more here.' He took out a tray from a drawer below the cabinet and laid it on the table.

'I collected some rough gems while abroad, but sadly I lost them,' James said, examining a beautiful specimen of amethyst.

There was a soft knock on the door. The maid entered and curtseyed.

'My wife is ready to see you now,' Mr Alexander said.

Davie was sitting outside James's door when James returned to his chamber after seeing his patients. He followed him inside, and sat on the floor while James arranged his desk and wrote some reports. When he finished he turned and faced Davie.

'Are you sure you saw Mr Lawson in the tavern with a stranger?'

Davie nodded. 'It was him, sir.'

'Your father. What did he say?'

'He was too busy to notice.'

'Anybody else? You're not making this up?'

'No, sir.'

'Did you get a good look at the other gentleman?'

'No. They sat in the alcove in the wee room. Dark there even in the middle of the day in summer. He was in the corner.'

'Then how do you know he was a stranger?'

Davie looked puzzled.

'Never mind. Look, let's just leave Mr Lawson to his business. And if you see him don't follow him. Is that understood?'

Davie nodded. James opened the door. The boy seemed to hesitate for a second before he left.

James listened to Davie's retreating footsteps on the turnpike. It was time for him to study. Pitcairne advised him to read widely. For a change he chose Herman Boerhaave's philosophical dissertation, *De distinctione mentis a corpore*. He was of a mind though that his main interests lay in botany and chemistry – the practical sciences. He worked on into the late evening. As the light gradually faded, he lit a cruisie lamp above his desk.

There was a soft knock on his door.

'Andrew!'

Andrew put his finger to his lips and crept in. He sank down on James's armchair. 'I need your help.'

James shifted his chair round. In the light of the lamp Andrew looked tired and pale. His face was drawn, and he seemed to have grown older. 'You're not well. In need of rest and good food. I suppose you have been drinking much, without good food to go with it.'

'I don't have time to rest. Tomorrow, first light, I'm off to Comiston with a merchant who requires somewhere secluded to stay. I'm asking you as my most trustworthy friend not to tell anyone else where I'm going. And keep that servant of yours out of trouble.' Andrew leaned back and closed his eyes, then continued. 'My affairs were poorly handled while I was away, as you probably know. The whole of Edinburgh knows.' Leaning one elbow on the armchair, he put his head in his hands. Then he looked up. 'Three weeks ago I left money to pay the crew of the *Lady Margaret*. That disappeared. Scarlett is on a voyage. Tom hasn't returned. I fear his ship is lost. Shipwrecked, or fallen into the hands of pirates, or taken by the French. I am all but ruined. I may even lose this tenement.'

'You left money for the crew?'

'I gave it to Scarlett.'

'I knew it. The man is a rogue,' James said.

'I wrote a letter for him listing my requirements – in detail. He was to pay the crew and other listed debts with the money I gave him. I told him to take the *Lady Margaret* and use his own money to trade. He has a lot of explaining to do when he comes back.'

'If he comes back.'

'If he doesn't, I'll find him,' Andrew said.

'You might find that difficult. Scarlett is slippery. He could disappear and assume another identity in the blink of an eye.'

'He has a wife here. That may be an unusual alliance, but I think they are fond of one another.'

'You could ask her for a loan.'

'I don't think so. I'm not welcome there – ah, you find that amusing.'

'It is amusing, though not unexpected.' James sighed. 'Anyway, how can I be of service in your current secret affairs? I suppose you're not going to tell me much about what you're involved in.'

'Mr Duff is handling my business. But he doesn't keep well, so please give him some assistance. You don't know a Mr Charles, but he told me he sent you a letter a few weeks ago. Anonymously.'

'I did get an anonymous letter. The writer implied you were involved with some trading for him and wanted your activities kept discreet.'

'That was probably from Mr Charles. I want you to be my eyes and ears around here. Report to Mr Charles. If he calls himself by another name, go by that. You may trust him.'

'Where can he be found?'

'Oh, he will contact you. Do not seek me out here or at Comiston. If I need your help I will see you myself, or pass a message to Mr Charles,' Andrew said, pulling out his timepiece. 'I must go now.' He stood up.

'One more thing,' James said. 'When you were away Brand was nosing around, according to Mrs Hodges.'

'He paid the crew and other debts, so I owe him. He seems to be settling in here, James. Everyone likes him. Except you.'

# 20

A t daybreak Andrew guided David Colville through the Grassmarket. With Colville's saddlebags neatly packed, they resembled two early travellers. The sky was dark and heavy with rain clouds. Loaded carts covered with heavy sheets appeared in the wide street, coming from all directions, splashing through muddy puddles. Andrew noticed the hood of Colville's cloak shielded his face from view, as well as giving protection from the cool wind and rain. No one paid any attention to them as they passed. Once clear of the market place, they mounted, and rode out of the burgh, south past Merchiston, through roads soft with mud. The rain eased slightly. Too much rain in the summer meant a poor harvest, and that meant poor trade for merchants.

Andrew's immediate concern was for his visitor. He was pleased Colville's journey so far had been trouble-free. He had been uneasy, though, about providing accommodation for the Jacobite with Rose and Bella Hunter. When Mr Charles had taken him to visit the Duchess of Gordon, and she advised him to lodge outside Edinburgh, he was much relieved. The home of Lady Comiston near the Pentland Hills would be ideal, the Duchess had suggested. She wrote a short note, sealed it and handed it to Andrew.

'Please deliver this letter to Lady Comiston with my good wishes.'

The road rose gently towards the Braid Hills. Water streaming downhill made the ground slippery. Progress was slow. Through the trees Andrew spied the tower house of Comiston on the spur of the hill, impressive and remote. Half hidden by trees, the castle provided good prospects to the west and south. Andrew's woollen cloak, damp and heavy, dragged on his shoulders. The trees offered little shelter.

Their arrival was announced by a chorus of crows in the trees. They dismounted. The iron gate at the entrance stood half open. The small courtyard beyond showed signs of neglect. From somewhere within the castle, a dog barked. Andrew handed his reins to Colville. He rapped on the oak door of the tower house, waited a few moments, then chapped again.

The door opened and a head popped round. A frail, elderly manservant with untidy hair peered at him through half-shut eyes. 'What do you want?' he said.

'We would like to see Lady Comiston, sir. I have a letter for her,' Andrew said.

'You can give it to me,' the manservant said, holding out his hand. The dog appeared, growling and sniffing around.

'I was told to deliver it personally to Her Ladyship,' Andrew said, pushing his way in.

'I am Lady Comiston.' A voice came from within the dark hall. Lady Comiston stepped forward. She took the letter. Her hands trembled as she read the contents. She looked up;

her face impassive. 'Gentlemen, you are very welcome,' she said. 'After you have attended to your horses, please join me for some refreshment.' She nodded to her servant.

The stables and barn were tidy and well equipped, and smelt of fresh, damp hay. Andrew glanced sideways at the French emissary as they rubbed down their horses. For the first time since his arrival in Scotland, Colville was beginning to look relaxed. But Andrew shivered in his damp clothes. He felt fear in this remote castle. The sooner Colville's business was completed, the better.

After seeing to their mounts, they sauntered back to the house. The manservant led them to the kitchen, where Lady Comiston had set out breakfast. The scullery maid, a silent girl of about ten years, was in attendance. She placed two large bowls of porridge on the table. Andrew draped their damp woollen cloaks over a chair in front of the fire. He was grateful to Bella and Rose, who had provided a selection of clothes as various disguises for himself, Colville and Mr Charles. The sisters were full of ingenious ways for them to dress discreetly and at the same time remain protected in all weathers. Andrew's eyes swept the kitchen and its contents: clean pewter and wooden bowls, polished silver platters, a girdle, and two pots on the fire.

Lady Comiston entered and dismissed the girl. Tall, silver-haired and plainly dressed, she wandered across to the fire and helped herself to some porridge. She sat opposite Colville at the table.

'I have a secret chamber on the top storey,' she said. 'You will be safe here, sir. We rarely have visitors.'

They ate in silence. As soon as he finished his meal, Andrew rose and retrieved his cloak. The heat had returned to his body. He was anxious to be on his way. He hesitated, curious about the secret chamber. Perhaps he would have a quick look before returning to Edinburgh.

Lady Comiston led them upstairs to the top of the house. The rain had cleared. Sunshine filled the guest's room; a corner chamber with windows on two sides. The south window showed a magnificent view of harvested fields, with the Pentland Hills in the distance. The east side faced the woods. Their hostess opened a closet door to reveal a cabinet with upper shelves full of books. She opened the door below, exposing back stairs under the shelves. 'These stairs go down all the way to the east-facing door, adjacent to the wood,' she said.

'How many servants do you have?' Andrew asked.

'Just the two.'

A little girl and an old man. Still, Mr Colville should be able to defend himself.

Andrew wandered round the chamber. In the distance he heard a dog bark. He opened a cupboard recess in the wall. It contained a large kist. It was unlocked. The lid was stiff and heavy. Inside were white linen sheets. Underneath he found priest's vestments, and an old quilt with brown marks that looked like bloodstains.

Heavy thumping on the outer door startled him. He dropped the quilt, and glanced round. Lady Comiston had gone downstairs. Colville was organising the contents of his saddlebags, and settling into his reclusive chamber. Andrew quickly replaced the contents of the kist, and closed the lid. He sped along the passage to the top of the stair, and pulled at the knob of a shuttered window. It came off. He tried another window, opened the shutter and peered down at the entrance. No one was to be seen. He heard Lady Comiston ascend the stairs.

She took a deep breath. 'The Countess Marischal and Mr Charles are here to speak with Mr Colville.'

Andrew kept a lookout while Colville followed Lady Comiston down the stairs. Voices from below reached his ears. Moving slowly down the stairs, he noticed the parlour door was ajar. He caught snatches of conversation as Colville raised his voice to make a point. The Earl Marischal had misunderstood. He was an emissary from France, here at the request of the Scots. The King of France wished to know how he might help the Scottish people. Andrew did not like what he heard. Why did the Earl Marischal not come to Comiston himself?

Andrew stepped down the stairs. He met Mr Charles coming up.

'I'd like you to stay here awhile with our guest, if you would be so kind,' Mr Charles said. 'And await further instructions.'

'I detect some uncertainty…' Andrew began.

'You will do as you are bid,' Mr Charles said. He took a couple of steps down, then turned to face Andrew. 'You may be called upon to escort our guest into Edinburgh.'

Andrew returned to the secret room. He paced up and down, glancing frequently out the window. The wind stirred the branches of the trees and rattled the windowpanes. Eventually, he heard the front door opening. From the window above the courtyard, he watched. The Countess Marischal was preparing to leave. The old man brought her palfrey, and was about to assist her when Mr Colville rushed out. He pressed a note into her hand, and bowed stiffly.

Andrew stayed at the window until the Countess and Mr Charles were out of sight.

He found Mr Colville and Lady Comiston in the parlour. Colville sat at a bureau, head bent, writing his journal.

'Please be seated, Mr Brock,' Lady Comiston said. 'It is kind of you to stay awhile.'

James studied the formal invitation, delivered earlier by a young manservant, to an evening of music in the company of Hugh Alexander and family, not sure whether it could be a pleasant experience, or a waste of time. He had given a short note of acceptance, thinking of the wealthy lawyer's generosity to the poor. He must go.

The day had been relentless, and tiring. He rose to dress for the occasion. His tailor had made a plain suit in good quality brown wool. A fine embroidered waistcoat, not new, but revived in the expert hands of Rose and Bella; gloves and hat completed his outfit. He dusted a bit of fluff off his waistcoat, feeling more confident than this time last year.

He strode down the High Street to the Canongate, taking care to avoid streams of water running down the road. At least it had stopped raining, though with a heavy sky, more showers threatened.

The same young manservant took his card at the door, and escorted him upstairs to the drawing room. The babble of conversation rose as he reached the door. Many guests had arrived, filling the large chamber. Several pairs of eyes looked in his direction as he entered but, to his relief, did not linger. He found himself being propelled to the far end of the room. There Mr Alexander was in conversation with a young lady poised nervously beside a spinet.

'My daughter, Anne,' he said, leading James forward. 'My dear, allow me to introduce James Lightfoot.'

The young girl curtsied. Her hands were tiny, the skin soft and white. Her blue eyes sparkled. She had golden hair piled high with delicate curls and ringlets. A strand hung loose. James felt the urge to put it neatly in place.

'I'm delighted to welcome you to our musical entertainment,' Anne said.

'My daughter plays and sings well. She is a very accomplished young lady.'

The girl's cheeks reddened. She lowered her eyes.

'Thank you so much for inviting me,' James said. It was inadequate but he couldn't think of anything else to say.

Anne turned abruptly and sat on the stool at the keyboard.

'Please take a seat. We are about to begin,' Mr Alexander said.

The music started. James glanced round at the other guests. He could see no one he recognised. Three young men sat near the spinet, eyes on Anne. She did indeed sing and play beautifully. James was content to relax and listen without any effort of concentration. His early apprehension had gone.

The audience applauded heartily at Anne's performance. Gentlemen crowded round her. After the refreshments were brought in, James wandered around, a glass of wine in one hand and an oddly shaped sweetmeat in the other.

Mr Alexander shuffled to his side. 'I thought I might just mention,' his host began, 'I am at this moment making arrangements to place a small fund, for the benefit of the College of Physicians.'

'That is most generous of you, sir. Very welcome indeed,' James said.

A servant poured more wine into his glass. Out of the corner of his eye James noticed an elegant lady who had just walked in. Eleanor, Jack Scarlett's wife. She joined a group of older ladies. Her husband wasn't with her. A pity. He would have enjoyed watching Scarlett toil his way through an evening of music and polite company. No need for anyone to embarrass him. Scarlett could do that himself.

Eleanor Scarlett noticed him, smiled and floated across.

'My sister, Eleanor,' Mr Alexander said.

'We've already met. A year ago,' Eleanor said. 'So pleased to see you again, sir.'

'I trust you are well,' James said.

'I am. I thank you.' She gave him a beaming smile.

'Your husband is overseas still?' James asked.

'He is abroad at present. And safe, I hope.'

'On the *Lady Margaret*?'

'He is. An unfortunate business. The loss of the *Louise Anne*,' she said. 'Mr Lawson's young apprentice. I'm so sorry.'

'What?' James said.

'You haven't heard? The wreckage was found at a remote spot off the coast of Norway. No news of the crew. All hands lost, I expect. Your friend, Andrew, must be devastated.'

'I didn't know,' James said.

'You haven't seen Andrew?'

'Not for several weeks,' James said. 'I've been fully engaged in my own affairs.' That part was true.

James was aware of Mr Alexander's piercing gaze. Where was Andrew? Did he know about the shipwreck?

'James?'

'Oh, my thoughts were miles away.'

'I was saying the musicians are ready to begin,' Eleanor said, ushering James to a chair.

She sat next to him. The folds of her silk gown overlapped into his space, emitting a strong lavender fragrance. He felt drowsy. He must make his apologies and leave. No. It was polite to stay.

Anne introduced the audience to two guest musicians; young men, probably students. They played lively dances on the lute and theorbo. James tried not to fidget. He tried not to peer at Eleanor's large bosom. He glanced at the door, wondering if he could slip out without anyone noticing. No, it would be unthinkable to do so. After the final applause he sought out Mr Alexander, muttered his thanks and then edged to the door.

Outside he ran through the Nether Bow and up the High Street. Heavy rain filled gutters, and soaked assorted debris of the day. He stood in a puddle and splashed a lady's dress. Her shouts faded as he ran on. His new suit was soiled.

He knocked on the door at Andrew's apartment. Hodges appeared. His face told James he had been informed of the tragedy.

'The master's no here.'

James stood still. He had promised not to seek Andrew.

'Mr Duff is going to tell the master,' Hodges said. 'He's at some merchant's house, I think.'

## 21

'I'm sure no one will recognise you,' Rose said. 'You look ten years older.'

James looked in the mirror. 'From a distance I may escape without notice, I suppose.'

The long grey periwig sat heavily, and made his head feel hot. He examined his dress. The coat, frayed at the edges, stretched across his back. His shiny breeches had a musty smell. He let his eyes wander round the chamber. The floor was covered in an assortment of gentlemen's clothing and other items. It was as if the sisters regularly supplied disguises. Perhaps they did…

'So who are you trying to avoid?' asked Bella.

James adjusted the wig yet again. 'A jealous husband.' It was the first pretence that entered his head.

'Oh.' Rose gasped.

James turned. 'I must assure you, I have not behaved inappropriately.'

'No, of course you haven't,' Bella said. The sisters smiled, and exchanged looks. 'We're ready to oblige. No more questions.'

Good, James thought. He glanced sideways, suppressing a grin. 'I will return these when I hear the gentleman has left town,' he said, dashing out before he became caught up in further invention.

'Good luck,' Rose called.

He packed an old satchel and set out for Comiston, managing to leave the city walls behind without bumping into any acquaintances along the way. There was no way to tell how effective his disguise was close up. Once out of town he strode along the narrow road, pausing occasionally to allow a cart to pass. Warm sunshine penetrated his coat and awkward wig. He began to perspire, but plodded on. Comiston, he thought, must be about five miles out from the city.

As he approached the hill, a well-dressed gentleman on horseback passed by, taking the road to Fairmilehead. The rider glanced briefly at James but didn't slow down. He soon disappeared out of sight among the trees. James took his coat off as he neared the spur of the hill. He was beginning to enjoy this adventure as he swaggered along. A path led to the castle gate. Crows screeched and scattered in the treetops at his approach. A dog barked from within the walls of the house. Feeling uneasy, he stopped and listened closely. A soft crunching sound in the wood. That could be an animal or a person.

A figure emerged from behind the wall and opened the gate. His left hand rested on the gate. His right shoulder leaned on the post. His eyes studied James. He looked about thirty years, handsome, and with the confident air of someone of high rank. Stepping closer, James's eyes took in a plain brown coat, over a blue waistcoat trimmed with gold. His lace cravat and shiny, curly wig defined his rank. He was the horseman who had passed about half an hour ago.

'Who are you?' the gentleman asked.

'I might ask you the same question, sir,' James said.

The gentleman drew his sword.

'I know that voice,' someone called from behind.

James's right hand went to the hilt of his sword. At the same time a hand whipped off his wig.

'It doesn't suit you,' Andrew said, looking at the wig in his hand and shaking his head. 'I assume you have come with a message from Mr Charles.'

James said nothing. Andrew moved toward the gentleman at the gate. He whispered to him, then walked back to James. The gentleman returned to the house.

'I've no message from Mr Charles. I came by my own choice…'

'What have you done?' Andrew stepped back and stamped his feet. His hands gripped his head. 'I told you not to come here. Not here, you understand?'

'Well, I'm here now.' James paused. 'I came with bad tidings about the *Louise Anne*.'

Andrew stood still, his face turning pale.

'The ship was wrecked off the coast of Norway, with the loss of all hands.'

Andrew turned his head away. 'Go back to Edinburgh,' he said.

A dog barked and ran to the trees.

'Get inside, quickly,' Andrew said, pushing James through the gate.

They rushed inside the house and closed the door. The hall was empty. Andrew took James up the turnpike to a small chamber at the top.

'Stay here, James,' Andrew said.

James looked out the window. The dog was still barking, and running to and fro. Two men sauntered past the house, going towards Fairmilehead. From the other window, the sun shone on rows of stooks covering the golden fields. Light clouds drifted over the Pentland Hills. He closed the shutter. Who was the finely dressed gentleman? And why was he here? Andrew wasn't going to introduce him. James had been putting to the back of his mind the possibility of Andrew's close involvement in Jacobite intrigue; more than delivering mail. And what about the sisters? Were they involved? And Louise? And what about Douglas and Francis? No. Not Francis. He was openly patriotic, and a pamphleteer, not involved in intrigue. He had said so.

James opened the door of the small chamber. He heard raised voices from below. He strained his ears to listen. Two men in heated discussion. Where was Andrew?

'Two thirds of Scots support the Stuart cause,' the handsome nobleman was saying. 'But we must be cautious. There are some among us who do not trust Hamilton. He's devious.' There was a pause. 'It's well known he is always in much debt, and in disagreement with his mother. Why is Hamilton thought to be so important anyway? His family are Presbyterian.'

'He has a large following among his supporters, has he not?' The other voice had the hint of an Irish accent.

'It is he who follows his supporters,' the nobleman said more softly. 'I acknowledge he is our leader, though in my opinion an incompetent one.'

James heard floorboards creak in the hall at the foot of the turnpike. He crept back up the steps to the wee room, thoughts rushing in his head. Francis had been telling him about progress within the Parliament; procedures for the appointment of commissioners to treat for a union. Everyone knew, Francis said, that the Duke of Hamilton had lands in England. How could the anti-unionists look to him as a leader?

At the top of the turnpike voices in conversation reached him, then gradually faded. He listened to the squeaking as the bolts on the outer door were closed, straining his ears for clues of what might happen next. He heard footsteps coming up the stairs. James closed the door and stood by the window, hoping to give the impression he had been there all the time. He turned round as Andrew walked in.

'Has the gentleman left?' James asked.

'He has,' Andrew said. 'I should return to Edinburgh as soon as possible. My absence will arouse much suspicion. But what to do? The seamen's widows…'

Andrew lowered himself onto the edge of the bed. James had never seen him this way. He was always a man of firm resolution, who made clear decisions. Very much in control.

After several minutes Andrew stood up. 'James, I want you to take my horse. Ride into Edinburgh and find Mr Charles, or rather, let him find you. Go to the usual places – my stable, the tavern, my house. He will introduce himself. Ask him to arrange another person as a guide for Lady Comiston's guest, so that I may return to Edinburgh as soon as I can.'

'What if I don't see this Mr Charles? He doesn't know me. Would it not be better to go yourself? I can stay here.'

'I don't want you involved.'

'But I am involved.'

'No, you're not. Remember this, James. You saw a gentleman at the gate. That's all.'

That was not quite all. James wasn't going to mention the conversation he'd overheard.

'No wonder naebody can find you, sir, dressed up like that.' Davie had chanced upon James in the stables at the Grassmarket, attending to Andrew's horse.

James hung up Andrew's saddle. He took off the wig and jacket, wrapped them up and stuffed them in his bag. Giving a last look at Andrew's contented horse munching away, he turned to face his inquisitive servant. He gripped the boy's arm, leading him into the street.

'I am trying to avoid someone,' he whispered into Davie's ear.

The lad gazed at him, wide-eyed, probably thinking he was some sort of hero. He wished he was.

'People have been looking for you, sir,' Davie said.

'Who?'

'Mr Atkins for a start, and Mrs Scarlett, and a well-dressed gentleman carrying a document case,' Davie said, walking two steps behind James up the steep West Bow.

'What did Mrs Scarlett want?'

'She didn't say. Mr Atkins will dine with you in the tavern. The man with the document case said he would keep looking for you, sir. I think he's a lawyer. Lawyers are always carrying papers.'

'Well now – maybe he is a lawyer,' James murmured. He paused to roll up his shirt sleeves and loosen his neckcloth. He meandered through the stalls in the Land Market, Davie following close at his heels. He wondered about going to his chamber first to see if any messages had been left for him, but he was hungry.

He headed down the steps into the darkness of the tavern. It was hot and steamy inside. A hand waved, and indicated a spare stool. James sat down.

'Good to see you, James,' Francis said. 'I can always rely on young Davie to find you. I am in need of sensible conversation and friendly company. My apprentice is looking after the shop. He can deal with the hawkies and chapmen for a change. I like to give the lad some responsibility occasionally, and have time to myself.'

James glanced round to see what others were eating and waved to Davie. 'Broth and a dish of chicken, and small ale, please, Davie,' he said.

'I'll have the same, if you please,' Francis said.

The boy smiled and disappeared. He returned quickly carrying two bowls of barley broth on a tray.

'I've been told by Mr Duff there aren't many details of the shipwreck,' Francis said. 'How is Andrew coping?'

James's hand shook and some broth spilled from his spoon. 'I haven't seen him since his return,' he said.

'Neither have I. There's only so much loss a man can take. He might have bolted.'

James felt Francis' eyes boring into his head. 'Aye, that's possible.' This was difficult. He must think of questions for Francis on other topics. What news kept him busy? Any new books? New pamphlets or pamphleteers?

'There's not much news these days,' Francis said. 'If truth be known, I'd rather have days of excitement. It's my work to inform men of matters of importance.'

'You do inform. You publish what people write, what matters to ordinary folk,' James said. He broke off a chunk of bread.

'You seem a little distracted today, James,' Francis said.

'Just hungry. That was good broth.' James pushed the bowl aside, and drew his attention to a platter of chicken and turnip.

'So what have you been up to this morning?' Francis asked.

'Oh, it's just been one of those mornings where everyone was demanding my attention.'

That was true anyway. Francis was watching him with a curious intensity. The printer seemed to have a nose for detecting anything interesting or unusual. James sighed with relief when they were joined at the table by a lively group of traders. The talk turned to street gossip. He didn't linger long. He paid his reckoning and rose to seek fresh air.

It was just as hot outside as in the tavern, as he crossed the street to head home. In the tenement turnpike stair sunlight never penetrated the tiny windows. The coolness was refreshing, as he climbed to the top. Opening the door to his chamber, he saw that a note had been slipped underneath. It was from Mr Alexander, asking if he could call on his wife later in the evening. It was near her time of giving birth, and she was anxious.

'James, is that you?' He heard Bella's voice.

He skipped down the steps, and faced a tall stranger.

'Ah, James Lightfoot, we meet at last. Robert Charles.' The visitor stood at the door of Bella's chambers.

'I was hoping to find you,' James said.

'The ladies told me you have been trying to avoid an angry husband.'

'Ah,' James said. 'A bit of invention. Come into my chamber, if you please, Mr Charles.'

He ushered his visitor in and closed the door.

'The sisters have realised your story is a fabrication, but they don't know about our special visitor at Comiston. I know you have been there this morning,' Mr Charles said, taking a seat by the fireside. He rested his arms on the chair, waiting to hear his story.

James related the details without mention of overhearing the heated dialogue. Mr Charles listened without interruption.

'Were you introduced to the gentleman at the gate?'

'No, sir. I don't know his name.'

Mr Charles nodded and stood up. 'It is best that you know little of this intrigue.' He paused as James opened the door. 'I will speak to Mr Lawson's lawyer. There may be ways to raise a loan for him. And I will see if another is available to take your friend's place at Comiston. Though I would prefer it if he stays.'

Mr Charles took a step back from the door, as if reluctant to go. 'Has Mr Duff talked to you about your father?' he asked.

'My father? No he hasn't.' Neither had Andrew. 'I never knew my father. I was taken away from my parents at the age of six. Stayed with an aunt.' He swallowed. 'That's all I know.'

Mr Charles rubbed his chin. 'Hmm…'

Did this gentleman know his father? Why had no one spoken about him?

'Stay here, or within reach. I will be back soon.' Mr Charles smiled and slipped down the stair.

James stood with the door open, listening to the footsteps retreat, and the thud of the outer door closing. He had questions for Mr Charles, but this wasn't the appropriate time.

## 22

J ames didn't have to wait long for Robert Charles to return.

'I have a letter for Lady Comiston's guest,' Charles said, handing James a tiny sealed paper. 'I must ask that you deliver this immediately. But take great care that no one follows you. There are spies about. I have reason to suspect my own activities are being closely observed.'

'I will need to improve on my disguise then,' James said, placing the letter in the pocket inside his waistcoat; another device created by Bella, and useful for securing prescription notes as well as letters for political conspirators. 'What message do I give to Andrew?'

'I've made arrangements with Walter Duff to secure a loan, to deal with immediate demands.'

'Thank you. I'm sure Andrew will be grateful. He's an impatient man though. He will want to honour the responsibilities of his own affairs.'

'I can't take the risk of providing another guide to replace him. You know now that Lady Comiston's guest is no ordinary merchant.'

'I've spent four years at sea, Mr Charles. There's no such thing as an ordinary merchant.' James closed his mouth tightly. He mustn't let any anger show. He would not mention the heated discussion he'd overheard at the castle. 'I'll be as quick as I can. I have a patient to visit later this evening.'

After Mr Charles left, James put on the grey wig. He needed a different outfit to avoid being noticed by Davie. The lad was likely to be hovering near the stables.

He called in on Bella and Rose. They had a wide selection of clothes on offer.

'How about some padding to make you look heavier?' Rose suggested.

'Hmm – perhaps. But not too much. I don't want to be overheated.'

He took Andrew's horse. His new clothes were cumbersome. Sweat poured down his neck and dampened his shirt. He pressed on, and didn't bother to check if he was being followed.

It was the first question Andrew asked when he arrived at Comiston.

'If I've been watched, we'll soon know,' said James.

Andrew took the reins of his horse, leading it to the stables. James related news of Andrew's affairs, while his friend attended to his horse.

'No further information about the *Louise Anne*?'

'I'm afraid not,' James said. He could sense Andrew's frustration at being distant from his own ventures.

'I must return soon. Charles could have sent another guide.'

'I'll ride with you. That is, if Lady Comiston can spare a horse. I have to see a patient this evening, and much to do before that.' He glanced round, then reached into his pouch. 'I have a letter for Lady Comiston's guest.'

Andrew took the letter, somewhat reluctantly, he thought. 'Stay here,' Andrew said.

James watched him enter the house, closing the door behind him. He paced up and down outside the stables. He had had enough of this. The secrecy, the disguise. No matter the nature of Andrew's commitment, he did not wish to be part of political intrigue. He was here only because of his concern for Andrew's business affairs. He strode across the yard and banged on the castle door. The dog barked. No one came. He thumped louder. Eventually the door opened. Andrew pulled him into the hall.

'I must go – now,' James said.

'You will not. You will stay here until just before dark, and then ride with me and our visitor into town.' Andrew added, 'There has been a change of plan.'

'I can't. I had a letter from Mr Alexander – a request to call on his wife this evening. I'll go now. Do you have any message for Mr Duff?'

'You must stay.' Andrew ushered James into Lady Comiston's parlour.

'Mrs Alexander is with child. The birth will be soon, all being well, and a midwife will be in attendance, but they are asking for me as well.'

'That's all right then. Your presence is desirable but not essential.'

'There may be problems with the birth. Therefore I am obliged—'

'Have you sent a message to him confirming you'll be there?'

'Well – no.'

'That's all right then. As far as he knows you haven't been home to see the letter.'

'You said this morning you didn't want me involved. What's happened to change your mind?'

'I haven't changed my mind. I—'

'I'm leaving.' James turned and headed for the door. He hurried across the yard, panting in the heat. He pulled off the heavy padding and wig. Andrew was following him.

'James, I'm asking you…' Andrew said.

The dog barked. Neither of them spoke. James listened closely to the rustle of the leaves.

'There's someone about,' Andrew whispered. 'You may be set upon if you leave now alone.'

Andrew was right. He was in no position to argue. There might be danger afoot. Perhaps he could wait a little. There would still be time to visit the lady. Mrs Alexander had been well two days ago when he saw her. They sat down in the parlour.

Lady Comiston put her head round the door. 'Would you like some tea, gentlemen?' she asked.

'That would be most welcome, Lady Comiston,' Andrew said.

'Where's your visitor?' James asked.

'He's in the chamber on the top storey,' Andrew said.

'I will see that the gentleman has some refreshment,' Lady Comiston said, closing the door behind her.

'Why must we wait until late evening for this outing?' James asked.

'That is the wish of our guest.'

'After dark it won't be safe.'

'That's why I need you with me.'

James suddenly felt cold. But he knew that Andrew was brave; and was also cool-headed, cunning and not prone to taking risks. 'Where exactly are we going?'

'Firstly, to a lady who lives in the Canongate. And don't ask me who he will be visiting. I don't know that either.'

They sat in silence. James looked around the parlour. Family portraits decorated the panelled walls. A porcelain bowl and candlesticks stood upon a walnut cabinet. Tiny ornaments placed round the room enriched the homely atmosphere, giving comfort to a lady living in solitude, unable to walk along the street to visit lady companions. In the winter, outside the snow and wind could do their worst. Here inside it would be cosy beside the fire.

Lady Comiston's manservant brought in a pot of tea, and served it sweetened with sugar. Tea drinking was a new experience for James, since coming back to Edinburgh. He fixed his eyes on the elaborately decorated silver teapot. He recalled his conversation with Mr Charles.

'What do you know about my parents?' he asked Andrew. 'I have often wondered why I wasn't told anything about what happened to them.'

Andrew sat stiffly. 'I was eleven years old when I saw you at Christmas 1689. I was told you were to stay with us. No one told me for how long. When you went to school – well, at first I didn't like you. You were smarter than me with books. I had no time for Latin and Greek.' Andrew smiled and sipped his tea. 'Then I found out, to my delight, that cleverness came in different ways.'

The dog growled and shuffled to the door. James exchanged glances with Andrew. The longcase clock ticked steadily. Outside the leaves in the trees rustled in the gentle breeze, casting flickering shadows on the wall.

James resumed. 'Did your parents say anything about me?'

'No. I didn't ask.' Andrew was staring at a finely decorated bowl. 'That Christmas, I wanted to put up holly and pine cones in the parlour. I didn't want you helping, so I threw away the holly you gathered.' Andrew leaned back. 'My elder brother was the favourite in the family. Then you were the focus of attention.'

'That was just at Christmas when I came. I remember people were all around me. Afterwards I was ignored,' James said. He paused. 'Robert Charles knows something. And Walter Duff.'

Andrew shrugged. 'Maybe they do.'

It was a long evening. James glanced frequently at the longcase clock. Its hands moved slowly, and it chimed reluctantly on the hour. Lady Comiston appeared and spread a clean linen cloth on the parlour table. Her servant brought in a large tray of cold meats and cheese for supper. 'Fine cheese from the farm in Bow Bridge,' Lady Comiston said. 'You need to eat well before you go.'

The kind lady treated them as if they were family visitors. Like the two sisters, Bella and Rose, she coped effortlessly with arrangements connected with actions of subterfuge, as if these challenges occurred every day.

They left at dusk. James resumed his disguise. He noticed that the visitor was suitably dressed. He wore a hood, and a black cloth partially covered his face. He stood by, ready to mount.

It was agreed that James would ride on his own a few yards behind Andrew and his companion. In the dimming light he followed the two horsemen as they picked their way down the hill and across the Boroughmuir. The air of the countryside was warm and smelt of damp hay. All the way to the Canongate he listened for signs of trouble, keeping apart from bushes and hedges. His nerves were on edge. Every rustle of a fox or other creature startled him. It was with much relief in his mind when they at last entered the Canongate by St Mary's Wynd, and made for the Nether Bow port. James still kept pace behind his companions. Their visitor, tightly wrapped up on a summer's evening, attracted occasional glances.

Andrew appeared to know his destination. The two riders had stopped and dismounted outside a pend. They walked through into a courtyard and stood outside the door of a mansion house. A maid emerged, holding a lamp. She disappeared into the house for a moment. Two men then appeared, and took their horses. Andrew waved to James. He stepped forward, and yielded his mount to one of the servants. The girl led him into the parlour.

Andrew was already seated in a fireside chair, looking relieved, when James entered.

'Lady Largo is with our traveller,' Andrew said.

'I wish you would give him a name. Even if it is not his real name,' James said.

'Just think of him as a merchant,' Andrew said. 'A stranger, like you were when you came here a year past.'

James remembered it well. He heard the creaking of floorboards, and the sound of a door being closed.

'He's slipping from us,' Andrew said. He was on his feet. 'You go by the way we came in. Through the courtyard. I'll go by the close.'

James dashed out. It was now dark and well past curfew but he knew how to feel his way around. He met Andrew at the pend.

'We've lost him. I've no idea where he might be going,' Andrew said.

'I think I know who he wants to meet,' James whispered.

'Who, James? Tell me.' Andrew gripped James and pushed him into a corner of the courtyard.

'The Duke of Hamilton.'

'Hamilton?'

'I overheard a heated discussion—'

'Let's go,' Andrew said. 'You can tell me later.'

James followed him down to Holyroodhouse.

'There they are,' Andrew whispered, pointing to two black shapes entering the courtyard, one holding a lamp. 'Now we wait. We have to be sure that he's with Lady Largo, that both come out safely. And then see what they do next.'

'If they don't emerge, there's nothing we can do anyway,' James said.

They sat down and leaned against the gate of a close. Something moved beside James. He felt a hand grab his leg. A drunken reprobate. He pushed the sleepy body away from him. It grunted, then lay still.

'I wish you'd told me you knew about Hamilton,' Andrew hissed.

'I heard his name mentioned. That's all,' James said.

A strong whiff of bad odour reached his nose. It was not the time to be out. The muckmen's cart passed them, trundling down the street full of the filth of the burgh, on their way to transporting the stuff outside the town.

'Is there anything else you would like to tell me?' Andrew asked.

'No.' James leaned back against the railing. His eyelids closed. He felt sleepy. He was dozing on and off, not aware of the time. He felt a sharp dig in his right arm.

'How can you doze off in this midden?' Andrew said. 'We have to keep sharp.'

'Are they still in there?'

'Maybe. I feel uneasy. The sooner I finish with this whole venture the better,' Andrew said.

James shuffled slowly to the left. A cold shiver ran through his body. 'My neighbour, the sleeping drunkard's gone,' he said. He was not so drunken after all. He stood up abruptly. 'We need to find another hiding place.'

'Agreed. He's maybe a spy,' Andrew whispered. 'We'll go back to the lady's house.'

James heard the sighs, murmurs and grunts of ne'er-do-wells as he groped towards the house, following Andrew's lead. He glanced back. The good people of the Canongate were asleep. There was a flickering candle in one window. He wondered if it was Mr Alexander's house. He should be there, not here.

Back inside Lady Largo's house he warmed up by the kitchen fire. The scullery maid arrived and dumped a bucket of water on the kitchen floor.

'Is your mistress in?' Andrew asked.

'No,' the girl said. She placed a large pot of porridge on the fire. James was eager to return to his chamber, but his eyes studied the pot and some bread on the table. Andrew had disappeared.

James had just finished enjoying a huge bowl of porridge when he heard the back door open. He heard voices but stayed in the kitchen.

'Our gentleman has returned and is writing some reports,' Andrew said when he entered the kitchen. 'He intends to stay here another evening. Then I'll take him back to Comiston on my own. I'm grateful for your support, James.' Andrew showed James to the door. 'Oh, and another thing: no mention of all this, not even to Mr Charles.'

James nodded. He strode through the pend and up the Canongate.

## 23

'I s that you, sir?' Mrs Hodges' voice came from below, as James stepped up the turnpike. He had removed his wig and padding, and carried them wrapped in a bundle. 'Mrs Alexander's maid was looking for you last night. Where were you? I had young Davie out searching.'

James tucked his bundle under his arm, and leaned against the wall. 'I was with a very sick person.'

'You dinnae seem bothered. Mr Alexander and his relations are well known in high places, mind. That's what Mr Duff says. Your absence won't go down well.'

'I know that, Mrs Hodges.'

Mr Duff was always giving these warnings. He had heard it all many times. The lawyer was prone to showing too much deference. A balance had to be maintained, James thought. The way was compromise. Was he learning from Andrew? Life was more than just profiting from trade. That led to greed. But being altruistic had its difficulties too.

Back in his own chamber, a wash, shave and change of clothes restored his confidence. He pushed aside thoughts of where his loyalties stood. What he needed to consider was the consequences of his actions. He would have to think of what to say to Alexander, a gentleman of influence and power. He set his mind to compose suitable untruths to explain his absence as he wandered down the High Street.

'The master's not available just now,' the manservant said. 'The midwife is with the mistress and her new son. She's much exhausted. We had to send for another physician…'

'Can I see Mrs Alexander?'

The manservant's face was severe. 'Certainly not,' he said. 'She's resting. You may know her needs are well provided for. Your services are not required.'

James hesitated. He shifted from one foot to the other. The man stood firm at the doorway. James turned and walked away. There was nothing more he could do. He strode up the street, feeling anger in every step. It was an unfortunate turn of events that the lady had given birth while he was engaged on a secret mission. Not a situation that occurred every day.

He slowed down, feeling tired from lack of sleep. A restful day alone was what he needed.

Back in his chamber, he kicked his boots off and lay on his bed. But sleep wouldn't come. He was in no mood for study either. Thoughts rushed through his head. Mrs Alexander's new son. Jacobite conspiracies. He would not be surprised if there were spies around, watching. Andrew's important person was, he suspected, in great danger.

He heard footsteps and a knock on the door. He glanced at the clock. It was past one. He had been asleep for hours.

'Mr Lawson is at home and ready to dine, sir. If you would please join him and Mr Duff,' Hodges said.

'Thank you. I will be down in a moment.'

So Andrew had left his visitor in the care of Lady Largo for the day, and was back in control of his own affairs. He appeared in good fettle when James joined him, a bottle of claret in one hand and a glass in the other. He put the bottle down and waved James to a chair at the dining table, just as if it was a normal day. No one would guess, from Andrew's casual manner, the unpredictability of his activities in recent weeks.

Mr Duff sipped his wine slowly. His skin was pale and drawn, his eyes red and baggy. 'I'm no so bad,' he said curtly, in answer to James's question about his health. He was not being truthful. His appearance showed otherwise.

Mrs Hodges brought in chicken and barley broth. James filled up his bowl.

Mr Duff took a small portion. 'I don't have much of an appetite,' the lawyer said.

Hodges addressed James. 'There are two young ladies requesting to see you, sir. In private.'

Andrew grinned from ear to ear. Mr Duff looked up from his plate, casting an enquiring glance at James.

'Miss Anne Alexander and companion. Shall I escort them to your chamber?'

'Please do, Hodges.' James frowned. 'Tell them I'm engaged on pressing business, and will see them in a short while.' He would make them wait. This was unexpected. He needed more time for invention.

Andrew's longcase clock ticked the time away. Andrew's agreeable mood continued well into the afternoon. 'Well, James. You mustn't keep the ladies waiting too long,' Andrew said. 'Though perhaps to face up to ladies, you need a bit of extra courage from the bottle first.' He refilled James's glass.

'I'm in no hurry to see them,' James said, taking a sip. He enjoyed his dinner as always.

'Tell them you came to see me last night,' Mr Duff said. 'I collapsed, and you stayed the night with me.'

'It's a useful fabrication,' Andrew said. 'We won't think worse of you for it. Rather, it is expected. To survive and stay ahead, tricks in deception and cunning are worthwhile.'

'Life is full of devious twists and turns,' Mr Duff said. 'You must form your own path.'

'Without a care for others? These deceptions are no better than the ways of the self-serving politicians you criticise,' James said.

'James, I don't think you are aware of the danger we are all in,' Andrew said. 'It's fine to have noble ideas and good intentions. But in the end we all do what suits our own interests.'

James was about to ask why Andrew was taking risks, neglecting the concerns of his trade and people dependent on it, but he said nothing. He was not sure of the extent of Mr Duff's involvement either. The conversation ceased and James was left to contemplate how he would deal with the young ladies.

It was with slow steps that he made his way up to his chamber. Miss Anne was sitting on the armchair and her maid sat by the window, perfectly at ease in her role as chaperone.

'I do not like to be kept waiting,' Miss Anne said.

'You wished to see me privately. Therefore you wait till I'm available. Had your visit been a social call you would have been welcome to join us after the conclusion of our business,' James said. 'I'm not treating you differently from anyone else.' He drew up a chair and sat down.

Miss Anne jerked her head and sniffed. 'That's just the thing. You have been treating us differently – with a lack of respect.' She shifted her body and leaned forward slightly, sitting upright in a rigid position. 'The nurse has been with my stepmother since she gave birth in the early hours. The baby looks poorly, and the physician who came – his manners were unpleasant. He said my brother may not live, yet barely glanced at him.' Anne paused. 'And he had dirty fingernails.'

'Well, I can't do anything from here. I'm not welcome at your house, apparently.'

'I know. Father was angry. We expected to see you last night. A message was sent to you when she was in the early stages of giving birth. You didn't call.' Her large brown eyes were moist.

James avoided her gaze. 'My lawyer took a bad turn. Quite suddenly. I stayed with him all night at his house. I didn't receive the message.'

'You will not be paid. And don't expect my father to support the progress of the College of Physicians,' Anne said. 'His opinions may have turned.'

There was no more to be said. James stood up, hoping they might decide to leave. Anne remained seated.

'Why did you come here?' he asked. 'You have another physician now.' He opened the door. Miss Anne and her companion stood up and shuffled towards it.

'I thought we might have been friends,' Anne said. She left without looking back.

James guessed that she had not come of her own wishes, but at the suggestion of someone else. She had attempted both indignation and flirtation, and achieved neither, due possibly to a lack of experience.

James descended the turnpike, and met Andrew coming up to see him.

'Come this evening, James. After ten o'clock, outside Lady Largo's house,' he said.

## 24

James left his chamber just before curfew. He wore a brown wig; lighter than the grey one and made with coarser hair. It made his neck hot and itchy after just a few minutes. He crossed the courtyard and entered the close at the far side. A tall man blocked his way. In the gloom it took a moment for him to realise that he wore a mask. Only his eyes were visible. James's hand went to the hilt of his sword. He felt a heavy shove from behind. He fought back in all directions but there were too many of them. One of them removed his wig and stared at him. James struggled. A cloth was tied round his eyes and another covered his mouth. The foul taste made him gag. They kicked him on both sides, dragged him by the arms, and deposited him on the ground. His hands were tied behind his back. He felt he was being lifted onto something, and then covered with a soft, damp blanket. The cart wheeled him a short distance. He was lifted and shoved down steps, pushed to the ground and a rope tied round his ankles. They left him.

James shivered in the stiff breeze. He guessed he must be on the steep north side of the burgh. He tried to move sideways. There was grit in his eyes. He wanted to rub them. He struggled with his wrists, trying to free the cord. It was too tight. He lay still; frustrated, angry.

Then he heard a rustle. He was not alone.

'If you try to make a sound, you're a dead man,' a voice whispered in his ear. 'Your body will be dumped into the North Loch down there. It will disappear among the filth, and will never be found.'

Hands lifted him up and carried him up steps. He heard the scrape of a key in a lock, and the creaking of a door being opened. The passage smelt of dampness and stale wine. The cloths were removed from his eyes and mouth, and he found himself staring at two men wearing face masks. One held a lamp in front of him. He glimpsed the shadow of a man on guard at the door. The chamber was small, with a table, chairs, and a bed in the corner.

'This won't take long,' the man with the lamp said. 'Quicker if you are agreeable.' His voice spoke of education and fine breeding. He faced James. 'I regret the rough treatment, sir. We can proceed now without pain if you wish. Some information and your collaboration are all we ask.' He pushed James down onto a chair, and moved closer. 'Now,' he said. 'First of all we want to know where you're bound after curfew.'

James did not answer.

'It's not a time to be on the street. Robbers and assassins are about.'

'So to which party do you belong? Robbers or assassins?' James asked.

He felt a sharp sting on his right cheek. This was followed by kicks in the shin. He stared at his inquisitor. His adversary's eyes indicated a resolute disposition. Definitely someone he had never met.

'We could have followed you,' his interrogator was saying, 'but we would rather you talked to us. Saves a lot of time.' He nodded to his companion.

James received another blow on the side of the face, followed by kicks on the same side. He kept moving his wrists to loosen the cord. His hands would soon be free.

'I don't think we have been introduced. May I ask the name of my inquisitor?' James asked.

His chair was couped. He rolled over on the floor, and ended up lying face down. He was hauled back into the chair. He could have taken the men if his legs had been free. He had seen mutiny and piracy at sea, but this was different. Unpredictable. He guessed they wouldn't kill him. He had to invent a story. About an old man who was poorly perhaps; or an affair with a married woman; or pursuing the young lady of his dreams. He smiled at the thought.

Another blow. This time the other cheek, and with a sharp object. Blood trickled down the side of his face. He thought of Jack Scarlett. This might be his revenge. None of the three men had Scarlett's physique. Of the ones who ambushed him in the close, he couldn't tell. But if Scarlett were here now he would relish the attack on James's face.

'Who are you protecting?' the man with the lamp asked.

'Myself at the moment,' James said. He waited for the next punch. It didn't come. 'I was going to see a young lady, if you must know. Not that it's any of your business.' He had to convince them he had nothing of importance to tell them.

'A young lady, eh?'

'Someone's coming,' the man at the door whispered.

James heard shuffling in the passage, dragging sounds, and heavy breathing. Smugglers perhaps? Contraband could be transported in boats on the North Loch, and stored conveniently in cellars on the north slope of the city. Who knew what went on at night? The sounds receded into the distance.

The two men pulled him outside the main door. One of them delivered a heavy punch. James sank to the ground. He heard the clash of metal objects being thrown down beside him. James lifted his head. They were his sword and dagger. The men disappeared.

After a struggle he pulled his hands free, reached for his dagger, and cut the cords on his ankles. His hands trembled. They were sticky with blood. His legs wobbled but, he managed to shuffle along to examine boxes at the entrance to the passage. Bottles of wine. James listened. He heard clattering and bumps in the cellar. He crept back from the entrance so that the men wouldn't trip over him when they came out. He lay still, listening.

After a while all was quiet. He had to go. His adversaries might come back and interrogate him further, or throw him in the loch. His whole body was sore. He stumbled along. He slipped. He was sliding down the hillside. He dragged himself onto a ledge and heard the creaking of a gate. A man emerged and relieved himself. James crept up, and managed to squeeze through the gate.

The man turned and asked, 'Are you a chapman?'

'No. Are you?' James said. His head was sore. He tried to think. His legs gave way again and he sank to the ground.

'That I am. If you're no a chapman, what are you doing here?' The man edged away.

James had a sudden thought. He must be near the printer's workshop. 'Do you know Francis Atkins?'

'Aye.'

'You have to help me. Find Francis or his brother Douglas. Tell them… Tell them…'

'Are you a spy?' the man asked coldly.

'No,' James said slowly. 'Just go. Find them.' He laid his head down.


The nightmares woke him up. His enemies were dressed in purple and singing loud, bawdy songs from massive printed broadsides. A skeleton tumbled off a bookshelf and fell on top of a pile of books. He felt the desire to sneeze, but couldn't. He opened his eyes. A hand touched the side of his face. Douglas was examining the wound on his cheek.

'Don't speak. I'm just about to dress this wound,' Douglas said. 'It's not deep.'

He felt a sharp sting, then a coldness. He closed his eyes and dozed off.

When he awoke he cast his eyes round the poky chamber. Books and pamphlets were piled up in boxes from floor to ceiling. Shelves on one wall were covered with papers. Francis was sitting on a stool in a corner reading a book, illuminated by a streak of morning light through a tiny window. There were papers everywhere. He sniffed the sheets on his bed.

Francis looked up. 'You're lying on a mattress of papers. And there are broadsides neatly folded between the linen, to prevent your body being covered in print. They make good insulation.' Francis kneeled down beside him. 'Welcome to my secret chamber of banned pamphlets. How do you feel?'

'I don't have much pain.'

'Douglas gave you a heavy dose of laudanum.'

'How...' He was finding it difficult to speak.

'A chapman came to my door late last night. I don't like hawkies loitering about the close, but this time I was grateful. I was cautious because he didn't know your name. It could have been a trap. The chapman found you at the north entrance to the close. So we brought you here. When you feel like it, you must tell us what happened. We want to know who did this to you.'

James dozed off again. The troubled dreams returned. He awoke with a jolt, eased himself into a more comfortable position and raised his head. Francis brought a couple of books to prop his head up, placing them under his pillow of crushed paper covered with linen.

'There was a group of them,' James began. 'I don't know how many. All wearing masks. They attacked me, bundled me into a cart, and I was dumped somewhere. They left me. Then I was taken to a chamber and questioned by three others, also disguised. Fortunately they were interrupted by a band carrying bottles of wine. This was in a close not far from here.'

'Where were you going when you were set upon?'

'That I can't tell you.'

'Hmm.'

'I've got to go.' James attempted to rise, then fell back.

'No. Stay here. At least until you recover. Your enemies, whoever they are, won't find you in this cellar. And you're not fit to do whatever's on your mind.'

'Well – if you see Andrew, can you tell him about this incident? But don't report it to anyone else. And please send a message to Archibald Pitcairne. Say that I will not be available today. If he asks why, tell him I'm unwell or something.'

'I'll do as you say, but you must tell me more when I return. I'm going to have to lock you in here.' Francis looked around and grinned. 'At least you'll have plenty to read.'

James sighed. He was too weak to move. He was not even hungry. Andrew would come to see him, if he was not at Comiston. It was going to be a long day. He cast his eyes round the chamber. Why were there so many books here, he wondered? His mind was muddled. He tried to recall the nobleman, Lady Comiston… He became drowsy, unable to focus his thoughts.

He lost track of time. At last he heard the key in the lock. It was Robert Charles. He came straight to the point.

'Francis Atkins said you are unwell. He was a bit vague,' Charles said, taking a seat on a small stool.

James related his account of being ambushed. He made no mention of excursions to Lady Largo's house and nightly meetings.

'I rather doubted the truth of the report I received from your friend,' Mr Charles said. 'How do you fare?'

'I've had worse treatment. Do you have any idea who would want to question me?'

'I was wondering if you might know.'

'There is one person from my past who would delight in making me uncomfortable, if paid well to do so, for revenge. But he would not interrogate me. These men were seeking information. You may be reassured I did not comply,' James said.

'Good. Excellent.' Charles nodded.

James tried to stand up. He wobbled a bit.

'Pitcairne sends his regards,' Mr Charles said. 'He said not to be concerned about your absence. He will manage.'

'He's not curious?'

'He's inquisitive, I think. Were you going anywhere in particular late at night?'

There was a knock on the door. It was Francis Atkins. 'You asked about John Scarlett,' Francis said. 'I heard that he returned to Leith the day before last, apparently after a successful venture. He has now taken off with a cargo bound for Shetland.'

'Take me back home,' James said.

'I suggest we take you for a meal first,' Mr Charles said. 'And no more outings after curfew.'

James was shaky on his feet to begin with, but by the time they arrived at the tavern he even felt a bit hungry. He managed a little mutton broth.

He recalled when he had first met Francis and Douglas more than a year ago when he returned to Edinburgh from overseas. He was a stranger and they were wary. Now he faced a different threat. He had to be on guard. He didn't want Francis being too inquisitive. He had to steer his interest elsewhere.

'So tell me about all those books and pamphlets,' James began.

'Books?'

'The books, pamphlets and broadsides in the cellar.'

'They are papers and broadsides that escaped the hangman, and are no longer newsworthy. They will be burned anyway. Some were smuggled in. Others were stored to go abroad. The papers tell their own stories.'

Mr Duff joined them. 'I heard you were unwell,' he said, studying James's face with curiosity.

'Tell me about John Scarlett,' James said. 'I heard he had arrived at Leith.'

'Aye, and wealthy too,' Mr Duff said. 'He was running his own cargo. He has paid Andrew generously for the use of the *Lady Margaret*, and donated some of his own profits to help with compensation for loss of the *Louise Anne*.'

'And what of Brand?'

'Andrew seems quite happy with the way Brand is handling his affairs. He was with them today.'

James frowned.

'Trading is like that, James. One day you're rich; the next you're out of luck. You take the risks.' Mr Duff took a sip of wine. 'Andrew is taking the news of the loss of Tom quite badly.' He lowered his voice. 'He's still caught up with his other ventures.'

James knew exactly what Duff meant.

Davie appeared at the table and handed James a slip of paper. 'A note for you, sir. From Mr Lawson.'

## 25

James turned the key to his own chamber. He was feeling sore. The effects of the laudanum had worn off, but it was not a good idea to take another dose. A clear head was needed to reflect on recent events. The best way to do that was here alone. Taking out Andrew's note, he opened the shutters to catch the remains of the evening light. He leaned carefully against the side of the window. Andrew's writing was careless, with scores through, as if written in haste. He was sorry for what had happened to James. He would be travelling frequently until his mission reached its completion. For now, they should avoid each other. The best course of action for James would be to be visible in his usual work. He must be vigilant. Dangerous enemies were about. Finally, on no account was he to visit Lady C – meaning Lady Comiston.

James lit a candle and burned the letter. He eased himself gently into his comfy armchair, feeling the positions of his bruises. Andrew's advice to focus on his own life confirmed what he wanted to do anyway. But it was not that easy. It is better to know who your enemies are. How did Andrew become involved in Jacobite intrigue? What did he have to gain?

The door opened and a head appeared. 'James, may we come in?' Louise asked. 'Mr Atkins asked me to call on you, to attend to your wounds.' She walked in, followed by Janet.

'I'm all right, thank you. No real damage. Mainly bruises and minor cuts.'

Louise stepped forward. Her face was slightly flushed, her eyes big and wide. Her small hands were soft against his skin as she examined the cut on his cheek. He felt the tension ease from his body.

'It's not deep,' he said.

Her hair fell partially across her face, but did not hide her frown.

'I don't know what the brothers have told you, but please keep any knowledge to yourself,' he said.

'I assure you, I know when to be discreet,' Louise said. 'I know nothing of your scrapes. Henry says you have a reputation for brawling—'

'Brand doesn't know me at all. But you do.'

Louise blushed. She stepped back and stood up straight.

'You didn't come just to examine my wound, did you?' James asked. 'I can see you have something pressing on your mind. Please sit down.'

She pulled up a stool and sat close to him. Janet settled at the table by the window.

Louise looked at her hands. 'I am going to be married to Henry.'

A cold shiver passed through his body.

'I would like you to be friends with him. He does want to get to know you.' She raised her head and held his gaze.

He closed his eyes, and felt a dull ache in his stomach. His legs were shaking. This was too much to take in. It had been a long day, and he was still weak, but resolute in his opinion of Brand. 'I see no reason to be friendly with Henry Brand. Our paths do not cross.'

'That's because you take steps to avoid him. He manages the shop now. You may pass some conversation with him there. There are often idle moments.'

'I have no idle moments. All my time is valuable to me, and to those in my care.'

Louise reddened, clearly affected by his words. 'You cared for my father. He thought kindly of you. "A man of deep intelligence who knows his own mind," was what he said. I enjoyed those evenings with just the three of us in conversation.'

'I enjoyed them too. I wanted your father to be comfortable and make the best of his remaining days.'

'When you came here first, I thought we could be friends. Anyway Henry and I are to be married,' Louise said. She stood up, walked to the door and turned round.

'I don't like your choice of husband.'

'That's regrettable. I thought you might wish us well.'

James closed the door behind them. He heard their footsteps on the turnpike gradually receding before they reached the bottom. He was jealous. He realised that now. His mind had been so much on his work that he had given Brand every opportunity.

A loud knocking at the door startled James. He crawled out of bed. The sun was well up. He was late for the Greping Office. It was good, though, to have this routine start to the day. It made the events of two weeks ago seem like a bad memory. He unlocked the door. It was Davie with a note from Mr Alexander, requesting James's company in the afternoon. This was a surprise. He wandered across to the table, took a quill and searched for a scrap of fresh paper. He scribbled a short reply, dusted the paper and folded it.

'Take this to Mr Alexander's house,' he said. 'Oh, and Davie, be mindful who you speak to. If anyone threatens you, let me know.'

'Are you in bad trouble, sir?' Davie asked.

The lad's concern touched his conscience. 'I hope not. But take care anyway.'

Davie nodded and was off.

James made haste to prepare himself for the day. He hobbled down the turnpike, still in some pain, and shuffled awkwardly along the close. Henry Brand was opening the shop. Dressed in a fine tailored suit and a new powdered wig, the merchant was proudly arranging the display at the front of the booth. He flicked a speck of dust off a bolt of cloth and placed it on the counter. Standing erect, he cast admiring glances at passing ladies. James's stomach turned. He looked the other way to avoid him, but it was too late.

'Good morning, James,' Henry said. 'A fine prospect of a day.' He grinned.

'Good morning,' James said.

'I haven't seen you in a while. I thought you might have come to congratulate me on my engagement to Miss Louise.'

'I've been... I've been rather preoccupied with many pressing matters,' James said. This was true, if rather vague. 'And if you'll permit me, I have consultations.'

He was being too brusque. He could have at least made an attempt to offer his congratulations. But why should he? He didn't really want to. He turned quickly along the arcade, and collided with a fat woman carrying a large basket of carrots.

'Clumsy young folk,' she shouted. 'They have no care.'

She was wrong. He did care. About the sick. About the spread of disease. About people. About Louise. He shifted his thoughts to Andrew. Was he here or at Comiston? Twice he spotted him, meandering up Castlehill and entering the Duchess of Gordon's house, high up on the hill near the castle. Andrew was still in a secret conspiracy with the nobility, he guessed, and managing his business at the same time.

A tiny window in the corner of the consultation room allowed just enough light to illuminate a patient in the corner. The rest of the chamber was dim. As the morning progressed the emerging sunshine made patients appear in better health than the early-morning visitors. Pitcairne, as ever, was full of enthusiasm for his work. Curiously, he had asked James no questions about his absences, and was even eager to allow him time off as suited his will. James hoped Andrew's secret mission would be finishing soon. His hands became sticky with the heat as the morning wore on. He was glad to be outside walking in the sunshine after the clinic.

As soon as his work was finished, thoughts about Mr Alexander crowded his mind, as he recalled his meeting with the lovely Miss Anne. At Mr Alexander's house, the servant showed James into the cool, empty, north-facing library. He wandered round to get a measure of the wealthy gentleman from the variety of books in his collection. He didn't have to wait long. Mr Alexander smiled as he entered.

'Please be seated.' Mr Alexander indicated a chair by the window.

James noticed an awkwardness, an uncertainty, quite unlike his previous encounters with the man.

'I apologise for rebuffing your efforts to make amends. I believe I have been mistaken. I realise now that others may press on your services urgently.'

This was unexpected. James had imagined he was to be on the receiving end of a severe reprimand.

'I accept your apology, sir,' he said. 'I have been—'

'Good. Then we move on.' Mr Alexander rose and picked up a small bell by the window. A servant appeared. 'We'll have the rest of the claret, if you please.'

The servant nodded and brought in a bottle and two glasses. Mr Alexander poured the wine and handed James a glass.

'My wife is visiting friends this afternoon, with my son. He is well. A fine boy, though quite small. The nurse assures me he takes milk eagerly.'

'Excellent. And Mrs Alexander? She is well?'

'Yes, she is, I thank you. She has more colour, and is in good fettle.' Mr Alexander sipped his wine. 'My sister, Eleanor, would like to see you. She says she has been feeling out of sorts, but she looks all right to me.' Mr Alexander eyed James. He leaned back. 'I do not approve of her husband. Don't trust him. I don't know what possessed her to marry him.' He shook his head. 'He has some sort of trading partnership with Andrew Lawson. Am I correct?'

'They are joint owners of the *Lady Margaret*,' James said. This fact was well known.

Mr Alexander's eyes were studying him. He was waiting for James to continue.

James said, 'I have met John Scarlett, but know little about him.' In some ways this was true.

'Hmm. It seems that little is known of his background. I am informed his wealth is considerable.'

Mr Alexander shuffled in his chair and crossed his legs. James glanced sideways to break the gentleman's constant gaze. He scanned the rows of books.

'Eleanor mentioned that you and Lawson are close, like brothers.'

'I've known Andrew a long time. I have lodgings in one of his chambers, but we rarely see one another. We move in different circles.'

'Do you not dine with him?'

'Occasionally we have dinner or supper together.'

'So you will have met some of his acquaintances?'

James was ready for this. 'When I dine with him, it is usually at home. Just the two of us, and sometimes other residents in the tenement. I don't meet the merchants he deals with.'

Mr Alexander continued his close scrutiny, his eyes piercing as if trying to penetrate his mind. James wondered if there had been rumours, or if Andrew was being watched. Whatever was going on, he had to make an escape. But he did not want to appear anxious. He leaned back in his chair, in casual relaxation. He glanced at the wall clock. He rose and edged towards the door of the library.

'I shall have time to see Mrs Scarlett this afternoon if she's available. Thank you for the excellent claret,' he said, draining his glass and setting it on a shelf, ensuring that Alexander noticed his hands were steady. He would not show signs of any discomfort.

A walk to Leith might be a pleasant diversion, and ease his mind. That encounter with Alexander had been uncomfortable. He felt the sun on his back and a gentle breeze soothed his body as he traipsed down to Leith to visit Eleanor Scarlett.

A narrow line of light indicated a slight opening at the door of his chamber. James pushed the door violently. Papers lay scattered on the table and chairs, and spilled onto the floor. His medicine cabinet had been burst open; the section holding his coins was empty. He picked up a jar labelled *Cumin*. The few coins within were untouched. Books lay open on the armchair. The lock of the door was undamaged. Someone must have a key.

The intruders may have been the men who interrogated him, or their master. Andrew must have some idea who they were. Or perhaps Mr Charles. But first he tried Rose and Bella's chambers. They were not at home. He tried Andrew's chambers next.

'Is your master at home?' James asked, pushing past Hodges.

'I'm here,' Andrew shouted from the small parlour.

'Has anything unusual happened?' James asked. He strode across the hall and tripped over the carpet.

'No. Whatever is the matter, James? Come in. Sit down before you explode.'

'Come with me.' James turned abruptly, marched to the door and waited for Andrew to follow.

Andrew rose slowly and followed him upstairs. He allowed Andrew a few moments to examine the scene in his chamber.

'Whoever did the damage had a key,' James said, thinking of Scarlett.

'The spare keys to the tenement are kept locked in my closet, along with my papers. I suggest you keep your papers locked up too.'

'Too late for that now.'

'Has anything been stolen?'

'Some coins. That's all. They were looking for information. What do they want to know?'

Andrew was silent.

'And another thing: Hugh Alexander has been asking me questions. He's seeking information about your acquaintances.' James shifted some books and sat down. He tried to focus his mind. 'Scarlett used this chamber once and had a key,' he said.

'Anyone who has occupied this room in the past could have made a copy of the key, I suppose.'

'I visited Eleanor Scarlett today. She said her husband is at sea. She was a bit vague. Is he ashore? Have you seen him?'

'He's in Eyemouth seeing to repairs on the *Lady Margaret*. I've just had a letter.' Andrew walked round looking for clues. 'I think the intruder was searching for more about you. Your interests, clients, friends.'

But James was not for dismissing Scarlett. His motive for searching the chamber would be for some reward or favour. But for whom? James didn't trust his wife either. 'Mrs Scarlett has grandgore,' he said.

'Really James, I thought that everyone knew that.'

'Well, I suppose it's no surprise, considering the man she married.'

'You may be wrong there. Scarlett himself told me they're married on paper only.'

'You mean…'

'I mean she's only one step away from being a lady of the night. But enough of Eleanor.' Andrew sat down on the armchair. 'I want to tell you that I will be going north; not sure when, possibly in the next few days. I can tell you our visitor is still at Comiston with another guide. His business here is nearly complete. He's waiting for some letters.'

'This venture north, is it a covert affair?'

Andrew nodded.

## 26

'John Scarlett's back in Leith,' Francis said. 'Already, he seems to have annoyed another merchant. He said Scarlett had pressed his crew. One thing's led to another. I've heard Scarlett has been thrown out of more than one tavern.'

James smiled and sipped his wine. 'I told him once he would never cope with refined Edinburgh society. He can't even manage to stay out of trouble in Leith.'

'Your own position is not too good either, James. You could say being a victim is more dangerous than being the perpetrator.'

James nodded. 'Especially when you have no idea who your enemies are.'

'It would be wise to stay away from Scarlett. I hear he is being disagreeable to all.'

'He's always disagreeable. Let's see that broadside you're holding,' James said, indicating the bundle that Francis had just brought into the tavern.

'Oh, it's nothing much.' Francis grinned.

'No? I can see you're eager to sell them. Must be important.'

'It's about the reports on negotiations for a union. Rumour has it, and these are just rumours, mind, that money has changed hands. How else do they change their minds?'

'Not everyone is like that,' James said.

'Politicians are,' Douglas said. 'I wouldn't trust any of them.'

'You're not near any of them,' Francis said. 'They make decisions that affect us all. Those in favour of a union state that it has to be an incorporating union – a merger. While those against fear loss of independence. A union would be best for trade, I suppose.'

James swallowed the rest of his wine and stood up.

'You're not going to Leith are you?' Francis asked.

'I am. The sooner the better. I must see Scarlett,' James said.

'Wait a bit. His dealings with Andrew are not your concern,' Francis said, following him to the door. 'You mustn't interfere.'

'I am involved.' James strode off down the High Street.

'We're coming with you,' Douglas said, quickening his step to keep up with him.

'I am. You're not,' Francis said, turning to his brother. 'If James doesn't succeed in provoking Scarlett, you will.'

'I don't provoke people. I give support and assistance,' Douglas said.

'All right then. You can help me with these broadsides,' Francis said, pressing a bundle to his chest, forcing Douglas to grip them.

James smiled. He couldn't help noticing that Francis displayed more cunning than his elder brother. They couldn't be more different. Francis, outspoken though he was in political matters, had good sense. James turned to face Francis.

'You're right. Andrew's trade deals have nothing to do with me.'

If only Scarlett had returned last week while Andrew was still in Edinburgh, then his mind would be at ease. There was no way of knowing when Andrew would return from up north, if that's where he was. Or he could be at Comiston. Anyway, there was the matter of the key.

'Someone had a key to my chamber. I've asked Rose, Isabella, Mrs Grant and Louise. Scarlett could easily have had more than one copy of the key. I think he's the one who searched my chamber. I want to know why, and who paid him.'

Francis stopped outside his shop. 'I'll get more broadsides,' he said, and disappeared inside.

James cast his eyes across the display of books on the counter. He picked one up – *The Perfect Accountant*. He quickly put it down again.

'I share your suspicion about Scarlett. I wouldn't trust his wife either,' Douglas said.

'Exactly. Then we are of similar mind.'


By the time they had walked to Leith, James had resolved to ask Scarlett about the spare key, in the same way as he had asked the residents in the tenement. Not a confrontation, merely an enquiry – if he could find him. The taverns were overflowing. Men crowded at the doors and stood outside. A group of well-to-do passengers gathered, waiting for a ferry, and nearby a tall trader waved his arms, directing the loading of coal.

Sitting at a table at the door of a tavern was Scarlett, engaged in earnest conversation with a merchant whose embroidered blue jacket with white lace facings and silk cravat indicated his wealth. James walked up to the table and held out a broadside. Scarlett waved him away, then recognised James and grinned.

'Reduced from doctor to chapman then, sir,' Scarlett said, leaning back in his chair and grinning from ear to ear.

'I'm bringing the news to the worthy gentlemen of Leith,' James replied.

As he singled out a broadside, he contemplated what kind of response his carefully chosen words would provoke. Instead he faced Scarlett's impassive gaze. The broadside slipped from his hand, and the breeze carried it round the corner of the tavern. He picked it up and pinned it to the wall. Scarlett's expression still hadn't changed. Clearly the man was minding his manners, eager to impress his client. The merchant showed a sardonic smile, shuffling in his seat and drumming his fingers on the table. Looking sideways for support, James spotted Francis and Douglas in a heated discussion with a group of seamen.

'Well, James.' Scarlett hesitated. 'Haven't seen you for several months. I've been much occupied overseas. Trade has been good.'

'I'm pleased to hear it,' James said. Thoughts rushed into his head; of Andrew almost ruined, the loss of the *Louise Anne*, the angry seamen's wives. He had questions, but not here in the presence of this wealthy merchant. He didn't want Scarlett quizzing him about Andrew's covert activities either. It might not have occurred to Scarlett that Andrew had been unexpectedly absent.

James took a deep breath. It was best to come straight to the point. 'Life for me has not been so fortunate. A week ago someone with a key entered my chamber and upset my belongings. Papers and books were scattered about.'

He studied Scarlett intently. He had a slightly quizzical look. Then he frowned and leaned forward.

'I know what you're implying. I handed your spare key back, remember. Are you accusing me?'

'I have been asking other residents in the neighbourhood as well.'

'He's pointing a finger at you,' the gentleman in the embroidered jacket said. 'He insulted you, and must apologise.'

'I will not,' James said. He looked around. A few men glanced in his direction, sensing a quarrel. He shuffled the bundle of papers balanced on his arm, keeping them straight so that none would fall loose.

The rich merchant leaned on his elbow, looking directly at Scarlett. 'You must call him out, for attempting to damage your character. Swords to first blood. I'll be your second.'

'I will not fight,' James retorted. 'Do not interfere, sir,' he said, addressing the merchant. 'I am seeking information. That's all.' James paused, and faced Scarlett. 'Did you have another copy of the key? Did you pass it on to someone? Do you know of anyone who would want to search my chamber and why?'

'I know nothing. You will apologise.' Scarlett stood up.

'I will not.'

To his relief Francis and Douglas had left the seamen and were at his side. Francis took his bundle of broadsides.

'Then you should answer his challenge. I'll be your second,' Douglas said.

'No. This is illegal,' James said.

Douglas took James aside. They walked along the quay. 'If you don't,' he whispered, 'Scarlett will haunt you. If you do, you will see that he is bluffing, and that will be an end to it.'

'I'm not so sure,' James said.

'I did warn you not to provoke him,' Francis said. 'You should mind that Scarlett has a partnership with Andrew. Seek a satisfying resolution.'

Scarlett joined them. 'St Anthony's Chapel. Tomorrow. First light,' he whispered.


'Andrew must stop this madness from happening.' James hurried on, hoping he was still in the city. Douglas and Francis kept pace with him as they walked back to Edinburgh. He tried not to think of the possible consequences. This encounter must not take place.

The door to the back stair in Andrew's apartment opened before James reached it. Hodges handed him a note.

'Thank you, Hodges.' He took a deep breath as he unfolded the paper.

'I noticed you hurrying through the back court, sir,' Hodges said.

James wasn't listening. He focused on the contents of the note. Andrew was going north to take a letter to *a merchant who is soon to take goods for shipping*, so must make great haste.

'I'm afraid you're too late. The master left after dinner,' Hodges said.

James considered the view as if for the last time. An orange glow filled the fields around the city. The slopes of the hills were in shadow. Beyond the chapel of St Anthony lay a long depression between Arthur's Seat and Whinny Hill. It was peaceful here. Calm. This was where they would fight. His stomach ached. He was tired from lack of sleep, and a sinking feeling of events spiralling out of control. He had faced danger before, many times. But this time he'd had hours of contemplation of what the day might bring. He might die. He might have to go into exile. All his expectations for the future gone.

It was too late to regret seeking Scarlett yesterday. He couldn't turn back the clock. Would the duel be to first blood, or worse? Scarlett was quick-tempered and unpredictable. Or he may have cooled off a little. A thought suddenly occurred. Scarlett might not show up. Another idea took hold in his mind. What if he were the one to take absence? He could cross to the steep side of Arthur's Seat, to St Leonard's and then to Dumbiedykes.

Too late. He spotted Francis and Douglas climbing the hill.

'We'll wait here,' Douglas said.

James could only hope for a resolution. With a little compromise on both sides that was possible. He eased the tension in his shoulders. His hands felt damp. He took off his gloves and rubbed his fingers.

He noticed Francis deep in thought. Douglas was surveying the ground with practical efficiency. The apothecary had set down a full package of surgical instruments and medicines, seemingly enough for any mishap or injury.

They did not have long to wait. James spotted his adversary at the side of the ruined chapel, with his second ambling along behind. They appeared in no hurry as they descended the gentle slope.

Scarlett's second walked up to James. 'We can call this off, if you apologise.'

James let out a sigh. 'I meant no insult. I was trying to find out who rummaged my belongings.'

'I know nothing. You questioned my honesty and worthiness,' Scarlett said, pacing up and down.

The seconds examined the swords. Scarlett gripped the one handed to him, and whipped the air with fury as he tried the measure of his weapon.

James's hand was trembling as he gripped his sword. He exercised his wrists. With Scarlett's temper up, he was likely not to follow the rules. James needed Andrew's support right now. He would have had a few words of encouragement and practical hints. He tried to recall the practice he'd had with Andrew but his mind went blank. He couldn't remember the words of advice. Was fear affecting his memory? He shivered. Francis and Douglas were watching him.

'I accept your word that you have no knowledge of the disturbance to my chamber,' James said. Was he being a coward, or trying to be fair and sensible? If Andrew were here he would stop this.

Scarlett paced up and down. James's whole body was shaking. Uncertainty was the greatest fear.

Scarlett stopped suddenly and turned, pointing his sword at James. 'These words come too late. Let's get on with it.'

At the signal from Douglas they started. Scarlett lunged forward, forcing James back onto rough grass. James backed up a gentle slope, giving him some height. He jumped down. Scarlett shuffled to the side, and stumbled; not used to the uneven ground. James sensed a rise of confidence, and attacked with vigour. He felt a kick in the groin.

'That's against the rules,' Douglas shouted.

'What rules?' Scarlett replied. He made to circle James. 'Come on then.' He gestured with his sword. 'Or are you the coward I think you are?'

'I'm no coward.' James stood on guard, waiting for Scarlett to make the next move. 'And unlike yours, my business dealings are fair.'

'What do you mean by that?' Scarlett swept his sword to and fro, circling James.

'Your ventures with Andrew Lawson. You neglected to pay the crew—'

'My trade deals are not your affair.'

Scarlett made his move. He stumbled, regained his balance and thrust forward. James whipped the sword from his hand, and nicked his forearm. James threw his own weapon down. It was finished.

Scarlett stooped to find James's sword with his left hand. Francis and Douglas rushed forward.

Douglas stood on the sword. 'Enough. It's done.'

Scarlett pushed them off, and retrieved his own sword. His second drew his firearm.

'Drop it.'

Scarlett eased his grip and let the sword fall.

## 27

A manservant led Andrew into the great library at Slains.

'My lady is with another visitor, a stranger.' He bowed and withdrew.

Andrew glanced at the longcase clock. It was noon. Some refreshments had been set out on a side table. He poured a cupful of small ale, and took a long draught. He had to tell the Countess of Errol about an urgent package for David Colville. Was he too late? Had the agent already departed for France? He paced up and down the large chamber.

He had to inform the Countess that Colville had left Edinburgh before receiving papers from the Earl Marischal. The delay had been due to the Earl's tardiness; some indication of the noble's indecisive nature or level of commitment perhaps. The longer the postponement, the greater the risk. Security was ever a problem. Had Colville arrived here, or had his cover been ripped open?

Andrew stopped at the window and opened the shutter, a sudden draught of cool air stinging his face. He scanned the horizon. The sea was blue-grey. Light clouds drifted across from the west. No sight of the French ship.

The door burst open and the Countess rushed in. 'Welcome, Mr Brock. I do apologise for not greeting you personally on your arrival. I've just been engaged in dealing with a stranger who has been in the neighbourhood for several days. A most unworthy person.'

She took a key from her pocket, slid back the small panel in the bookshelves, and inserted the key. The door opened. Sea air from the wee window filled the secret closet. Papers fluttered in the draught.

'Mr Carron tells me this stranger was trying to seek a passage to France on *L'Audacieuse*, pretending loyalty to the King. I have spent an hour of my valuable time with him. I fear his only motive is to escape the pursuit of his creditors. If he goes aboard he may be a danger to Colville. Indeed, his presence threatens the security of us all.'

The secret study was just as Andrew remembered from his last visit. He removed a pile of books from a chair, placed them carefully in the corner and sat down. He took the parcel from his satchel and handed it to the Countess, feeling the lift of a heavy weight of responsibility. So Colville hadn't sailed yet. He watched Lady Errol unwrap the papers.

'*L'Audacieuse* arrived a week ago,' she said. 'She was forced out to sea by the weather. We've had strong winds for three days.' The Countess arranged the bundles on her desk. 'We are expecting her return any time.'

'Then we're grateful this time for unfavourable weather. Colville would have missed letters from the Earl Marischal,' Andrew said.

'Indeed.'

'I hope this gentle breeze stays with us.'

Lady Errol opened a letter. As she read it, her hand shook a little. Andrew could not see the expression on her face.

'Robert Charles reports he's most satisfied with your service and loyalty to our cause.' She paused. 'But I am much troubled with the conversations and conflicts within...' She put her letter down and picked up the bundle for Colville. 'My maid will deliver these immediately.' She stood up quickly and knocked some papers off her desk. 'Mr Colville is at a safe place near the girl's family home.'

The Countess withdrew, leaving him to his own reflections. He felt the tension ease from his shoulders. He gazed out the library window. The sun broke through the clouds. He stretched out on the armchair. His eyelids were heavy. He eased his head back and closed his eyes.

A thump in the chamber above the library disturbed his rest. He heard shouts from a distant part of the house. He scanned the sea. A ship had appeared on the horizon. He took out his glass and watched it approach.

Lady Errol burst into the library, carrying a bundle of white sheets.

'It's *L'Audacieuse*, my lady,' Andrew said.

'Then we must show the signal,' the Countess said. 'Two sheets at two windows above one another.' She gave Andrew a white sheet. The manservant brought forward a chair for him to stand on. 'This shows the commander that we are aware of the ship's arrival.'

Andrew reached up to fasten the sheet to the shutters, and jumped down. 'Shall I fetch Mr Colville?'

'I will bring him here. I would rather you observe the ship approaching.' She gave Andrew a paper. 'This is Carron's list of signals, for us to communicate with *L'Audacieuse.*'

The servant led Andrew to a bedchamber above the library. The room was chilly and smelt damp. He read Carron's letter while the servant fixed the sheet to the window. There was a list of fourteen signals – warnings and instructions to cover all possible situations and difficulties, and to ensure safe arrival of the frigate.

Andrew heard shouting from below. He handed his glass and the letter to the manservant. 'Observe the signals from the ship,' he said, and ran down the stairs.

A gentleman in the passage spotted Andrew and rushed towards him, the servant at his heels. Was he the unworthy stranger the Countess mentioned? Andrew stopped in front of him, blocking the way. The gentleman was tall, with a thin face and piercing black eyes.

'I must speak with the Countess of Errol,' the gentleman said, addressing Andrew.

'I told you, sir, she is not at home,' the girl said.

'May I be of assistance, sir?' Andrew asked. He walked towards the stranger and, gently gripping his elbow, steered him through the hall to the entrance of the house. 'You may leave a message for Her Ladyship with me.'

The gentleman shook his elbow. Andrew dropped his hand, and softly laid an arm on his back. The man turned round fiercely.

'Take your hands off me, sir. What right have you? You're a stranger to me,' he said.

'And I know you not,' Andrew said, holding his gaze.

'I ask you to listen, sir. Please. Please allow me an interview with the Countess. There is a French ship out yonder.' His eyes appeared to soften. 'She must persuade the commander to grant me passage.'

'You're a scoundrel, sir,' Andrew said. 'The Countess of Errol wishes you to be gone. This instant.'

'I swear to you my loyalty to the King.'

Andrew caught a slight movement out of the corner of his eye. He turned round. The manservant appeared at the foot of the stairs.

'Mr Brock, sir. All is well.'

'Very good. And you, sir – you will depart. If not, you will find me joining your creditors in your pursuit.' Andrew stood with his right hand on his hip. 'I would delight in a hunt for quarry of your kind.'

The stranger flinched. His eyes widened.

Andrew stepped forward. 'It would be a pleasure indeed,' he added.

The stranger turned towards the entrance hall. Andrew twisted his arm and eased him out the door. He watched the unwelcome visitor cross the courtyard. A boy emerged from the stables with his horse. Andrew retreated to his chamber, watching the stranger ride south until out of sight. *He won't be back*.

The unworthy gentleman was long gone by the time the Countess returned with Colville. *L'Audacieuse* lay at anchor. Carron had come ashore. Andrew looked on as supplies were loaded onto the frigate: beef cattle, sheep, poultry, pasties, artichokes and wine.

'You are very generous, my lady,' Carron said, as he sat down at the dining table.

'For your safe voyage,' Lady Errol said. 'Mr Colville will join us shortly. He is just finishing one of his reports. He's such a meticulous writer. He was so relieved to receive the Earl Marischal's parcel from you, Andrew. Another day and he would have missed it. He is now composing his replies regarding these matters.'

'If all is well we shall sail early morning with the tide,' Carron said.

A fresh breeze cooled his face and invigorated his spirit as Andrew rode south to Edinburgh. The ship carrying Colville was on its way to France, and Andrew's mission was nearly complete. He had secret letters to deliver in Edinburgh, and then he would be free to concentrate on his own affairs. There was a lot of catching up to do. For the past two and a half months his time had not been his own. But firstly he would have to contact Mr Charles.

As it turned out, Robert Charles soon got word of his arrival in Edinburgh.

'You did well,' Charles said. 'It was important that Colville received the Earl Marischal's letter.' The Jacobite agent sighed, and put his feet up on a cushion embroidered with white roses. He appeared quite relieved.

Andrew leaned back comfortably on Bella's favourite scarlet chair. The sisters had gone to visit acquaintances, giving Andrew and Mr Charles the privacy of their cosy parlour.

Charles spread his hand across the bundle of letters on the table by his side. 'David Colville has, I think, been very thorough in his work. I will distribute these letters,' he said. 'Then we wait.'

It seemed to Andrew that Charles was revealing more about the conspiracy than he should.

As if reading his mind, Charles said, 'I feel more at ease regarding your loyalty and commitment than I did two months ago. Your friend, James, however...'

'James?' Andrew shifted his legs and sat up straight.

'Aye. I have worries about those he associates with socially.'

'You've been spying on James?'

'Not exactly.'

Andrew leaned forward in his chair. 'James is slightly naive; in another world. He is very much his own man.'

'I don't think so,' Charles said. 'I fear he may fall under the influence...'

'What do you mean?'

'To put it plainly, he may betray us.'

'Not at all. He is loyal to our cause. I know it.'

'I hope you're right.'

'The master would like to speak with you, sir.' Hodges popped his head round the door to James's chamber. 'He's in a bad humour.'

James put down his pen and turned his chair sideways, resting an elbow on the desk. 'It will soon pass, Hodges.' He smiled. 'Tell him I'll be down in a moment.'

Andrew's up-and-down moods were much exaggerated, varying according to his day-to-day fortunes. He'll be requiring the rest of the rent money. James opened his accounting book and reviewed the recent entries. All his charges were neatly entered. Several payments were overdue for drugs and treatment. He didn't overcharge, yet the money was slow to come in. Last week he was down to his last shilling. He opened a small drawer in his cabinet. Nothing. He would like to buy another cabinet for his coins and papers, but that purchase would have to wait.

Hodges led James into Andrew's small parlour at the far end of his chambers. Andrew's head was bent low over a bundle of papers on his desk.

'Sit down, James,' Andrew said, waving his arm in the direction of the fireside chair.

James watched Andrew pick up a sheet of paper, dip his pen into the well and then write vigorously. He dusted the paper, and when he raised his eyes he met James's gaze.

'Hodges told me you arrived back late last night,' James began. He wasn't going to ask about the journey. 'I'll have the remainder of the rent money just as soon as I can. I'm disappointed with the slowness of some gentlemen regarding their reckoning. Even some of the wealthier clients have bills outstanding.'

Andrew waved his arm. 'I am aware that you gave some moneys to Walter Duff six weeks ago. You may pay the rest when you are able.'

Andrew left his desk and sat in the armchair on the other side of the fire opposite James. 'I want to discuss another matter with you,' he began. 'This quarrel with Scarlett has to stop.'

'I wasn't seeking a quarrel with him.'

'You provoked him, and fought a duel.'

'I didn't call the duel.'

'But you sought him in Leith.' Andrew leaned an elbow on the armchair. 'Fortunately the fight remains a secret.'

'Many seamen lost their lives through his greed and ruthlessness. He has a grudge against me, from a while back.'

'You've already told me. Besides piracy is not that far removed from legitimate warfare. You could argue similarities. But anyway, that's in the past.' Andrew loosened his neckcloth, closed his eyes and then opened them. 'Listen to me, James. I have no particular fondness of the man. But I need him. He's a good moneylender. Don't know how he does it, but he's a survivor. He has the ability to deal easily with money matters.'

'He's unscrupulous, and a troublemaker.'

'There is something else. Before I left I warned you that there are those searching for knowledge of Jacobite intrigue. I know that you are acquainted with certain persons of power and influence who—'

James stood up. 'What are you suggesting? That I will betray you?'

'Of course not. I'm not suggesting that at all. But you must take care. You seem rather distracted often.'

James felt the heat in his face. 'I have the confidence of my patients. I do not discuss their private affairs. Nor do I discuss politics. You warned me yourself, remember – more than a year ago. Stay neutral. Do not get involved in politics. Now here you are. Up to your eyes in intrigue.'

'No one is entirely neutral. And I haven't forgotten you took a beating...'

'I didn't reveal anything...'

'I know you didn't.'

## 28

OCTOBER 1705

Louise felt tense with excitement. The wedding was tomorrow. She glanced round her bedchamber. It was no longer her own. All that remained was a bed. Her possessions had been packed for transport, except for some clothes she'd donated to the hospital. The other chambers, too, had been cleared. A new tenant was probably ready to move in. What would her father have thought of her leaving? A large tear trickled down her cheek before she could stop it. As Mary stepped forward, she turned her face away, but not quickly enough.

'You should be happy. You're moving to a better life,' Mary said. 'A house much grander than this.'

'But this is my life. Here,' Louise said. A shiver ran through her body. 'I thought Henry liked Edinburgh. I thought he wanted to stay. His desire to move came quite suddenly. I don't understand...'

'He has an estate down south. It's natural he wants to settle there.'

'Mm… he described his mansion house; formal gardens, and surrounded by parkland with sheep grazing. There are oaks, yews, chestnuts, beeches and lime trees. Sounds wonderful.'

'It does indeed.'

'But what will it be like living there? Away from friends?'

'You'll make new ones.'

Louise put aside feelings of unease. 'You're right. A future to look forward to.' She put on her new blue cloak, a present from Rose. 'I'm fine really.'

She was grateful that Mary had made the arrangements for the wedding. But not having to attend to details was making her anxious as her mind drifted to the coming marriage. Henry was not here. He had left Edinburgh on some business for Andrew – last-minute details, he assured her. She would spend the night with Mary in Mrs Grant's lodgings.

'Now shut the door for good,' Mary said, ushering Louise out into the close.

Louise closed the latch and turned the key. She grasped her bunch of keys firmly in her hand. Walking briskly, with Mary following behind, she climbed the back tenement stairs and knocked on Andrew's door.

'Thank you, my dear.' Mrs Hodges took the keys.

'We've taken out my own belongings,' Louise said.

'The master is not at home.' Mrs Hodges spoke softly, her eyes wide. Soft wisps of brown curls escaped from under her white cap. Lines on her brow deepened into a frown. Louise wanted to remember the details of the kind housekeeper; the features that made up a mature, confident, hard-working house servant, loyal to her wayward master.

Andrew took too many risks, but that was the uncertainty of the life of a merchant. He was a moneylender, and more besides. But for all that, he was a good friend and she trusted him. She would lose her companionship with James as well.

But she loved Henry. That was what mattered now. But why couldn't she persuade him to stay here?


James stepped out of the shadows into the courtyard to read the letter again. Mr Alexander was offering regular funds for the poor, and a loan towards his education at Leiden. But what had James to do in return for this? Alexander had been asking about Pitcairne's friends; probing for information on their interests and activities. Not that he knew much about them anyway. No. He would refuse the money, and fund his own education. He would continue to work for those in need. His success would come from hard work and honest friends.

He turned back into the shade of the close and came face to face with Louise.

'I've moved out,' she said, opening the stair door. She lowered her head to avoid meeting his eyes.

'You sound disappointed. That's not the way it should be. You're marrying a wealthy man; a young lady's dream.'

Louise stiffened and stood at the entrance to the stair. 'I'm not marrying Henry because he's rich,' she said. 'Though there are those who seem to think so.'

'You can't tell me you love him. He's much older than you.' He regretted his words as soon as they were out. Brand's charm was superficial. Any gentleman offering wealth and stability would catch a lady's eye. No woman would look at a man in his situation, no matter how worthy he was. What could he say? Wish her well? He didn't like Brand and there was no use pretending.

They reached the landing at Mrs Grant's lodgings. Tomorrow they would go their separate ways, and he would be unlikely to see her again.

'I won't forget your kindness to my father, James,' she said, avoiding his eyes.

The door was unlocked. She lifted the latch, and pushed the door a little. He wanted to stop her going inside. He wanted her to cancel the wedding, but he didn't say any of this.

'I wish you all the best. And do come and visit us sometime,' James said.

James found a note had been pushed under the door of his chamber. Andrew wished to speak with him in private. He found him seated in an alcove at the back of the tavern. The smell of cabbage and warm bread made him hungry. He rubbed his cold hands. Loud laughter came from Andrew's dining companions at the table. Andrew smiled meekly. James watched him swallow a cup of wine, pour another glassful, and swiftly devour it.

'Come, join us James,' Douglas said, indicating a chair. 'How do you feel... how do you feel now that Miss Morton is Mrs Brand, eh? She's gone now.' He waved an arm, accidentally dropping the piece of bread he was holding. 'I know you had an eye for her. You kept quiet about it. But I could tell.' Douglas took a sip of wine, spilling some of it. 'A lovely bride. You think so?'

'I did not attend the ceremony. Last week I was fully engaged. First at the Greping Office, then to Cramond, then to—'

'You missed the wedding?'

'That's enough, Douglas. James, place your order,' Andrew said.

James turned round and faced Willie Bell. He looked at the landlord's grubby apron. 'It's about time you wore a clean peenie,' he said. 'I'll have chicken pie with vegetables, if you please. And some bread.'

Willie strode off in a huff.

'Never mind, James,' Douglas said. 'Let me tell you that marriage is not the best situation... situation to find yourself in. Your life is not your own. You—'

'If your life as a husband and father is not agreeable to you, it is because you made it so,' Andrew said.

'And what would you know... what would you know about living with a tiresome, ungrateful wife—'

'We don't want to hear your complaints,' Francis said. 'Let's rejoice in the good news. Freedom of movement in the wine trade.'

'I'll drink to that,' Andrew said, raising his cup.

'I have good tidings as well,' James said. 'The College of Physicians have agreed to improve services for the sick and poor.' He glanced round the table as he spoke. Heads nodded in approval. He took the opportunity to steer the conversation to more pleasant matters. Everyone had an opinion to express. With the aid of wine and ale, there was no shortage of ideas round the table of how to right unpleasant wrongs.

James was anxious to remove Andrew from the tavern while he was still upright. He had a sense that all was not shipshape with his trade. He caught Andrew's eye. Andrew appeared to sober up momentarily, and James seized his chance. He paid his reckoning and gently eased Andrew from his chair. Andrew swallowed a last mouthful and put his cup down, not wanting to release it from his fingers. James linked his arm in his.

Andrew pushed him off. 'No need to fuss about me,' he said.

'I'm not. Just in a hurry to get home. You wanted to see me about something,' James whispered, steering Andrew out the door.

Andrew shoved him off again. The wind caught Andrew off balance, but James pushed him on through the crowded street.

'You were right about Brand,' Andrew said. He muttered a profanity, and an old woman kicked him in the shin. 'She must have good hearing,' he said.

They reached the close. James guided him through and up the spiral stair. Hodges took over and, initiating what seemed to be a well-practised routine, deposited Andrew in his favourite armchair. James sat down beside him and waited to hear the story.

'You warned me about Brand.' Andrew leaned back. 'He… he cleared me of my cash last week before he left.' Andrew closed his eyes and then opened them again, appearing quite sober. 'I had been going over the accounts with Duff when I came back from Aberdeen. I have a sneaking feeling all is not as it should be. Brand may have been manipulating the figures. I suppose Louise knew nothing of this.' Andrew eased forward in his chair. 'The man's a scoundrel. He's a betting man. Douglas told me. Thankfully we're well rid of him.'

Hodges knocked, and entered carrying a cupful of liquid. 'Your favourite medicine, sir,' he said.

'Ah, thank you, Hodges.' Andrew attempted to rise, then changed his mind. He swallowed the draught. 'One of Douglas's recipes. Tastes awful. But effective.'

'I used to give the seamen half seawater, half fresh water.'

'Did it work?'

'No. But they thought it did. It made them sick.'

Andrew smiled. 'You're an unscrupulous mountebank.'

'Only with drunkards.' James leaned forward. 'You said Brand took some cash?'

'Aye. Don't know how. Mrs Hodges said she had been at home all day.' Andrew paused. He sat up straight. 'So I think you owe Scarlett an apology, about the payment of seamen's wives when I went north to Aberdeenshire last July. Louise should have paid them.'

James couldn't think straight. Louise was honest. And who searched his chamber? Scarlett or Brand, or someone else?

'Did Bella come to see you?' Andrew asked suddenly.

'Yes. With a message from Robert Charles, thanking me for my help. Bella said he has left for France. I don't suppose you would have told me.'

'You're right. No.'

'I will tell you this. Mr Alexander is not using me to gain information. He has offered me a loan for my education. I declined, of course. I will not betray you or anyone else. But don't think I've changed my mind about support for the Jacobite cause. I remain neutral.'

## 29

It was the salt on the gentleman's boots that attracted James's attention. Common enough in Leith, but not here in the Canongate. This man strode in haste. James followed him as he turned into the courtyard at Lady Largo's house. Could it be David Colville? James entered the pend. He keeked round the corner. At the door of Lady Largo's mansion on the far side of the court the stranger was talking to a housemaid. James could see only the back of his head, but, yes, possibly Colville. The woman led him inside.

James turned and pressed on to the apothecary's shop. He had a parcel of drugs from abroad to collect. Douglas Atkins, despite his failings, was an efficient dealer in imported drugs.

The Jacobite agent had been far from his mind. It had been more than a year since he last saw him. He'd had no more visits from Mr Charles, and no further threats from adversaries. He had never found out who'd interrogated him back then. He'd thought that the conspiracy had come to nothing. Now he wasn't so sure. Maybe covert Jacobite meetings were being held. Andrew was absent from Edinburgh often, and was as secretive as usual. But if their opponents suspected a conspiracy, he would find himself in danger as well as Andrew. His involvement had started when he came back to Scotland with the secret letter. Had he been watched since then?

'My troublesome brother has been looking for you,' Douglas said, handing over the package. 'He has the intensity of a man with a story to tell.'

'Oh, he always has a story.' James opened his bundle, laid it on the bench, and studied the labels of the small parcels within. He gazed at them. Should he tell Andrew about the gentleman at Lady Largo's house? He must. But he wasn't sure. He didn't see the man's face.

'Is there anything amiss?' Douglas asked, as James fumbled with his medicines.

'No… no, all items requested have been supplied,' James said. 'Thank you.' He gathered his bundle and made for the door of the shop.

'James?'

James glanced round.

'About Francis…'

'Oh, he knows where to find me.'

Francis's news and political gossip would have to wait. He must find Andrew.

He wasn't at home. He left a note with Mrs Hodges, asking to see Andrew urgently on a personal matter. He pushed on up the stair to his own chambers, closed the door, and cast his eyes round, delighted that he now had two rooms. He was happy to remain in Lawson's Land. The larger room was James's bedchamber and parlour. In the other he furnished with a press and a bed for young Davie.

He unlocked the press and dumped his package on the top shelf. He would organise his purchases later. The drugs were expensive, but he could afford them now that he was charging more for his services from gentlemen of means. This was justified. He had more experience now after all. Care for the poor and needy would still be his priority though.

Davie had swept the parlour and covered the fire. A couple of lumps of coal lay on the hearth. It was working out well, employing Davie as his servant, teaching him manners and a little mathematics. Above Davie's bed James had attached a shelf for books. The boy was a quick thinker but not bookish. He merely wanted so hard to please, and tried to copy him. James had sent the boy on a round of delivering prescribed medicines. Straightforward but time-consuming work he was pleased to pass to the boy.

The tavern was busy. Francis waved James over to a table where a heated discussion was in flow, and pulled up a stool for him.

James looked around. 'Is Andrew here?'

'I don't think so,' Francis replied, handing James a handwritten sheet.

James held it towards the window and squinted. 'I can't read your handwriting.'

'I scribbled this quickly,' Francis said.

The man next to James bumped his elbow and spilled small ale onto the paper. Francis rose quickly and snatched it. He tried to blot the ink smudges. 'I have to write and produce a broadside.' He glowered at the man, who seemed oblivious to the inconvenience. He tugged James's arm. 'Let's go.'

They pushed through into the noisy street. Small groups were assembling in closes, and women were leaning out of windows in conversation.

'What's happening to make people so excited?' James asked.

'Well, it's the uncertainty of the Union. It was meant to be an incorporating union... James, do you take any regard for what is happening around you?'

'Sometimes, when I have a spare minute or two.'

'Folk aren't happy. Representatives in Parliament will be reduced with the Treaty of Union.' Francis paused and faced James. 'The Duke of Atholl is concerned with the number of peers joined with the House of Lords. Scots peers' share in legislative powers will be very much reduced, and unequal to the English. That's not an equal union.'

'The rest of us are not equal to those in the House of Lords anyway, regardless of the numbers.'

'James, do you have to make an argument sound obtuse?'

'What I mean is, I don't think these people in the streets are concerned with the finer details of Parliament. What do they care about how many peers there are?'

'Well no, but—'

'Pitcairne talks much of political issues. I do keep informed. I know the Duke of Atholl and others have continued protests about the Union since last November, and – there he is!' James shouted.

Andrew had just passed by without noticing them and was heading for the tavern. James turned to go back in, Francis on his heels. Andrew was nowhere to be seen among the diners.

'Why does he seem to vanish when I need him?'

'What do you need him for?' Francis asked.

James snaked his way through the tavern, down steps to the far end. 'Some advice.' He paused. 'On a personal matter.' He felt the heat rise in his face.

Francis smiled. 'Oh. I see. A woman. A beautiful lady. Let me guess. She's married, and her husband is after your blood.'

'What are you blethering about?' James said, turning to avoid Francis's curious gaze. He opened the door of a small chamber at the back of the tavern. A scantily dressed woman faced him. 'I beg your pardon, madam,' he said, and pulled the door shut.

'It seems you are not having much success with the ladies,' Francis said still grinning. 'And don't look at me like that. Ah, over there.' Francis gripped him by the shoulders and swivelled him round. 'Over there!'

Andrew had joined a group of elderly men standing by the window. Tankard in hand, he was engaged in discussion with a thin old man whose face was blackened with coal dust. James strode over, Francis at his heels.

'I want the coal loaded by—' Andrew began.

James pushed in between them. 'There you are. I beg your pardon, sir,' he said, addressing the coal merchant. James pulled Andrew aside, almost knocking the old man off balance. He dragged him to a corner. 'I've just spotted a mutual friend – David Colville.'

'Who?'

'You heard.'

James took Andrew's arm and pushed him towards the door, ignoring the coal merchant. He noticed Francis following behind.

'I thought you had something important to publish.' James pointed to the smudged paper in Francis's hand.

'Who's this David Colville?' Francis asked.

Andrew grabbed the paper and cast his eyes over it. He thrust it towards Francis. 'We need reports like this published now, not next week. Should you not be at your printing press?'

Francis stared at him.

Andrew put on his persuasive voice, as if securing a trading contract. 'The people of Edinburgh need the facts. They need books, pamphlets, broadsides. They need you, now more than ever.'

Francis's eyes widened. He opened his mouth and closed it again. He took the paper. 'I'll see this is printed straight away.'

'What's his report about?' James asked, as they entered the close at their tenement.

'I've no idea. There are smudges. He has short names for politicians; "Q" for "Queensberry", for example. It looks like important political stuff, about the Treaty of Union I suppose,' Andrew said.

'Anyway we got rid of him,' James said.

'Don't be too sure,' Andrew said. 'Francis can spot a story a mile off. Anyway, are you certain it was Colville you saw?'

'No, I'm not. The gentleman entered Lady Largo's house after talking with a servant.'

'A letter for you, sir,' Hodges said as Andrew led James into his chambers.

'Thank you, Hodges,' Andrew said, taking the note. 'Please see that we are not disturbed.' Andrew unlocked the door of his private chamber and ushered James inside. He placed the letter on his bureau. He locked the parlour door, and opened his cabinet. He selected a decanter of brandy and two glasses.

'Should we be looking for this gentleman?' James asked. 'If only to confirm he is Colville?'

'And then what?' Andrew said. 'Besides he may not want our help. He's probably arranging a secret meeting with the Duke of Hamilton.'

'Or merely staying at Lady Largo's house, as safe lodgings.' James took the brandy offered and settled into Andrew's soft armchair.

Andrew took the other chair opposite the fire. He rested his arms on his chair. Deep thinking was not Andrew's style. He must be considering some kind of action.

'I've not heard from Robert Charles for several months,' Andrew said at last. 'I think he is in France.'

James felt Andrew's eyes trying to bore into his mind.

'There has been a fair amount of mail between here and our friends in France. Something is afoot. I know that. I only pass on correspondence.' Andrew sipped his brandy. 'I expect to hear from Pitcairne soon. He is down south visiting patients. I think he passes on information and letters under cover of sending prescriptions.'

James nodded.

'Let me know if you see Colville again. Other than that, I ask only that you take care.'

After James left his chamber Andrew picked up the letter on his desk. It was a note from his agent saying that a merchant had delivered a crate of bottles of wine for him from the

Countess of Errol. This was unexpected. It did not seem right. He must be on his guard. It could be some sort of trap. He took up his quill, dipped it in the pot. He would pretend he didn't know the Countess of Errol. He wrote to his agent. It was a mistake. The wine was not for him, and was to be returned to the merchant. He sealed the letter and called Hodges.

'Take this to Leith right now.'

'Right now, sir.' Hodges nodded, taking off his apron.

Andrew listened to his servant close the door. He picked up his pen again, and wrote a letter to the Earl of Errol. He wondered if a merchant, a mutual acquaintance, was back in town. It had been nearly a year and a half since their last venture. Andrew sealed the letter, enclosing it within a letter to the Duchess of Gordon. He had some fine silk to sell, assorted shades and colours. Maybe she would be interested in first offers.

The Earl of Errol disliked the Duke of Hamilton, and didn't trust him. If the gentleman James saw was indeed David Colville, the Earl of Errol would be desirous to know if he was meeting with the Duke of Hamilton. Andrew remembered – rumours though they might have been – that the Duke of Atholl had broken links with Hamilton. If true, that meant Atholl was now the Jacobite leader.

Andrew tucked the letter inside his waistcoat. He strode up the hill to the Duchess of Gordon's mansion. He had met the Duchess only once, when accompanied by Robert Charles. In all likelihood she would not remember him.

A tall manservant with piercing eyes answered the door of the mansion. 'Mr Lawson, am I correct, sir?' he asked.

'Correct,' Andrew said, impressed by the man's recollection. Had they met before? Never mind. It made his task easier. 'Would you be so kind as to give this note to the Duchess of Gordon, with my compliments? I have some fine silks on offer.' He suddenly realised that he would have to find silks to bring. He would think about that later.

'The Duchess of Gordon is entertaining a small party to dinner. Will you please wait a moment, sir?'

He was shown into a dark chamber. There was a chair in the corner, but he stood, pacing up and down the small space.

The servant returned with a note, and an apology from the Duchess. 'Her Ladyship thanks you for the offer of silks, and regrets that she is engaged. She extends her good wishes.'

The servant handed Andrew a sealed note, bid him good day, and closed the door, too abruptly for Andrew's liking. He stuffed the note into his pocket, looked up, and caught the eye of a man who had been watching him emerge from the doorway of the house. The stranger looked away.

Andrew took a turn down the steep West Bow and ventured through a back close. He knew another way to the tavern, through a passage at the back, but the door was locked. He checked to see if he was being followed. He wasn't.

He made his way back to the Land Market. He stood at the edge of a close and cast his eye around the busy market. A woman was making her way toward his house. She staggered with the heavy bundle she was carrying. She wore a heavy brown coat over a fine linen dress, soiled at the edges. Her long brown hair escaped from her hat. He glimpsed her face as she turned sideways before vanishing into the close. It was Louise.

## 30

'Is that you, Mrs Brand? Come in lass, for goodness sake.' Mrs Grant took her bag, placed an arm round her waist, and eased her inside.

Louise leaned against her. She collapsed into an armchair in the parlour. Her head was aching. She lay back and closed her eyes. She wanted to speak but the words wouldn't come.

She heard the landlady's muffled voice from the kitchen, as she gave instructions to the maid. Mrs Grant returned to her side. 'Here, have some mutton broth.'

A bowl and spoon were placed in her hands. She sipped the broth. Her stomach ached. She put the bowl down.

'You can have more of the same later. Look at you. If you lose more weight you'll disappear.'

The sounds of someone attending to the fire woke her. She didn't know how long she'd slept. It must have been a couple of hours. The servant crept around, probably thinking she was asleep. Her feet were cold. She shuffled her body to a more comfortable position.

What was she going to tell Mrs Grant? She had left her husband. She was ashamed to say her marriage was a failure. And now she was in trouble. She mustn't show her fear. And how could she tell Mrs Grant, or anyone, how she came to be in this desperate state?

The heat from the fire reached her feet and slowly spread through her body. When the servant left, Louise rose and arranged her clothes as well as she could.

Mrs Grant burst into the chamber. 'I don't have a spare room. You'll have to find somewhere to stay,' Mrs Grant said. 'That is, until your husband comes. I expect he'll be searching for you.'

'I don't think so.' She realised these were her first words to the landlady since her return.

Mrs Grant looked at her sideways. 'Why did you leave him? Or has he thrown you out?'

Louise stared at the carpet.

'Don't worry, I'll see that you're cleaned up and well fed. I suppose you can sleep on the chaise for the night. Do you have a clean petticoat?' Mrs Grant glanced at Louise's bundle of clothes. 'No, I thought not.'

Mrs Grant fussed and chatted about the residents in the tenement. The rooms where she had lived with her father had now been rented out to a young family from the north. Lodgers come and go.

'Is James Lightfoot still in residence here?'

'Aye, but he's moved from the garret. He's now in south-facing chambers on the fourth storey.'

Louise could see that the landlady was regarding her with some curiosity. She was grateful though. She felt warm and comfortable now. Overwhelmed by exhaustion, she managed to mumble her thanks as she settled down for the night.

In the morning Louise ate her breakfast in silence, listening to the clock ticking and wondering about her next move. She would have to find lodgings first, and look for work to pay the rent. She remembered that James had been in a similar predicament three years ago, when he returned from far-off places.

'My dear, I see that you are troubled,' Mrs Grant said. 'Your husband will take care of you. Mr Brand is a kind gentleman. You must go back to him.'

Mrs Grant's change of mood surprised Louise. If only she knew her husband's true nature. The landlady flustered about, clearing the table, clattering the plates and replacing the table cover. She arranged some cushions, and put a lump of coal on the fire, poking it vigorously. She hovered around. Louise could see she wished her to be gone, but she was reluctant to face the cold.

She left the landlady to her chores and made her way up the spiral stair to visit Bella and Rose. It was clear that Mrs Grant, though kindly in some ways, was not going to provide lodging for a woman who had deserted her husband. It was obvious she had no means to pay rent. The sisters, on the other hand, might have work for her, and allow her the use of the chamber they used for storing their cloth. Though she had never been inside the chamber, she could ask if a bed was available.

'I'm looking for work. Any kind of needlework,' Louise said as she stepped into the sisters' cosy parlour. She thought about what to say next. Her mind was a blank.

The sisters exchanged glances. Louise had the vague feeling she had interrupted something and wasn't welcome.

'Is this an awkward time?' she asked. She blinked and a tear trickled down her cheek. Her vision was blurred. She stood there, trying to focus.

Bella and Rose were watching her as she wept silently. Rose extended a hand, offering a delicate embroidered handkerchief. It smelt of fine perfume. She dabbed her eyes. Rose led her to the large crimson armchair. It smelt of tobacco, and reminded her of her father. For a brief moment she thought of him and wondered if he were here. Anxiety was confusing her mind. But there was a distinct smell of snuff, not unlike the kind her father used to have.

All the familiar sights and smells of days gone by brought back memories. The delicate chimes of the parlour clock reminded her of happy days, sewing by the glowing fire. She couldn't turn back the clock and start again. That's what was really painful.

Bella drew up a chair, sat down and leaned forward. She spoke gently. 'Unfortunately, we're not busy just now. If enough work comes our way in the future, we may have something to offer you.' She paused to let this sink in. 'But please tell us why you are here. When you're ready.'

Louise wiped her nose with the wet handkerchief. She sat erect, forcing an effort of self-control. 'I had to leave our current lodgings,' she began. 'I had no money to pay the rent. And strangers turned up, demanding money. They... They wouldn't go away.'

'And Henry?

'I haven't seen him for a month. The money he gave me last, I used for food and some coal.' Louise gazed at the heap of coal in the scuttle beside her chair. 'I don't know where he is.'

'He has many debts?' Bella asked.

Louise nodded, and lowered her head. She looked up to find Bella and Rose watching her, waiting for her to speak. She cast her eyes round the chamber. The door to the garret was closed.

'May I bide in your garret?' Louise asked.

'We have a guest here just now,' Bella said. 'We had to clear out our materials and offer the bed to our visitor. A relation who arrived unexpectedly.'

'A second cousin on our mother's side,' Rose added. Bella glanced severely at Rose. Louise was puzzled.

Bella leaned forward again. 'You must go home to your husband. He must settle his debts...'

'But I have no home.' Louise took a deep breath. 'It's complicated. I mentioned in one of my letters that my husband is not as rich as I thought he was. I have to explain. He... he has not been honest. There was no mansion in Yorkshire. He took me to a bleak cottage near Eyemouth. It was only an overnight stop, he said, but we stayed there a month. It was cold and wet. Then it snowed. A blizzard kept us there. I realised much later that he was hiding from people... people...'

'People demanding payment,' Bella said.

Louise nodded. 'Aye. That was it.' She felt her face burn with anger. 'He didn't even have a proper home. I mean not even an ordinary permanent house, far less a large one.'

'We had no idea from your letters it was so bad. You must have been very unhappy.'

'I was happy to begin with. Henry was kind and loving. It took a while for me to realise he was deceiving me. He kept saying it wasn't his fault he had money problems.'

A knock on the door gave Louise a chance to pause. Rose answered. Louise heard her talking to a man. She tried to listen, but their voices were low. Rose closed the door and returned.

Bella stood up. 'Andrew Lawson will see if there is a room for you for a few days,' she said. 'And then maybe you could stay with your sister for a while. You could help with her children. But you must eventually return to your husband.'

Bella was easing towards the door, indicating it was time for her to leave, but she remained as if glued to the chair. She had not responded to Mary's letters because she felt shame. It was bad for the family.

'I now know my husband's a cheat and a liar. He was running away, I think, when he left Edinburgh.' She paused. 'I'm so sorry. I had to sell the silver teapot you gave me. I sold other wedding presents too—'

'You must see Andrew,' Bella said, easing Louise from the chair and guiding her towards the door.

She was being rushed out gently. If they were not so busy, why were they in a hurry to see her out? No one wants to know anyone who is down on their luck. She was being rejected.

As Louise stepped onto the landing, Rose handed her a purse. 'A loan, until you find work, as I'm sure you will.' She smiled.

Louise took the purse and thanked them. She wanted to say more about her misfortunes, and about how Henry had deceived her. They had been constantly on the move. Henry kept promising things would get better. That was her mistake. She believed him. She was slow to see the reality of her situation.

She stepped down the turnpike, one slow step at a time. She hesitated at the door. The thought of having to beg for work from Andrew was painful.

Mrs Hodges hugged her and tears filled her eyes. She stood back and fumbled in her pocket for a handkerchief.

'The master's not here, but please come in. Mr Duff is working in the office,' Mrs Hodges said, indicating the open door on the right. 'It's good to see you. But you look ill. Please tell me about yourself.'

Louise followed Mrs Hodges, glancing briefly into the office. Mr Duff raised his head. His pale face turned purple. He took off his spectacles and regarded Louise with horror.

'You!' he shouted, pointing a finger at her. 'You dare to show yourself here? Where's your husband? Is he here?' He stood up. His hand accidentally brushed a bundle of papers onto the floor. He stood on them as he walked round the table.

Mrs Hodges rushed into the office. 'Sit down, sir. Please. You'll make yourself ill.'

Mr Duff staggered and gripped the edge of the table. Louise watched as Mrs Hodges led him back to the chair. She suddenly felt sick, and covered her mouth. Her heart was racing. She resisted an urge to escape down the stairs, but to where? She had nowhere to go. Mrs Hodges closed the door of the office. Louise was alone in the parlour. She sat down and leaned her elbows on the dining table.

# 31

The smell of cooking greeted James as he opened the door of his chambers. Davie was at the fire, stirring a pot.

'Rabbit stew, sir.'

James moistened his lips. He was hungry now. It had been a productive morning at the clinic. Depositing his satchel by the desk, he picked up a bundle of letters. One was a note from Mr Alexander asking him to see his wife. She had been poorly during the night. Another letter was an invitation to dine privately with Andrew and Walter Duff – an urgent matter required his attention.

Was this about David Colville? James had been watchful, but there had been no more sightings of the mysterious gentleman. He wondered if he really had seen the French agent, or if it had been someone else of similar size and build. Hopefully it was another. He had his work to think about, and despite Pitcairne's sympathies and sometimes persuasive dialogue, he had no leanings towards the Jacobite cause.

'I will be dining with Mr Lawson, Davie,' James said.

Davie lowered his eyes and frowned. Then a smile slowly appeared. 'That'll be more for me, then.'

James was about to ask where he got the rabbit, then changed his mind. 'The more you eat, the more work you'll have to do. You get nothing for nothing.'

It was good to keep the boy on edge. Walter Duff, on the other hand, should not work so hard. Not good for his health at his age, as he often told him. He could do with a tonic. He didn't look at all well when he bumped into him in the close yesterday. James cast his eyes along the shelf and selected a recently prepared cordial of herbs from a recipe given to him by Douglas. He took the bottle with him.

Andrew and Walter Duff were already seated at the dining table enjoying a glass of claret when he arrived. Andrew waved him to the table. The atmosphere was cool. No smiles or pleasant conversation. He would rather have been with Davie, enjoying the rabbit stew.

'I'm much better today, thank you,' Mr Duff said in response to James's enquiry.

Something had upset the lawyer. James placed the bottle in front of him, and sat down opposite. 'Please try this cordial. It comes highly recommended.'

Mr Duff nodded his thanks. Hodges brought in a large fish pie, and dishes of cabbage and carrots.

James smiled as he piled fish and vegetables onto his plate. 'Hmm. Excellent meal, Hodges,' he said.

Andrew was watching him. Mr Duff lowered his head, his eyelids closing. James noticed he ate little, leaving most of his pie untouched. The conversation seemed unnaturally subdued. Andrew enquired politely about his work at the clinic. Had he seen much of Archibald Pitcairne? Had Pitcairne travelled south in recent days?

'There's stewed gooseberries with custard, and cinnamon biscuits to follow,' Hodges said.

'Thank you Hodges,' Andrew said, watching his manservant retire to the kitchen and close the door. Sitting down at the table, he poured himself another glass of claret and looked directly at James.

James helped himself to another portion of fish pie.

'Miss Louise, I mean Mrs Brand, is here in town,' Andrew said.

James almost choked on his claret. Despite his many queries, no one had spoken to him about Louise. It was not surprising, perhaps, considering the rogue she married. 'How is she?' he asked.

'I'm afraid it's not good news, James,' Andrew said carefully, setting down his glass and looking straight at James. 'We think... we think that Louise, as well as her husband, has been involved with misdeeds against our company. What I mean is, they have been working together. We have kept this from you. We couldn't believe this of Louise ourselves. This knowledge came to light after their marriage, from exchanges of letters with our partners.'

Mr Duff nodded in agreement, his eyelids drooping.

James put his fork down. His second portion of fish pie looked less appetising now. He lifted his fork again and poked at it. 'But Louise is honest. Surely you know that?'

'Apparently she is not,' Andrew said, fixing his eyes on James.

'But—'

'Louise worked conscientiously for me for years. She was a canny soul. That is, until she married Brand. That was her undoing.' Andrew paused, still staring at James. 'She has deceived us.'

'She has not. It's her husband. He's a scoundrel,' James said. 'From the day I first met him, I knew he was bad. I did warn you.'

'I know that.' Andrew stabbed at his pie crust.

'Anyway, you seem to survive these losses and setbacks reasonably well,' James added.

Andrew's eyes flashed with anger. He pushed back his chair.

Mr Duff put a hand on his arm. 'Be at ease. Let us think sensibly,' he said.

James watched Andrew in silence as his friend drained the remains of his wine from his glass.

Andrew resumed. 'Because of my regard for Louise, I was prepared to forget the loss, humiliating though it is. But now that she has appeared…'

'Where is she now?' James asked.

'I've no idea. She was here yesterday. She had the audacity to come to this house,' Andrew said.

'She fled when I lost my temper,' Mr Duff added.

'So that's what was bothering you.' James shook his head. 'But Louise – why would she come to your chambers?'

'She is pretending to be innocent,' Mr Duff said.

'I will find her,' James said. He finished his pie and stood up.

'Stay for the next course, James, please. Gooseberries and custard. Sweetmeats,' Andrew said, waving his arm towards the sideboard.

'I thank you. No,' James said.

'Stay, James. There is another matter of importance I wish to discuss with you,' Andrew said as he spooned gooseberries and custard onto a porcelain plate.

James sat down. Andrew placed the plate in front of him.

'When she arrived, Louise apparently stayed a night with Mrs Grant. Then she visited the Hunter sisters yesterday. Rose and Bella were quite shocked at her appearance. She told them her story. Like you, they think of her as a victim,' Andrew said, helping himself to a portion of pudding. 'I'm wondering if Brand will come here to search for her. We need to be ready to confront him if he does. There is the question of proof. For instance, we think Brand took the coin that was payment for the seamen back in July 1705, but we're not sure. It was Louise who signed for the purchase of fancy wares that didn't exist, and for wine…'

'Are you sure?' James asked.

'We're sure,' Mr Duff said. 'No wonder I'm no weel.'

'You need to rest now,' James suggested.

Andrew nodded. 'We can talk again tomorrow.' He gently eased the lawyer from his chair and guided him to the door. After seeing him out, Andrew returned to the table and poured another glass of wine for James and for himself.

'What is this other business you wish to discuss?' James asked. 'Is it about Louise?'

'No.'

Hodges entered and gathered platters from the sideboard. He picked up an unopened bottle of wine.

'No – leave it,' Andrew said. 'Let's go through to my private chamber,' he suggested, taking the bottle.

The chamber was cool and dark, the fire nearly out.

Andrew poked the coals until a faint glow appeared. He poured generous measures of wine and set the bottle down.

'I am being watched closely by a stranger,' Andrew began. 'From outside Lady Gordon's house. I've seen him in the street from the windows here. For the last two days I believe he has been around the Land Market and Castlehill area, maybe for longer.' Andrew sipped his wine. 'There's something else puzzling. I had a note from my agent about bottles of wine supposedly from the Countess of Errol. I left him to deal with it.'

'Do you think that was wise?' James asked.

'I would prefer to deny knowledge of my acquaintance with Lady Errol. I instructed my agent to reply saying it was a mistake and to return the goods.'

'And what if the wine was from the Countess of Errol? A serious insult that would be.'

'I think she'd understand.'

James wondered how many others of the nobility Andrew was acquainted with, and what was making him so touchy.

'In the meantime I am staying clear of the Canongate,' Andrew said. 'Have you had any more sightings of David Colville?'

'No.'

'I've had word from on high to avoid communication with him.'

So it was Colville James spotted in the Canongate. 'But you would like me to spy on him?'

'The general view is that Colville may consider acting on his own if he is indeed in Edinburgh right now. I am telling you more than I should, but I think it wise that you are informed. Think of what you overheard when he stayed at Comiston. Well, anyway – I would like you to let me know if you happen to notice him.'

James nodded slowly. Andrew's unease was obvious. As it happened, he had visits to make in the Canongate that afternoon. He felt Andrew's gaze as if he was trying to read his mind.

'With the possibility of an unequal union, more and more people will be leaning towards the Jacobite cause. I don't think many in this country will favour the prospect of a Hanoverian king one day,' Andrew said.

'So are the Jacobites planning to bring back the Chevalier and disrupt the Union?'

'With French backing, perhaps.'

'But what of Colville?' James asked.

Andrew shook his head. 'Who knows where he stands? He may be having secret meetings with the Duke of Hamilton.'

James was as puzzled as ever. Politicians might be inclined to argue for hours over details, but somehow Andrew seemed to sum up the practical notions neatly. Always in a hurry to get the words out of the way, and on with the action. James was not sure of Andrew's motives, or his own. The reality was that Andrew had become too deeply immersed in intrigue.

'Anyway – about our stranger, who is lurking around,' Andrew resumed. 'I think we should try to snare him. We need to find out what he's after, and who he is working for.'

'I don't like this "we". Exactly what do you have in mind?' James asked.

'I'll let you know.'

It seemed to James that as soon as his work was progressing smoothly, something came along to turn things on their head. David Colville was back in town, and now Louise. James disliked Brand, but he could not have foreseen Louise's great misfortune.

James needed to find Louise, but where to look? First he had to visit Mrs Alexander. He ascended the stairs to his flat.

Davie was standing at the top landing, leaning over the rail, fidgeting nervously. 'You have a visitor, sir,' Davie whispered, as James eased past him. 'Louise Morton – I mean Mrs Brand. I beg your pardon, sir.'

James smiled, pleased with the lad's good manners. He slipped Davie a farthing and asked him to leave. 'Not a word to anyone about Mrs Brand, mind,' he said.

Davie nodded and smiled. He probably misunderstood the situation for a romantic dalliance. If only it were.

Louise was settled on the armchair, her head bent, when James entered his parlour. She jumped up, her eyes, tired and red, resting on his briefly before looking away. Her face was pale, and her arms were thin. Her green woollen dress was soiled.

'Please sit,' James said, waiting for her to be seated, and taking a chair opposite. He glanced at the remains of the pot of stew, now set aside. 'Have you eaten?'

'Yes, thank you. Davie's tasty rabbit stew and small ale.'

They sat in silence.

'I've just been with Andrew this afternoon—' James began.

'I know. Davie told me. I expect he talked about me.' Louise took a deep breath. 'I was shocked at my reception. You must believe me. I worked honestly on the accounts.

Always. I don't understand. I think... I think my husband is to blame. He took over, that time Andrew was away a lot. I told Mr Duff that he could trust Henry to look after the business. So, it's my fault.' A large tear trickled down her cheek. She pushed back a strand of hair.

James felt an urge to rush over and comfort her, but held himself in check. He still had feelings for her. But, in the back of his mind, some doubts too.

'Can you tell me more about how you and your then-husband-to-be managed the accounts?' he asked. He did not like to say the man's name. He wasn't sure how he would act if he came face to face with the rogue at this moment. He listened carefully to Louise's story; how she slowly came to know her husband's true character.

'But he's not a bad person really,' she said after a long pause. 'He is weak and unable to resist gambling. So he lies and cheats. And then people come searching for him.'

James was not convinced. His years at sea had taught him to recognise the differences between weakness and criminality. Brand was thoroughly bad, and Louise could not see this even now. But what to do next? He was shocked that neither Mrs Grant nor Bella and Rose would give her lodgings.

'Your sister. You must go to her...'

'Her husband won't have me, despite the fact that he knows I would be of useful service in the house, and with the children.'

'Does your husband know you've come to Edinburgh?'

'I left a note saying I was going to stay with Mary, so he thinks I'm there. That is, if he cares.'

James needed time to think. 'I have people to see,' he said. 'You can stay here until I return. Do not let anyone in, except Davie.'

He took his bag and closed the door behind him. He took his time. He meandered slowly down the High Street. It was dreich. There was a chill in the air and not enough wind to dispel the smoke which drifted horizontally along the rooftops. After his visits he would have to think what to do to help Louise. He needed some sort of plan.

Mrs Alexander was with child again. She was getting too old to bear children without complications, James thought. She looked pale and tired.

'You know you should rest. Put your feet up—'

'I cannot. I had to dismiss my housekeeper. She… she… I will have to engage another. In the meantime, there is much to arrange.'

James thought of Louise. She would be well away from Andrew's wrath.

'I know of someone who may fit your requirements,' he said. 'On a temporary basis.' He began to construct a vague story about Louise. He was treading carefully. Mrs Alexander had not met her, so he could avoid any mention of a husband.

'I will see her,' she said.

James sensed she was not quite convinced of the story. He descended the stairs to wait for her husband in the library. He was engaged. James took out his watch and studied the dial. The watch was a luxury gift from Andrew. It had a second hand. He rose from the window seat, and cast his eyes along the middle bookshelf labelled *D*. Each book on this shelf had the letter D and a number – its position on the shelf. If James were fortunate to keep a library, he would organise his differently: books arranged on shelves by subject. To keep a library is to assemble your known world around you; your own sense of identity and independence.

His thoughts were interrupted by the manservant. He placed a tray containing a bottle of wine and two glasses on the side table. Mr Alexander entered, greeted James, and held up the bottle. James shook his head. Mr Alexander poured himself a glass of wine. He appeared to be in good fettle and exuberant mood.

'I thank you, sir, for your continued support of our welfare fund,' James said.

Alexander inclined his head, took out his snuffbox and fiddled with it. 'Anne tells me you are hoping to go off to Leiden soon.'

'That's correct. I have managed to set aside sufficient funds.' James was uncomfortable with this untruth, but didn't want Alexander to renew the offer of a loan he had made more than year ago.

Alexander walked across to the secretaire, removed a key from his pocket, unlocked a drawer, and searched among the papers within. He paused for a moment, sharpened a quill and dipped it into the well. He wrote a letter, enclosed it within another, and then sealed the small bundle. He rose and handed the papers to James.

'If this is a loan…'

'It is not a loan. It is an offer of employment to an eminent politician.'

James held out his hand, then hesitated.

'You would be wise not to refuse. It's an excellent opportunity.'

# 32

'There he is,' Andrew said, 'leaning against the wall just beyond Effie's wool stall. Wide-brimmed hat, with his head down.'

Andrew had been watching the busy street from the open window in James's chamber. From four storeys up facing the Land Market, the room offered a commanding view of the bustling market below, and the rooftops of the houses opposite and beyond.

James exchanged places with him, leaning sideways against the open shutter, peering round the edge. 'If he could just raise his head a little...' he said.

'It's our tenement he's watching – sometimes from the Land Market, sometimes from James's Court.'

'What about Lady Gordon's house?' James asked. 'Has he been lurking there again?'

'Aye, he's been around Castlehill and the West Bow. But I think he's probably more fearful about spying on the nobility. It's me he's observing, I'm sure.'

'He's lifted his head now,' James said. 'I haven't seen him before. He looks anxious.'

'Let's go,' Andrew said, opening the door.

James closed the shutter, locked his chambers, and followed Andrew down the front stairs into the crowded market. He kept close to Andrew, weaving in and out of the customers and traders, narrowly avoiding a collision with an overloaded drapery stall. The stranger had spotted them coming his way, and dashed off. James saw him bump into two women carrying bundles of linen over their shoulders. Their bundles toppled, one sending ribbons flying from a haberdashery stall. The haberdasher raged at the women. Seizing the opportunity, Andrew rushed forward and grasped the spy by the left shoulder. James appeared at his right side.

'We would like to have a quiet conversation with you,' Andrew said through gritted teeth. 'And don't attempt to call for help.'

The stranger looked around. James gripped him tighter. The man yielded, and gave little resistance as they marched him towards the apothecary's shop.

A huge man with a dark beard suddenly appeared in front of James. He pushed against him, forcing him to release his hold on the spy. The giant dragged James into the close. James glanced sideways in time to see Andrew and Douglas pull the spy through Douglas's front door. James kicked and punched, broke free and dashed across the courtyard. Another huge figure appeared, and grabbed him. The man suddenly released his grip. James's eyes scanned the courtyard. A man stood at the entrance to each of the houses. Four of them in all. Friends of Douglas and Andrew, planted at strategic positions. The huge man ran out of the courtyard.

George opened the gate of the back garden. James hurried through, and opened the door to the laboratory. The stranger stood in the middle, shivering, his clothes soaking wet. He was held by a man at each side. Douglas was examining a selection of bottles on a small table. Andrew and Francis were staring at the stranger, face to face.

'I ask you again. Who hired you?' Andrew said.

'I told you.' The man tugged against the straps that held him at the wrists. 'I told you. I don't know. I don't know his name.'

Andrew turned to Douglas and inclined his head.

'Now watch this carefully,' Douglas said.

James watched Douglas as he inserted a dropper into one of the bottles. He withdrew some liquid and added a few drops to a thick substance in a dish. The mixture fizzed and bubbled. Francis released the spy's hands. Douglas stepped towards the man, holding the bottle and dropper.

'You're English, aren't you?' he said.

The man nodded.

'Don't like Englishmen much,' Douglas said. 'Why are you here?'

The stranger stared.

'Why were you spying on us?' Andrew asked.

'I wasn't.'

Andrew hit his right cheek hard. Tears welled up in his eyes.

'You were lingering outside my house.'

'I wasn't watching…'

Andrew punched him again. Douglas applied a few drops of liquor to a piece of paper. A brown spot appeared. Within less than a minute the spot developed into a wee hole. He slowly advanced towards the man, and held up the paper. 'Your fingers next,' he said.

Francis placed the man's right hand on the table. Douglas dipped the dropper in the bottle, withdrew some liquid and held it suspended over the man's finger.

'I wasn't watching you. I was looking for a woman.'

Douglas stepped back and laughed. 'A woman? A lady of the night?'

'No… no.'

Andrew smiled. The stranger's body was shaking.

'Ask anyone and you'll be pointed in the right direction,' Andrew said. 'I could recommend—'

'No… no. Not just any woman.'

'Oh, he's particular,' Andrew said, walking round the man. *Is Andrew enjoying this?* James thought.

'I'm searching for a Mrs Brand.'

'Mrs Brand?' Andrew moved closer to the man's face, almost touching.

James felt his body go cold. His legs turned to jelly.

'She used to live in Edinburgh. So I understand. Before she married that villain who… Before she married a merchant by the name of Henry Brand.'

Andrew nodded to Douglas. The bottles were removed. Francis pulled forward a stool. The man sat down and scanned the room, fear in his eyes.

James could not believe this. He, like others, was sure the stranger was involved in anti-Jacobite activities; a political spy. He had to go. He had to find Louise and warn her. Yet he was curious to see what Andrew would do next.

'Now then,' Andrew said, dragging over a chair and sitting opposite the stranger. 'Tell us what your business is with Mrs Brand.'

The man appeared confused by this change of attitude. He mopped his brow with a dirty rag.

'We might be able to help you.'

'You're not Brand's men?'

'No. We are not.'

The man sighed, and looked down at his hands. He raised his head. 'My master. He's a merchant.' He paused.

'Tell me about him. He does have a name?' Andrew asked.

'My master wants back what Brand owes him. He will stop at nothing. He's ruthless with his enemies. And with Brand he's angry. Very angry. He told me I might find Brand's wife at a place they call Lawson's Land. That is, if she's left her husband.'

'Well now,' Andrew said. 'It looks like your master and I have something in common.'

James had heard enough. He had to see Louise now. She had to stay indoors. The Alexanders would probably dismiss her at any sign of trouble. 'I could use some of your ointment, for bruises,' he said to Douglas. He opened the door leading to the shop and shuffled through.

Douglas handed James a small tin.

'That corrosive liquid...'

'I wasn't going to burn his fingers.' He grinned. 'I switched the bottles. I thought he was a political spy.'

Mrs Atkins burst into the shop, clutching her basket tightly. 'There's a riot in the street out there. I'm feart. Go and see what it's about, husband.'

James followed Douglas out of the shop. Shouts came from the Tron where a mob was gathering. James separated from Douglas, and pushed through the crowd to reach Mr

Alexander's house. He spotted Davie running towards him. The boy stopped, breathing heavily.

'Well, young man?' James said.

'The Union, sir,' Davie said. 'There's a riot about the Union.'

James took a deep breath. 'Listen to me, Davie,' he said. 'Mrs Brand is in trouble. There are men looking for her. I cannot tell you where she is, but if you see her on the streets, warn her, and then let me know.'

'Aye, sir.'

'Right now, please go to the shop, and order this.' James handed him a recipe. 'Wait until it's prepared, and then take it home and put it on the top of my drugs cabinet.'

'Aye, sir.'

'And Davie…'

The boy fixed his eyes on James.

'Do not, do not, under any circumstances, talk to Mr Atkins or Mr Lawson about Mrs Brand. If you see her, do not tell them. You understand?'

'Aye, sir.'

'Good man.'

James placed a farthing in the palm of his hand. Davie's fingers closed tightly over it. The boy nodded, and James watched him head towards Douglas's shop. He turned and pressed on down the Canongate.

The manservant led James into the library. 'The mistress is with guests in the parlour. You said she not expecting you?' he said.

'No – this is just a courtesy call,' James said. 'I can return later when convenient.'

He was about to turn to the door. His path was blocked by a young girl servant who showed him to a seat in the library. He remained standing, shuffling from one foot to the other.

Mrs Alexander breezed in.

'Good day, my lady. I was just passing, so I thought to make a quick call. I apologise—'

'No need to apologise. We are all well, thanks to your care. It's bath time in the nursery… You are troubled, sir?'

'It is nothing,' James said. Were his feelings that transparent? 'I… I was wondering how your new housekeeper was settling in. I recommended her, so I feel responsible.'

'She is efficient. Hard-working. I'm pleased.' Mrs Alexander frowned. 'She doesn't talk much about herself. The other servants say she's sad. If so, she hides it well.' Mrs Alexander walked over to the window and looked up and down the street. 'She is out on an errand. You may wait for her return, if you wish.'

'I thank you, but no. I will intrude no further. You may give her my regards.'

James hurried out. The riot was over. The crowd had dispersed; bairns rummaged around the arcades picking up spilled goods, fighting over morsels of bread. He shuffled homewards, uncertain how to proceed.

At the Land Market some stallholders were wrapping up their goods at the close of business. He spotted Louise browsing over a haberdashery table.

He gripped her arm. 'Quickly, come with me.' He pulled her to the outer stair entrance of the tenement, and opened the door to the turnpike. He noticed Andrew in the street.

'You are in great danger,' he said, leading her up the stair. He fumbled for his door key.

He wasn't quick enough. Andrew was halfway up the stairs as he led her inside. He barged in and closed the door with a bang.

Andrew turned to face Louise. 'Sit down,' he said, pushing her into a chair. He stood over her. James saw the tears rise in Louise's eyes. She took out a kerchief and dabbed the wet corners. *Good*, James thought. *She's keeping her composure.* Andrew strode to the window and turned.

'Please let me—' James began. Andrew held up his hand to silence him. He fixed his gaze on Louise.

'I have made many errors,' Louise began, looking directly at Andrew. 'A bad choice of husband, it seems. But I never planned to do you wrong. I did not undertake any fraud.'

'We have proof otherwise,' Andrew said.

'I don't know how...' Louise began. She screwed her kerchief into a ball.

'Maybe your husband forged your signature,' James said.

'I trusted Henry. I loved him.' Louise raised her kerchief to her cheek. 'I suppose he could have—'

Andrew turned to James. 'Can I have a word?' He opened the door.

James followed him down the stairs, closing the door behind him. They stopped at the landing on the floor below.

'Now do you believe me?' James whispered.

'Hmm... I'm not sure. Walter Duff said the letters are in her writing, and the deception is deliberate in every case. I can show you.' Andrew leaned against the wall. 'I wish it were otherwise.'

'We have to protect her. From Brand and from those who seek him.'

'We need to find Brand. Our stranger gave a name of one of the pursuers, but I think he's reluctant to work with us.' Andrew leaned over the banister with his head in his hands.

'We have to give Louise support. Can't you see she's suffering?'

Andrew looked up. 'We could use her as bait to get Brand. She will help us. She has no choice.'

# 33

J ames rushed upstairs to Andrew's chambers. He banged
on the door.

'Can't you knock quietly, James? I'm not deaf,' Andrew
said.

'Louise has left with Brand,' James said, striding through
the chamber.

Andrew punched the wall. 'We've let the rogue slip away.
Did no one spot him?'

James shrugged. 'He's too slippery.'

Andrew led James into his office. He removed a bundle
of papers from a chair in front of the desk, looked around
briefly, then dumped them on top of another pile. Some
letters and documents spilled over the side of the desk and
scattered across the floor. James stooped to retrieve them.
He assembled them carefully, scanning the contents, mainly
lists and sums. Andrew was watching him. He snatched the
papers.

'Sit down, James. As you can see, several matters occupy
my attention.' He swept his arm across the documents.

'Perhaps you can tell me how we have managed to miss them.'

'What?'

'Perhaps you can tell me about Louise leaving with her husband.' Andrew sat down and leaned forward, fixing his eyes on James, as if it were his fault. He suspected there was more on Andrew's mind than Louise and Henry Brand. Other problems.

'I don't know,' James began. 'It was a complete surprise. Mrs Alexander told me this morning. Louise has taken all her belongings, left one letter for her employer, and one for me – written neatly as if she were in no hurry at all.'

Andrew continued to stare. 'So, Louise has bolted. Still with him.'

'Against her will.'

'James, she's his wife.' Andrew leaned back in his chair and stretched out his legs, his face still tense. 'We have to try some way…'

'Without harming Louise.'

'Walter Duff has a friend, a lawyer, who undertakes special investigations. Duff suggested a year ago that we engage this gentleman to find out more about Henry Brand – his background, previous activities, people he has associated with – and even exert extreme pressure on him, if we have to. I had thought about this, but my time has been consumed with other matters. The problem is, the gentleman is quite expensive to take on, even for a short commission.' Andrew sat upright in the chair. 'We could employ him now. No matter what it costs.' He frowned.

'What do you know about this gentleman?'

'I haven't met him. Duff assures me he delivers results. We have to be discreet, of course.'

'Ah. You're wondering what Brand and his associates may find out about your activities,' James said. 'Anything that might be – well, out of the usual ways of business.' His eyes swept the papers on the table. He tried to read something upside down.

Andrew stood up. 'What do you mean?'

'I mean… I mean…'

'I have several interests at the moment.' Andrew walked around his desk, turned and faced James. 'How did you manage to let Louise slip away? I thought you were close.'

James felt the heat rise in his face. 'She was the housekeeper at the home of Hugh Alexander. It was impossible to see her and be discreet at the same time. Mrs Alexander gave me the letter after she left. She thought nothing unusual about her departure, apparently.' He looked down, fumbling in his pocket for the letter. 'Perhaps someone discovered where Louise was biding and contacted Brand. Someone close to us.'

'Or Louise wrote to him herself,' Andrew said.

'No. I don't think so.' James studied the letter.

'Any idea where they might be?'

'No clues in the letter. She has mentioned a cottage near Eyemouth.'

'Could you find the house?'

'Louise wasn't precise about the details.'

'I'll contact Duff about that friend of his,' Andrew said. He rose and opened the door. He looked around, then closed it again. Lowering his voice, he continued, 'Another thing, James. You were right. That was indeed David Colville you recognised entering Lady Largo's house. He has now left Edinburgh. That's all you need to know.'

Andrew was staring at James as if expecting some response from him. James had never declared himself loyal to the Jacobite cause, yet here he was, once again, with knowledge of a conspiracy. He believed his involvement had begun when the sea captain gave him a letter to deliver to Andrew four years ago. No matter what he felt he would not betray Andrew. But what were his real feelings? With growing protest at the Union, more and more people were giving thought to anti-union sympathies and Scotland having its own king. Now Presbyterians were declaring support for the King Over the Water.

Andrew traipsed along The Shore, smiling and nodding to acquaintances. There was a slight breeze. The bitterly cold air of the sea at Leith invigorated his mind. He had been careful not to tell James much about David Colville. James did not need to know that the Jacobite agent had now sailed for France. The Earl of Errol had been interested to hear that James had spotted him. The nobleman had guessed he had taken lodgings with Lady Largo, and feared the agent might have had further talks with the Duke of Hamilton, and sensed betrayal. Andrew was surprised that the Earl openly expressed his fears to someone of lesser rank.

But James was vulnerable. His mentor was Archibald Pitcairne. He also accepted the patronage of Hugh Alexander, a staunch Unionist of anti-Jacobite persuasion. James was a scholar of complex mind and imagination, but was not familiar with the workings of political intrigue. It was unfortunate he had noticed the list on Andrew's desk.

At last John Scarlett emerged from the Customs House. He had just returned from a venture. With a mariner's swagger, he ambled along The Shore towards Andrew. They turned towards the Kirk Gate.

'I've made my report,' Scarlett said, keeping his eyes straight ahead.

'And…'

'It's done. The waiter has been paid. He thinks the "extra cargo" is iron ore and some other assorted goods. They will be unloaded at the ports as agreed.'

'Good,' Andrew said quietly. 'It all sounds too easy.'

'Comes with experience.'

'You are more at ease than I am.'

'Attention to detail. All the packages will have specific addressees. It took a while to organise though. We know it makes sense to vary the load of disguised cargo. I would like to know what some of the heavy goods are. You know of course.'

Andrew did not reply. Scarlett was clever, and utterly ruthless. He would be capable of guessing arms and ammunition were hidden within, and not care anyway.

Scarlett led Andrew into his house and through to the parlour. He uncorked a bottle of claret, and poured a generous measure for Andrew.

'I have the uneasy feeling there is a spy in our midst,' Andrew said. 'Someone close, within the city.'

'As you know, I am often away – Eyemouth, Berwick, Newcastle.' Scarlett sipped his wine. 'Your friend James, perhaps?'

'No. Definitely not. Anyway, let me know if you suspect anyone. Be on your guard.'

'As always. Your gentleman said you have another project in mind,' Scarlett said.

'Indeed I have. The sale has not been finalised yet,' Andrew said. 'It would involve a charter for coastal waters around the east coast. I am awaiting instructions.'

## 34

MARCH 1708

A ndrew read the brief note. *Come at once.* It was from the Earl of Errol at Slains. He smiled, slipping the paper into the inner pocket of his coat.

Could there be fresh hope of another attempt to restore King James? It had been nearly a year since he had assisted with importing a consignment of arms. There were suggestions then of a landing near Montrose, or perhaps somewhere in the west. No ships came in the summer. Then the long winter months, with rumours of an invasion. Only rumours. But he had not been idle. Far from it. The Union had created opportunities for illegal trade across the border. Many hands, dissatisfied with the Union, had been happy to assist. Jack Scarlett, Andrew knew, was among them. The rogue enjoyed using his skills to outmanoeuvre customs officials.

Now lighter days were ahead. The weather had been calm for several days. Andrew glanced out the window at the clouds scudding past from the east. A storm was coming. He finished the dregs of ale in his tankard, rose and swept his eyes around the room. No one took the slightest notice of him. He was just another merchant in an inn at Stonehaven.

Andrew stepped outside, the fresh wind stinging his face. He relished the salty taste. The harbour bustled with fishwives, carters and pedlars. He walked along the quayside. Suddenly the wind increased. Violent gusts caught traders off balance. Sleet, snowflakes and sea spray blew in, pounding the townsfolk and their houses. Huge waves battered the harbour walls. Andrew weaved around children who darted about between bundles of cargo, helping to load the remaining goods and retrieve scattered boxes. All the local folk, taken by surprise by the sudden storm, were now engaged in frantic activity. His attention was drawn to a small party leaving the inn. He must not be conspicuous. He turned down the narrow lane towards the stables. He must be forever watchful. Stormy weather or no, he must make haste.

Andrew dismounted in the courtyard at Slains, and handed the reins to the waiting groom. He took a kerchief and mopped his brow.

'Good to see you again, my friend.' Robert Charles stepped forward. 'I arrived here on a fishing boat. The frigate that brought me from France, *Le Cigalle*, is at sea. As ever, the Earl and his dear mother have been most generous in their hospitality.' He guided Andrew through the lobby to the library, talking in a constant stream of preparations for invasion. 'It required much secrecy to assemble troops, and order battalions to Dunkirk. Sailors to man the privateers and other vessels had to be ready.'

Refreshments were brought in. A servant handed Andrew a letter.

'The French fleet are expected to arrive in the Firth of Forth within the week,' Charles said.

The Earl of Errol entered, smiling as he welcomed Andrew. He sensed optimism and confidence in the nobleman's manner. 'We must act with haste,' the Earl said. 'I have a dispatch for you to take to Mr Malcolm of Grange, a Fife laird of known allegiance. His instructions are to have a boat and pilots ready to go on board the first ship that arrives in the vicinity of the Isle of May at the entrance to the Firth of Forth. The ship will show a special prearranged signal.'

Andrew nodded, absorbing all the detailed information. He could barely believe this was happening. With this zeal and commitment, they must surely have a successful campaign.

'Mr Malcolm will also order burghs and villages along the shores of the Forth to have vessels and pilots in waiting for offloading and disembarkation. You understand that speed is essential?'

'Of course, my lord.'

It was like a dream. More details and instructions followed. Andrew's mind was focused, his heart thumping.

'You must depart as soon as you're refreshed.' The Earl rose.

When he closed the door behind him, Andrew asked, 'Did you come with James Carron?'

'Ah, no. He was not available,' Robert Charles said.

'It would have been good to have him with us. I have much confidence in his intimate knowledge of the east coast.'

Mr Charles frowned. 'That may be so, but I have been saddened by changes in him. He has upset officers in the French Navy as a result of his fondness for the bottle. He's in much disarray.'

'I see.'

'There have been delays because of him. It's enough that we have to deal with spies, changes in weather, and other hazards.'

The strain on Robert Charles was beginning to show. Andrew turned his attention to his letter. It was a dispatch from Walter Duff asking him to return to Edinburgh immediately to attend to domestic matters of utmost urgency.

The serving maid deposited a platter in front of James. She smiled. His eyes swept to admire the soft skin on her arms. Then he transferred his gaze to a huge portion of fish pie.

'Mr Duff sends his compliments, sir, and requests your company at your leisure.' Davie had appeared at his side, with his eyes fixed on his pie. 'He means right now, I think, sir.'

'Thank you Davie,' James said. He stabbed the pie with his fork and took a mouthful. 'Delicious,' he said, grinning at the boy.

The lawyer would have to wait, whatever the business. Maybe Louise had returned. Over the past few months he had tried to forget about her. He recalled the last time he saw her, sitting in a chair in his parlour, sad and distressed. Did he feel pity, or was it love?

A heap of broadsides were dumped on the table in front of him. Francis sat down opposite. 'I've been listening to the latest gossip,' Francis began. 'There have been hints – just hints – from my contacts.' He winked. 'The French may be coming with troops to join the Jacobites.'

'Oh.'

'James, you're not with us, as usual. I'm telling you...' Francis stopped, and regarded three strangers who had entered the tavern. Their dress was rough plaid, and their boots were caked in mud. They slumped down at a nearby table. Seizing the opportunity, Francis picked up some broadsides and shuffled over to join them.

James would have liked to hear more about the latest turn of events. Maybe later. He ordered more ale. He took his time with his meal, determined to enjoy it before facing Andrew and Walter Duff. Drawing out his purse, he had just enough coin to pay the reckoning. He remembered his rent was overdue. Andrew had previously collected it himself on the term days, but James had not seen him since the New Year. Relations between them were cool. Was it because of Louise? Andrew could have shown more sympathy for her. Then again, Andrew was as secretive as ever, probably because of dubious trading ventures.

James returned to his chambers to collect the rent money, then headed up the turnpike to Andrew's office. He had meant to pay on Candlemas, but had accumulated several unpaid fees from wealthy clients. They needed to be reminded. Often. The money from them enabled him to continue his work with the poor without payment. It was necessary. An assistant or clerk attending to menial tasks would be grand, if he could earn enough to employ someone. That was a thought for the future.

'You took your time,' Walter Duff said. He was sitting upright behind Andrew's large desk, his eyelids drooping. He placed two papers in front of him; his satchel and an empty bottle also lay on the desk. There was no sign of Andrew's usual jumble of documents.

'I apologise for my tardiness,' James said, taking a chair opposite, and dumping the rent money on the table.

Mr Duff's hand shook as he wrote a short note and placed it with the money on a side table. 'For Mr Lawson's clerk. He's due to return soon. I must be gone in a few minutes. An appointment with a client.'

James took the receipt for the rent money. No mention of Andrew's whereabouts then. He had no intention of asking.

'I have here a short communication,' Mr Duff began, holding up a letter. 'It seems our Mr Brand was already married before he met Louise Morton.'

'Married? Are you sure?' This was a possibility that had not occurred to him. He gripped the arms of his chair.

'Definitely.'

'Does Louise know?'

'I don't think so. My gentleman has been unable to find her. I have a letter here,' Mr Duff said, pointing a finger at a paper on the table. 'The investigator has been putting together clues about Brand's activities. He has assumed false identities. Brand is not his real name. We know for sure that he has a wife and a family of six living in a house in London.'

'So why did he marry Louise?' James asked. 'He would gain nothing by it.'

'Perhaps he wanted respectability in the eyes of Edinburgh society. Who knows?'

James closed his eyes. He was trying to think. 'How do we know this man's information is accurate and reliable? He may be happy to take your fee and—'

'We can, and we must trust him. As I said before, he comes highly recommended.'

Duff stared into James's eyes. James let him continue.

'In addition, he has been trying to find out if Brand has any major political contacts. Perhaps you can help here, along with Francis Atkins. Find out more about the people he met when he stayed here.' Mr Duff stood up, and straightened slowly. 'I must go now. We can meet again tomorrow.'

James shuffled to the door, and turned. 'What about Andrew? Does he know?'

'I sent him a brief message several days ago.'

James traipsed back to his chambers, unable to settle his thoughts and emotions. He picked up a couple of letters on his table that were awaiting replies. Glancing over the first one, he took a sheet of paper and dipped his quill into the pot. He put the pen down, stood up and paced the room unable to concentrate. He sorted out some bottles on a shelf, and arranged them in a neat row. He opened the shutters. The lantern clock chimed the hour. It was a present from Louise. It reminded him of their friendship. Just a friendship. It could have been more had Brand, or whatever his name was, not existed. A draught ruffled the papers on the desk. He slammed the shutters tight. He would go and see if Francis was still at the tavern.

The hostelry was buzzing with excitement, the air thick with smoke. James peered through the gloom, and spotted Francis deep in conversation with a small party in the cosy alcove at the back. Several pairs of eyes stared at him in silence as he approached. James recognised them as the highland gentlemen who arrived while he was having his meal. The table was littered with empty plates, upturned glasses and a bowl with some leftover cabbage. Scraps of pie crust lay on the table and scattered about the floor. These men were merry, but not yet drunk. It would be difficult to prise Francis away.

'Ah, James. Pull up a stool. Allow me to introduce my new acquaintances.' Francis smiled, his face glowing, as it usually did when good stories and intrigue were on offer.

'You are a loyal Jacobite, I assume.' A burly figure leaned towards James. He wore a tartan highland plaid, kilted and tied loosely around his waist. Out of doors his plaid would be wrapped around his shoulders for warmth. His sharp eyes peered from under heavy brows.

James caught a whiff of his foul breath. 'I am indeed.' But was he deep down? He would think about that later.

'Excellent.' The big man pounded James on the back, his voice as large as his body. He grinned to his companions. The conversation resumed, loud and boisterous.

'If I may interrupt…' James addressed Francis.

A maid brought wine. James waved her away.

'If I may interrupt, there may be spies about,' he whispered. 'We…' James wasn't sure how to continue.

'Aye. We must be cautious,' Francis said.

'Is the King coming?' one man asked.

'I hope so,' Francis said.

'Of course he's coming,' said another.

'We don't know if, or indeed when or how, matters will be arranged,' Francis said.

James noticed that, for once, Francis was struggling for the right words.

'Can we go somewhere quiet?' James asked.

Francis nodded his understanding. 'If you will excuse me, gentlemen. It was a pleasure.' He shook hands with those round the table. 'My work awaits me.'

'I do have a lot to catch up on,' Francis said as they ambled down the High Street. 'Help me sober up at the workshop, and give me your news. You have something pressing on your mind. I can tell.'

The apprentice was busy at the printing press. Francis handed James two embroidered cushions, picked up a lantern, led him downstairs and unlocked a door in the basement. The smell of ink and dampness penetrated James's nostrils and throat. He felt a pang of fear. Francis shone the light on stacks full of books and broadsides.

'Reminds me of a certain event two years ago,' James said.

Francis nodded. 'You were in a secret cellar then. This is a different kind of store. Some of these books are currently in use.'

They set the cushions and lamp down. James told Francis of his meeting with Duff and the surprising knowledge about Brand.

'So our earlier suspicions were probably right,' Francis said. 'Perhaps he was a spy.'

'I recall once Mrs Hodges mentioned he was often in his room writing,' James said. 'He may have left some scraps of letters. We could speak to Mrs Grant.'

'That old, brainless gossip? Anyway, Brand probably cleared the room thoroughly.'

'Maybe. We could try.'

'I hope you have plenty of coin with you.'

'That's a difficult matter these days.'

'James, I'm surprised. Are you not well paid for your services?' Francis smiled.

'I don't find the topic amusing. Let's go to Mrs Grant's. Then I'm going south to find Louise.'

James stood by as Francis inserted the key into the lock. He caught a whiff of sweat and mixed spices as he followed Francis into the small chamber. Daylight from a high window lit one half of the room. A ewer and basin stood on a folding table. In the other half a ruffled blanket and sheet lay on the bed. A bundle of clothes lay on the floor. Francis knelt down and looked under the bed. He pulled out a chamber pot, turning his face away, his eyes screwed up in disgust. Then he took the poker and prodded about. Clouds of dust flew out. A mouse appeared and scurried across the floor. Francis pulled out various objects, prodding them with the poker and holding his nose with his other hand.

James watched as he examined them. 'You've done this sort of thing before,' he said.

Francis raised his head and nodded. 'Often traces of the previous tenant can be found. You'd be surprised.'

'But Brand was here more than two years ago.'

'And the old wifie said there has only been one tenant here since. A man with few possessions and filthy habits, obviously. Lucky for us he's not often here.' Francis was examining his dust-covered hands. 'Not the most pleasant of tasks.' He removed the keys from his pocket. 'Mrs Grant said to look in the press. This key.' He showed the smaller of the two keys.

The cupboard was stacked with curtains, blankets, linen sheets. Some packages wrapped in printed paper were stuffed in the corners. Under moth-eaten blankets lay a pile of pamphlets.

Francis examined them. 'In support of the Union. Probably written by Defoe.'

There was a rattle at the door.

'You've had enough time in there,' Mrs Grant said.

'And found nothing to tell us anything new about Brand,' Francis said.

'Just return the keys, please,' she said.

Francis fumbled inside his pockets and pulled out some coins and laid them on the bed. He took out the keys and handed them to the landlady. Her eyes followed the coins as Francis put the rest back into his purse.

'James would like to write to Mrs Brand, with the prescription for a new remedy he has for severe headaches.' He took out a crown and placed it on the bed. 'I understand they stayed at Eyemouth for a while.'

'Aye, Eyemouth.' Mrs Grant's eyes narrowed. She stood still, her left hand holding the door.

Francis removed another crown from his pocket and placed it on the bed.

'I ken a landlady who bides in Eyemouth,' Mrs Grant said.

'Let's go down to the baths,' Francis said. 'I feel dirty.' He examined his hands as they emerged from the close into the sunshine.

'Your hands are always dirty,' James said.

'Only ink stains and dust from paper.'

James said no more about it. There was no point in any reasoned, logical discourse with Francis. He always had his own view of life that was different from anyone else's. Like James, he was an individualist.

'Are you coming with me to Eyemouth?' James asked.

'I can't. There's too much going on here. We are ready for a Jacobite Rising.'

## 35

J ames descended the steep slope, taking in the view of
Eyemouth harbour. The recent storm had kept him
in Edinburgh, increasing his frustration. Now that the
wind had eased, the waves pounded the beaches with less
ferocity. He wandered along the shore. Three fishermen sat
on a wall mending nets. A dog barked but ignored him as
he wandered on. Near the harbour he found a house fitting
the description given by Mrs Grant. She had suggested the
lodgings to Henry Brand, as she was acquainted with the
landlady there.

'I'm looking for bed and board,' James said to the young
girl at the door.

She disappeared and he was left standing on the doorstep.
She returned, and pointed to the stair. 'Top floor, first room,'
she said.

As he opened the door, a cold draught from the window
filled the wee chamber with sea air and the smell of smoked
fish. Mice scurried from under the bed. James tidied the grate
and lit a fire. He rubbed his hands. It was cooler here than

outside. He glanced at the unmade bed and filthy sheets. There was a soft knock on the door.

'Will you be wanting supper, sir?' the girl asked.

'No, thank you. I've already eaten. Some bed sheets and a towel, if you please. Clean.'

The girl nodded. She brought clean linen and dumped the bundle on the bed. James closed the door and locked it from the inside. He removed his short grey wig, shook his brown hair and scratched his head. The wig and the extra padding under his coat were enough of a disguise. He felt cold even with the stuffed cloth padding. His tired eyes were drooping. He lay down, exhausted.

He was still tired when he awoke in the early morning. Shouts from the distance, and the excited blethers of women outside the lodgings, forced him from his bed. He poked the fire and put on a wee piece of coal. While dressing, he thought about how he would introduce himself to the other lodgers and the people of the town. He wished he had brought Davie with him to carry his bottles and jars. The lad would be useful while James explained to an eager audience cures for headaches, stomach ache, and the effects of too much drinking. Packing as much as he could into his satchel, he stepped downstairs to the board.

He nodded to other lodgers, picked up a clean pewter plate, and drew a stool to the table. He helped himself to a portion of bread, leaned forward and cut some cheese.

The man next to him passed the flagon of milk. 'What are you selling?' he asked, indicating the satchel James had set down in the corner.

'Some remedies for common ailments,' James said.

A woman across the board snorted, spitting out phlegm onto the table. 'A mountebank. We don't want your sort here. The kind who charge high prices for recipes that don't work.' She sniffed. 'My good man, now sadly in another life, had gout—'

'Be quiet, wife. We'll have none of your stories.' The speaker stood up, knocking his empty plate onto the floor. He left the parlour without picking it up.

James could not imagine Louise staying long in a house like this. Filthy lodgers with poor table manners. Food scattered on the board and about the floor.

'I've stayed hereabouts for over four years,' his neighbour said. He took a mouthful of milk. 'I can see you're just passing through.' He narrowed his eyes as if assessing James's character and figuring his intentions. 'The best way to trade is to offer your wares to the fisherfolk,' he said, 'when they're half fou.' He laughed, and nudged James.

James tried his luck. 'You haven't come across a young lady of about twenty years? From Edinburgh…'

'A young woman, eh?' The man brought his face close to James's, his foul breath reaching his nostrils.

'A friend.'

'Oh, a friend, eh?' His tone was mocking. They all laughed. James's neighbour looked him up and down, turned his back on him and set up a quiet conversation with the man on his left.

James took his leave of his ill-mannered table companions and picked up his satchel. Outside the fresh easterly breeze threatened to dislodge his hat and wig. He pulled the wide-brimmed hat down so that it almost covered his eyes. Thick cream on his face to lighten his skin and powder on his eyebrows completed his disguise, though his chances of meeting an acquaintance here were remote.

A group of fishermen gathered round the crew from a boat that had just come in. Other men at the quayside looked on with curiosity. James approached one of the idlers.

'Many ships,' the man said.

'From where?'

The seaman shrugged and walked on.

There was no chance of selling his wonder cures while the local people were distracted. He would be as well to return to his chamber and dump his heavy satchel of medicines, then ascend the cliffs to view the many ships. Should he go round by the bay, or cross the river to the cliffs on the east side?

A merchant leaning against a rail held the attention of a group of seamen. He glanced in James's direction and stood erect. Jack Scarlett. Had he recognised him? Scarlett was waving him over. So much for the disguise.

'Do join us, sir,' Scarlett said. We were just discussing—'

'He's a mountebank,' came a shout from behind. 'See his bag there? Full of fake remedies.'

'Not at all.' James dipped his hand into his satchel, and pulled out a small, dark bottle. 'This here is guaranteed to improve your success with the ladies.'

The men sniggered.

'And I have here a recipe for early morning following a night of entertainment. You all know how it is, when you wake up.' He held up another bottle of liquid.

Scarlett leaned back and folded his arms, a slow smirk emerging on his mouth, his ugly scar prominent.

'I have a few bottles left. Only—'

'I'll take a bottle,' Scarlett said, and slipped a coin into James's hand. He grabbed the potion, winked and sauntered off.

Scarlett was teasing him. The eyes of the other men wandered. James's hands were shaking. The seamen drifted off. So much for his skills as a vendor.

James plodded back to his lodgings, taking care that Scarlett was not around before entering the house. He dumped his medicines in his chamber and sought out the landlady.

'Henry Brand and his wife? No. I ken no folk of that name,' the landlady said.

James described them. 'They might have passed the winter here two years ago.'

The woman shook her head. There was no way of knowing if she was being truthful.

Back outside, James strolled along the road to the east of the town. He spotted a ferryboat approaching, ran down the steps and waited. The ferryman carried him to the east bank. He bounded up the steep, grassy slope. At the top he paused to look down at the rooftops of the town. He strode to the promontory, and glanced back. He was alone. Here at the extremity, a grassy slope overlaid horizontal stone. About halfway down, these layers covered rocks tilted on their sides as if some force had turned them over. He took out his glass and scanned the horizon for several minutes. Nothing. Then he saw sails. He strained his eye but the ships were too far away to be identified.

'Ah, there you are.'

James froze, reluctant to remove his eye from his glass. He turned round slowly.

'Thank you for the cure,' Scarlett said, holding up the bottle. 'I will try this to see if it works. As you know, I enjoy fine wine in select company, rum in the company of seamen. Often the next day, well, I'm not shipshape.' He put the bottle into his pocket. 'So if I need more, you're the supplier, eh?' Scarlett walked up and down, edging nearer to the cliff edge.

James's eyes followed his movement. He stood still, not wanting to step back and lose his balance. How did Scarlett get here? He was sure no one had followed him.

Scarlett eased forward to face him close up. Was he going to push him over the edge? He peeked at the upturned rocks.

'Why are you here? Are you a government spy?' Scarlett stared.

'I might ask you the same question,' James said.

Scarlett kicked a stone. It bounced down the slope. James took the opportunity to move away from the edge.

'I am a merchant—' Scarlett began.

'An unscrupulous one. A mercenary. A smuggler.'

'I may be any or all of these things, or none. But right now you're in my way. Poking your nose in, or threatening to.'

'Me threaten you? You've got that the wrong way round,' James said.

Scarlett shuffled backwards. 'No, I won't threaten you, as you are a friend of Andrew Lawson. Go back to Edinburgh. Don't interfere.' He pointed his finger and turned.

James watched him head back to the town. He stood for a few moments, then eased his way gently down the slope to the jagged rocks, and away from the burgh. Scarlett would be watching his return, observing him cross the river. So he would cross further upstream. But Scarlett needn't worry. He would stay out of his way.

After wandering about aimlessly, here and there, for most of the day, warm air and the smell of fish and smoke from the fire at his lodgings, welcomed him. He rubbed his sore knees, scraped while clambering over rocks. He spread his hands out in front of the fire in the parlour, and eyed the steaming pot of fish broth. Behind him three lodgers sat round the table.

'You have a rival. Another mountebank,' one of the men said.

James turned round. 'You mean another selling medicines?'

'A charlatan. And he has a hawker companion with a load of broadsides. They just arrived after midday, and set about selling their wares.'

'Oh,' James said, forcing himself not to smile. He picked up a bowl and ladle from the sideboard, and helped himself to fish broth. Keeping a serious expression, he ate his soup, then took a second bowlful.

'You have a good appetite.'

'The way to a healthy body.' *Poor quality meal though*, he thought. 'These men, the other mountebank and his friend, do you know where they're lodging?'

'Aye, that I do. We'll have no mischief here, mind. This is a peaceful town.'

'With talk of Jacobites, I think not,' James said, glaring at the man. He finished his food and made for the door.

'The two strangers are biding at the inn at the harbour mouth,' one man said.

James thanked them and wandered out into the cold evening, not caring if he were to meet Scarlett again. The two travellers had aroused his curiosity. The inn at the corner was full to bursting, and smelt of sweat and ale. No one paid him heed as he meandered about, glancing at the faces. Then he noticed the mountebank and the broadside seller. He ordered a tankard of ale and pulled up a stool beside them.

Douglas regarded him with curiosity, then smiled. 'Didn't know you at first. You've put on weight,' he said.

James opened his coat and tugged at the padding. 'The disguise wasn't good enough for Scarlett. He recognised me,' he said in a low voice.

'Scarlett's here?'

'Yes, and he's up to something,' James said. He looked across and frowned at Francis. 'Don't you think it's dangerous selling broadsides?'

'These are not political ones.' He held one up.

James nodded.

'Word is, French troops are coming,' Francis said. 'And we heard from travellers on the road that the army is assembled near Berwick, ready for action.'

'Fishermen here are going out to meet the French fleet,' Douglas said.

'We came to help you search for Mrs Brand,' Francis said. 'Have you found out anything?'

'No. People here either don't know her or are not saying. They don't trust me; suspicious of strangers. Though that's not surprising.' James leaned forward. 'Thank you for coming.'

'It was young Davie. He told us you had left on a journey. He was disappointed. Wanted to go with you. We guessed you might have come here.'

'It's too dangerous for the boy. I would have to be minding him as well as taking care of my own welfare.'

'We arrived this afternoon. Heard someone here was peddling medicines.' Douglas smiled. 'We might be more successful if we work together, eh?'

'So they've not been buying your wares either?' James asked.

'In a while maybe,' Douglas said. 'I'm not giving up. And we're not giving up on finding Mrs Brand. We need to have some sort of plan. What are your lodgings like?'

'Mice scurry out the door when you walk in. Bedbugs.'

'Food?'

'Inferior. Thin broth. Stale cheese…'

'Not what you're used to,' Douglas said.

James stood up. His limbs ached, and his right leg felt weak.

'I see you've had an accident,' Douglas said.

'I took a tumble. It was nothing,' James said. He finished his ale and stood up.

He limped back to his lodgings, tiredness catching up on him. It was now almost dark. Lights flickered from windows. James was used to feeling his way in the dark. The lodging house was easily identified by the shape of the gabled end. A shadowy figure hovered near the corner of the house and drew back as he approached. James's body was in no shape to deal with a robber. The door of the house opened and the landlady appeared, bearing a lamp and a pail of night soil. The light caught the face of the prowler, before he shrank back into the shadows.

'Andrew?' James whispered. 'Is that you?' He edged round the back.

'James!' Andrew tugged his arm. 'I'm cold. I'm on the run. I'll be imprisoned if I'm caught.'

## 36

The landlady had left the door ajar.
        'This way.'
    James stood for a moment to listen. Rough voices raised in excited discussion came from the parlour. He led Andrew up the stair just in time before hearing the landlady close the house door. He entered his wee chamber, lit a lamp and poked the fire. Only a couple of pieces of coal left. He put one on. While Andrew hunched over the fire rubbing his arms, James removed his coat, and the padded waistcoat beneath. Andrew took off his wet coat and exchanged it for James's padded waistcoat.

    'Clever. Looks like an ordinary waistcoat, with bulges. I know why you're here. Have you found her?' Andrew whispered.

    James shook his head. 'Francis and Douglas are here searching for her too. Oh, and Jack Scarlett's in Eyemouth.'

    Andrew frowned. 'I know somewhere we can talk in secret. Tomorrow. Right now, I'm tired.' He lay down in front of the fire.

James found a blanket and covered Andrew. He was curious to hear his story, but that would have to wait.

All night, through intermittent sleep, James turned to ease the aches in his body. He had some ointment in his bag, but was too weary to rouse himself. Anyway, a slight noise might wake others in the house.

The reflection of a flickering flame dancing on the wall and a scraping noise alerted his senses. He was still tired. He turned and watched Andrew tending the fire, putting the last piece of coal on. He swung his legs off the bed, feeling the cold air.

'The first light of dawn is beginning to appear,' Andrew whispered. 'We must move now.'

James was quick to detect urgency in Andrew's voice. Andrew was ready. James dressed and packed his satchel. He left the medicines. He smoothed the bedcover, took some coins from his purse and placed them on the bed.

They crept downstairs. The house was silent. The bottom step creaked. There was a soft rustle from the direction of the kitchen. James opened the door and pushed Andrew out into the cold. He followed him and closed the door.

James walked behind Andrew as they hurried along the quayside. The town was slowly beginning to stir. A gull on a rooftop squawked. Shadowy figures loaded cargo onto a cutter. James glanced backwards at them.

'They're in the fair trade. Just ignore them, and they won't bother us,' Andrew said, urging him on.

Andrew waved to a man in a small boat. They waited as the boat approached. The man nodded, and they climbed down to the boat. Andrew put some coins into the man's outstretched hand, and pointed to a spot across the river. He rowed them across in silence. Andrew jumped out and led James up the slope to three dilapidated cottages.

A head peeped round the half-open door of the first cottage. Andrew stooped and whispered something into the ear of an old woman. Andrew beckoned, and James walked behind him into the hovel. The woman wore a filthy brown dress. A ragged shawl covered her head and shoulders. She closed the door, lit a lantern and passed it to Andrew. She opened a press, and unlocked a small door within. Andrew passed through. James followed, blinking in the darkness. He kept his eye on the lamp through a tunnel with twists and turns. James tasted the dampness of the rocks. A gentle draught with a whiff of brandy came from somewhere.

They emerged at the edge of a cliff. James watched Andrew ease his way along, finally entering a large cave. Andrew disappeared, then re-emerged after a few moments. He waved James on. James stepped through the low entrance into a spacious cave neatly arranged as a living area, and furnished with assorted boxes and barrels. A pot of porridge simmered on a low fire.

Andrew took an empty bowl, filled it and handed it to James. 'Welcome to a different kind of home. I've sent a servant to look for Scarlett,' Andrew said.

They sat down on boxes in the corner.

'Does this house, if I can call it that, belong to you?' James asked.

'Oh, no.' Andrew smiled. 'I've lodged here occasionally, though.'

James told Andrew about his encounter with Scarlett. 'He suspects I'm a government spy.'

'It's more complicated than that, I suspect. Scarlett has many ventures. Anyway, I have my story to tell you.' Andrew helped himself to more porridge. 'In Aberdeenshire I was summoned to Slains, the home of the Earl of Errol. He was the gentleman you met briefly at Comiston. He said that ships bearing troops from France were on their way here. I was asked to deliver a letter to a Fife laird, James Malcolm of Grange. Errol also passed on a letter addressed to me from Walter Duff. It had been delivered to Slains. Duff wrote he had news of Brand and begged me to return to Edinburgh as soon as my business had been completed.

'When I met Mr Malcolm he told me he was delighted to be given the honour of going out to the flagship to greet the French when they arrive. He asked if I would go on board with him and assist as one of the pilots. Well, there was much to do before that. Messages to be delivered. I took some dispatches to Edinburgh, and while I was there Duff told me about Brand. James, I can tell you there was great anticipation among the citizens of Edinburgh. I did not delay. I returned to Fife. Then came news of the first ship. Lots of boats went out to greet them. I was on one of them, and boarded the French ship.'

Andrew stretched his legs, leaned back and continued. 'It turned out the first ship, *Le Protée*, was not the flagship. Malcolm told me this later after he spoke to the commander, Monsieur Rambures. On the voyage to Scotland, *Le Protée* had encountered a storm, and returned to Dunkirk for replacement anchors. When they arrived at the mouth of the Forth they thought the fleet would be there already. They were sure they must have been two days behind the admiral. On *Le Protée* we sailed back down the Forth, and saw lots of vessels. I was disembarked with other pilots at North Berwick.'

'So where were the other ships before *Le Protée* arrived?'

'They must have sailed north, I suppose. And then returned.'

'Why?'

'I never found out. When we met up with the rest of the fleet, we saw them engaged in battle with English ships. The pilots were put ashore then. Malcolm told me to stay concealed. Anyone disembarking from a French ship was at risk of being arrested.'

'You could have stayed on board *Le Protée.*'

'I wanted to find Louise. I...' Andrew stood up, peering at something behind James. His right hand moved automatically to the hilt of his sword.

'I didn't expect to see you both here,' a familiar voice said. 'I told him to go.'

James turned to face Jack Scarlett.

'James is with me. We're searching for Mrs Brand,' Andrew said.

Scarlett took a box and cushion and sat down beside the fire. He lit a pipe.

Andrew told him about Brand's illegal marriage. 'As for myself, I need to hide for a while,' Andrew said.

Scarlett sat for a few minutes. He tapped out the embers of his pipe, stood up and left without a word.

'We mustn't annoy him. You may find it hard to believe, but he holds considerable power here.'

'I can imagine,' James said. 'He can intimidate. No one wants to cross him.'

'Hmm,' Andrew said.

'What does he do here? You must know.'

'I ask no questions. He's in the fair trade, and engaged in moneylending. He prospered well a year ago. My guess is he is selling some of the goods he bought then, before the Union. He's selling them over the border… He's coming back.'

It was the manservant. 'Follow me, gentlemen,' the man said.

He lit a lantern and handed it to Andrew. The servant took another lamp and led them through a tunnel off the cave, through twists and turns. Like the other passage this one was also quite airy, with faint scents of brandy and spices. The servant unlocked a door. Inside was a long cellar, filled bottom to top with casks of wine and brandy. A passage down the middle led to another locked door. The servant knocked and held up the lamp. The door opened softly, and a lamp shone on Louise's smiling face.

James rushed in and wrapped her in a warm embrace. The servant retreated and closed the door behind him.

Louise broke free and pulled back. 'James! I'm a married lady.'

'There is a legal problem with your marriage,' Andrew began, stepping forward. Louise opened her mouth, but Andrew held up his hand. 'Let me explain. But first I should apologise for my behaviour. I should have had more trust in your motives and your character.' He took a letter from his coat pocket. 'Here is a letter from Mr Duff about the villain who deceived you and worse.'

Louise sat down on an armchair. James watched her smile vanish as she read the paper. He looked around the room. It was a small parlour with a table and chair, cabinets, armchair and a small bed. There were no windows, but it was well lit with lamps giving off an odour of burning fish oil.

Louise leaned back and closed her eyes. 'I thank you both for this, and I'm grateful to Mr Duff,' she said softly. 'Please thank him for me.'

'You may thank him yourself. You're returning to Edinburgh with us,' Andrew said.

Louise sighed.

James's joy and relief were replaced by a sense of unease. 'How are you managing here, in this place?' he asked.

Louise stared blankly before replying. 'I have Mr Scarlett's protection.'

'Scarlett? The sleekit rascal is your benefactor?' It didn't seem possible.

'Oh, Scarlett is good on blackmail,' Louise said. 'He knows how to extract revenge on his enemies – in the best way to do damage to them. With my husband, he kept demanding more and more money. I was affected too. So, in a way, Scarlett is actually paying me back. I don't owe him.'

James couldn't take his eyes off her. She had grown in maturity and confidence since her first encounter with Brand nearly four years ago.

'Scarlett could have told me more about Brand,' Andrew said.

'He's had us all running around,' James said. 'I did warn you from the start.'

'Yes you did. So you keep reminding me,' Andrew said. 'Anyway, now we must plan. We return to Edinburgh for news of the invasion.'

'Should you not stay here?' James asked. 'You could remain concealed for a while.'

'No – I must contact Robert Charles.'

# 37

J ames settled into the comfy armchair in Andrew's small parlour. Andrew locked the door, and set a bottle of claret and two glasses on the wee table. It was late. A single candle flickered. The red glow from the fire warmed the room. It was good to be home.

'I'm waiting for news from Robert Charles,' Andrew said. 'We hope that the King has made landfall safely.'

'Francis spoke about rumours going round,' James said. 'That the ships had to retreat, and the French left without landing troops.' He took the glass of claret.

Raising his glass, Andrew said, 'Here's to the King.'

'To the King,' James said. He set his glass on the table. 'You drink too much, I fear.'

The comment appeared to have no effect on Andrew. He said, 'The element of surprise had gone from the invasion. The English Navy arrived quickly. I fear they must have been informed. There seemed much confusion, and I suppose the English Navy had more ships.'

James sighed. 'It's not safe for you here. You should have remained in Eyemouth with Scarlett and his friends for protection.'

'No. On the contrary. I'm better here, conducting my business in the usual way. I won't be visible, except to friends. There's always a closet or cellar to hide in at a moment's notice; and disguises too.' Andrew smiled. 'I could be betrayed anywhere, I suppose.'

James admired Andrew's composure and resilience. Not everyone could adapt and manoeuvre so easily. He had to ask about Louise. 'So how does Louise fare? Bella and Rose say she won't speak to anyone. Not even me. I haven't seen her since we returned.'

'Bella says she's all right. The sisters' garret will suit Louise for now. For some time the chamber has been used for guests under cover of the dressmakers' workshop. Louise has the ladies for company, and employment as well.'

'Have you seen her?'

'No. Right now, I'm probably the last person she wants to speak to. She's not the first to suffer from being a victim of misfortune, though.'

'She'll need time to recover,' James said.

Andrew leaned forward, pressing his hands hard on the armrests of his chair. 'James, I'm going to ask Louise to be my wife, once Duff has attended to the legal matters of her marriage to Brand.'

'What?' James clenched his fists.

'My wife, in name only. For the security of both of us.'

James stood up. 'A marriage of convenience. I don't believe you would do this.'

'Sit down. Let me explain. If I don't survive these difficult times, she'll have Lawson's Land, the whole tenement. If I live in exile, I can return after a few years, and have a house.'

James paced up and down. He banged his hand against the wall, turned round, and faced Andrew. He wanted to rush at him, but held back. 'You scheming rogue! And I thought you were brave coming to Eyemouth to seek Louise with genuine concern for her. But you were only thinking of yourself.'

'Yes, I was. And with good reason.'

'But you gave no care to Louise. Think on it. The last thing she wants is another unfortunate marriage.' James tried to ease the tension in his body.

'You're not the man for Louise,' Andrew said. 'You're not ready for marriage. You're set on going abroad to further your education. Whereas, it's about time I considered matrimony.'

'But you don't love her.'

'And you do?'

James felt as if he had been punched. He sat down. Did he love Louise? Was he sure? He had lived for so long with the situation of Henry Brand as her husband. Andrew was watching him.

There was a knock on the door.

'Mr Duff to see you sir,' Mrs Hodges said.

Andrew took Walter Duff into the office. The interruption couldn't have come at a better time. He hoped that James would take time to consider, and see things sensibly. He knew James had his mind set on going to Leiden. Now was the time for him to go. On the morrow Andrew would seek out Archibald Pitcairne for his thoughts on the matter. Well, maybe not. Too many secret eyes about.

At this late hour the lawyer's eyes drooped, and his face was pale. 'I have the documents here.' Mr Duff passed them to Andrew, and sank wearily into the chair at the desk. 'I will send the letter for Brand to my colleague in London. He is informed of the situation.'

Andrew read the letter, laid it down and nodded. 'It covers the main points. Brand is not to set foot in Scotland. He is not to attempt to contact Louise.' He looked up. 'As long as we are sure these conditions are met, we will not pursue debts owed to us.' He folded his arms. 'I think we can make these arrangements work.'

Andrew watched Mr Duff as he folded the document case and placed it in his satchel. Was it too soon to ask Louise? If the Rising were to fail, there was the chance Andrew's days in Edinburgh were in short number.

'I will ask Hodges to accompany you to your house.' Andrew took his arm and led him to the door. It struck him that he may not see his lawyer for some time. 'Please take care,' he said.


'Miss Louise has not been receiving visitors, or going out. A pity. On a bright day like today, she would benefit from some fresh air,' Rose said. 'I do hope Bella is able to persuade her to come down, even for a few minutes. Some conversation will revive her spirits, I'm sure.' She sighed.

Andrew was prepared to wait patiently.

'She hardly talks to us. She works alone, seeing us only on necessary matters. We have given her some fine embroidery work for one of our best clients, to focus her attention and help restore her confidence. I fear she is absorbed with guilt and shame.'

'How is her appetite?'

'She eats little. She is silent and lifeless. We try to persuade her to talk, but tears begin to fill her eyes, and she retreats into her own world.'

'How does she feel about me?' Andrew asked.

'She's grateful to you and James for bringing her back to Edinburgh. With some encouragement and security I think in time she will settle here again. I do hope so. This is her home.'

'What of her sister and brother?'

'She has lost touch with her brother. He left to be a soldier more than four years since. Her sister has not come to her aid. Louise tells me that Mary has been poorly. It's her husband who prevents her, I think…'

Andrew heard the creak of floorboards on the stair, and soft footsteps. Louise entered cautiously, followed by Bella. Andrew stood up, noticing the paleness of her face. *She needs to go out more*. Louise gave him a thin smile. She sat on the edge of a chair, hands clasped and her head slightly bent.

'Would you like to go for a ride? It's turning into a mild spring. Quite pleasant outside.'

'I have no mount.'

'I know a gentle palfrey we can borrow if available.'

Louise nodded. 'Thank you. I would like that.'

'Come to the Grassmarket when you're ready.'

This was foolish, Andrew thought, as he walked down the West Bow; but worth it. It would go some way towards easing his conscience. He had sensed a change in Louise's mood when he suggested an outing. What were the chances anyway of him being recognised as someone who disembarked at North Berwick? Mr Malcolm was perhaps being excessively cautious in his warning.

Andrew stepped round the corner and almost bumped into James's servant leaving the stables.

'A fine day, sir,' Davie said.

'Aye. Grand day.' Andrew stared at Davie, daring him to ask questions. The boy opened his mouth and closed it again. He disappeared up a close.

'I saw you coming through the Grassmarket,' the stable boy said. 'I will have Marcus ready for you, if you wish, sir.'

'Thank you,' Andrew said. No one, it seemed, could wander without being conspicuous.

Andrew was able to arrange to borrow a palfrey for Louise. He led the two horses out, and to his relief spotted Louise coming down the West Bow. She had changed into outdoor clothes, looking smart and composed in a brown woollen jacket. Would he draw attention to himself, out riding with a lady unchaperoned?

'Just pretend you're not with me,' Andrew said. 'Go through the Cowgate, and follow me in the direction of Arthur's Seat.'

Andrew handed Louise the reins, and moved ahead along the busy road, not looking back until he passed Blackfriars, and into the park. Then he set off at a brisk canter towards Arthur's Seat. He slowed down a little. Louise was behind. He allowed her to catch up, and they stopped in the gap between the crags and Arthur's Seat. They dismounted.

There was no sign of troops being assembled in the park, Jacobite or Government. Andrew let his eyes wander over the landscape, across the fields, to the shore.

'You didn't ask me here just to enjoy the view,' Louise said.

Andrew turned to face her. He had to be straightforward. No delicate words. There was no time to lose. 'Louise, once the legal matters have been sorted I mean to ask you if you will be my wife. In name only, you understand. Not a proper marriage. You see, I'm not optimistic of the outcome of the Rising. In case of failure I may have to go abroad. Or—'

Louise held up her hand. 'No. I—'

'Or I may perish in the conflict. Of course, we may succeed without the aid of French troops. The King will gather the clans and raise forces. Whatever happens, you will have Lawson's Land.'

'It's property you think about, not me.'

There was a hardness in Louise's voice that Andrew had not expected. They sat down on a rock. Yes, the arrangement was for his own benefit.

'I am much to blame for some of your troubles. I was blind. I could have made enquiries about Henry Brand sooner. James, I recall, didn't like him from the start.'

'I've had time to think,' Louise said. 'It doesn't do to dwell on the past.' She fiddled with her gloves, put them on, then turned to face Andrew. 'I thank you for your kindness to see me settled and provided for. I must decline your offer. I think you feel you owe me, but you do not. It is me who is in your debt. But anyway, I've had enough of married life and intend to remain a spinster. The idea of living independently appeals to me.'

'And James? Is it possible you are in love with him?'

She made no reply, and turned her head to avoid meeting his gaze. They sat in silence for a while. Slowly rising to her feet, Louise stretched and approached her palfrey. Andrew helped her mount. He removed his wig and replaced it with a tousled brown one. They rode back to the edge of the city. He was offering her a reasonable, workable solution, and taking a risk being out here in the open. Andrew put these thoughts aside as they made their way through the Canongate. He needed to be watchful for their safety.

He made it back to his chambers without meeting anyone else, though there was no doubt a thousand eyes peered at him from all corners of the burgh.

'A servant brought a message from Mrs Scarlett,' Hodges said.

Andrew tore open the note. Eleanor wanted to see him on a matter of some urgency. This was unexpected. He had not seen Eleanor for a while. He hadn't heard from Jack Scarlett either since leaving Eyemouth. He did not trust Scarlett's wife, and feared a trap. For too long he had believed Eleanor had something to do with James being kidnapped and his chambers searched. That was more than two years ago. But not forgotten. Not forgotten either the raw passion she excited in him. So he had kept his distance for some time. Andrew shut himself in his parlour. He paced up and down.

Eleanor Scarlett was seated on a chaise longue in her parlour. He could have ignored her letter, but here he was. She wore a soft gown of green silk, with long sleeves, and revealing her lovely shoulders and neck. She gestured for him to be seated but he remained standing, watching her and uncomfortably aware his back was to the door.

'Well,' he asked, 'what do you want that's so urgent?'

'Come here and relax. Tell me why you've avoided me for so long. What have I done to disappoint you?'

'You know very well.'

'You speak as if we are enemies. We used to be friends.' She stood up and glided close to him.

He gripped her by the neck. 'You're a whore and a spy, and no friend of mine. I ask you again, what did you want to see me about?'

He heard a soft creak of the door, and loosened his grip on Eleanor. Two guards burst into the room.

'Andrew Lawson, you are under arrest.'

The guards bound Andrew's hands, and led him down the stair at musket point. He turned to see Eleanor watching from the top of the steps. Suddenly the door flew open and four men rushed in. Andrew kicked one of the guards, knocking him down the steps. Andrew lost his balance and slid down to the bottom of the stairway. Easing his body to one side, he looked up and saw the boots of a man dashing up to the landing. He sat on the bottom steps.

Hooded men had disarmed the guards, bound and gagged them. One of them rifled through their pockets, and found a set of keys. He fumbled with the keys, eventually finding one that unlocked the shackles that bound Andrew's wrists. He removed his mask. It was Douglas Atkins.

'We need to move fast,' Andrew said.

A shot was heard from upstairs. Everyone froze, and waited. A door opened slowly and Jack Scarlett emerged.

## 38

James awoke with a start. It was full daylight. He had to go to the Greping Office, and was already late. Davie had gone, leaving a basin, a ewer of water and a towel on the table. Beside the glowing fire lay a pot of steaming porridge. He was dressing when Francis arrived at his doorstep.

Francis wore his working clothes, his jacket stained with ink, and worn bare at the cuff and elbows. He took a rag from his pocket and rubbed his hands. He spoke rapidly. He had just finished printing pamphlets when Douglas burst into his workshop. Andrew had been betrayed by Eleanor Scarlett. She was now dead.

'Shot by her husband, I think,' Francis said. He explained that Eleanor had asked to see Andrew, and Andrew, fearing a trap, had engaged the assistance of Douglas and three others. Scarlett had apparently turned up out of the blue.

'So where's Andrew now?' James asked.

'Douglas came straight home after the fray. Jack Scarlett and Andrew have disappeared. The guardsmen will wake up with sore heads.'

James would have to wait till later in the day to find out more. He had told Andrew to remain concealed in Eyemouth. If only he had listened. He was always the smart one. *And now he's gone.* He could be hiding in Leith, or Edinburgh, in one of the cellars beneath the tenements. Or in Francis' store for banished pamphlets.

James locked the door and dashed down the turnpike. A scene bordering on chaos filled the High Street. Individuals hurrying to and fro merged with customers and vendors dawdling about the market stalls. A fight had broken out amongst the rabble at the narrowest point of the High Street, obstructing his passage. James pushed through. The guards appeared from nowhere. One of them stood in front of him, blocking his way.

'I'm a doctor,' James said.

The guard scowled and gave way. James zigzagged through the crowd and rushed down the steps, passing a long queue to the clinic. When he arrived he set his bag down in the corner. Pitcairne waved the next patient to join him.

It was a long morning. As well as the regular complaints and ailments, there were several who'd suffered minor injuries as a result of scuffles in the streets over the last few days. Unrest and panic had penetrated the minds of the city folk, and unleashed the worst in behaviour of some. At the end of a packed morning there was no time for a students' post-clinic discussion. Pitcairne had vanished anyway. James lost no time in heading to the apothecary shop for news.

Mrs Atkins was serving a frail old lady. 'My husband left early this morning,' she said. 'I don't know where he is. I'm busy. Would you oblige me by lending a hand in the shop?'

'I can't. Maybe later,' James said. He left before waiting for her reply.

Francis was not in his workshop, and, not surprisingly, his apprentice had no idea of his whereabouts. Back home, Davie was waiting for James, stirring a pot of mutton stew and turnip.

'Good man,' James said, as he dumped his bag on the chair. 'I'm hungry.'

'You're always hungry, sir.' Davie set a huge platter of stew on the table. 'Miss Bella Hunter called.'

'Well? What did she say?'

'She's been poorly, with stomach trouble, she says, but she looks fine to me.'

'Don't worry about it, Davie,' James said. 'Women's problems. Women are complicated. I'll go and see her, after another dish of stew. Has anyone else been asking for me?'

'No, sir.'

'No one?'

'No one. Are you in trouble, sir?'

'No, of course not.' He glanced sideways at the boy. No need to alarm him. The lad was beginning to mature, but there was a rebellious streak in him. 'I do hope your conduct has been satisfactory. I have been distracted of late, and do not want you to disappoint me.'

'I won't disappoint, sir.'

'Good man.'

James rose from the dining table and stretched, suddenly feeling lethargic, as if the joy of life had gone. He sat down and rested his elbows on the desk. Too many questions rushed into his head all at once. It was overwhelming. What if Andrew was in prison? What of Louise? Did he love her? What kind of life could he offer her anyway?

He turned his head. Davie was holding his bag. He grabbed it and headed for the sisters' chambers.

'I am well,' Bella said as she ushered him into her parlour and closed the main door. 'We must be discreet. A loyal friend wishes to see you.' She handed James a note and keys. 'He's in the basement.'

*Please come to my chamber*, the message read. There was no signature.

'Thank you.' He was about to ask about Andrew, but changed his mind.

James recalled the chamber. He'd stayed there on his first night when he returned to Edinburgh four years ago. The keys he held now were for the outer door, which was surrounded by railings and entered from the close. He unlocked the gate, and inserted the other key into the door lock. He lifted the sneck as softly as he could, and stepped in, his right hand instinctively finding its way to the hilt of his sword. He turned quickly to face Robert Charles standing behind the door. Charles stuffed his dirk into his belt, gripped his shoulders with both hands and led him to a chair by the fire.

The basement chamber was dim, daylight showing obliquely through the wee window. A low fire and two candles added some colour. James watched Mr Charles as he poked the fire. His hands were listless, his face drawn.

'I was expecting to find tidings of Andrew Lawson on my arrival at his chambers today,' Charles whispered. 'I had heard he was a pilot on board *Le Protée*, and is now lying concealed somewhere. I hope you have news of him, and are willing to convey a message from me'

James shook his head. 'He is at present in hiding. I know not where.' He related the events as told to him by Francis.

Mr Charles frowned. He perched on the end of the bed. 'I'm afraid our cause is all but lost. It saddens me to say so, for there were opportunities to be seized. French ships, though fewer in number than the English, were much faster. Victory at sea should have been easy. It puzzles me how attempts at landfall have failed. Meanwhile, English troops have assembled on land.'

'And our troops?'

'We have a sizeable force, I'm told. The enthusiasm has been considerable. Defeat, I fear, will come as a great disappointment to them.'

'And the King?' James ventured to ask.

'I spent some time in Dunbartonshire waiting for news of the King's arrival. Rumours came to me that His Majesty had landed north of the Tay. So I travelled north discreetly through various routes in Perthshire. I was buoyant. Then I heard the bad news. The English fleet were in the Forth. The French had not landed their troops, and, I guessed, returned to France. It was later I heard more details of what happened, and that the King was on his way to Dunkirk.'

Mr Charles picked up the poker again and stabbed the coals. 'Had the King landed, and raised forces in the north, there's no doubt that the English troops would have been outnumbered and forced to retreat. The castles in Edinburgh and Stirling had not enough powder and ammunition to defend themselves.'

Charles turned his head, and James felt his gaze. 'Meanwhile here in Edinburgh, we are in danger. You must be cautious. Hugh Alexander will be initiating enquiries about his sister's death.'

James felt his stomach turn. Was it fear, or confusion at the turn of events? 'He'll be asking me…'

'A word of advice. Do not try to be too smart. The bravest of men eventually yield under pressure. Betrayal can be forced.' Mr Charles sat on a cushion and leaned against the bed. 'If you haven't thought of it already, now is the time for you to go overseas, for your own safety. Pitcairne tells me you have a promising future as a physician. He says you're keen to learn.'

'I can't afford to go just now, sir.'

There was a soft rustle outside the window. James rose and sat down on the floor next to Charles.

He lowered his voice. 'I mean to go to Leiden sometime, when I have sufficient funds.'

'But you have patients who pay well?'

'Most of my time is spent in the clinic or at the hospital. I give much of my time to the poor.'

'I know. But do gentlemen of means pay promptly?'

James hesitated. 'They are troublesome. They claim that I supply poor recipes. But that's not true. Pitcairne will confirm.' He felt the heat in his cheeks. He had not betrayed the Jacobite cause, and was suffering the consequences of prejudice and intolerance.

He watched Mr Charles as he turned and fixed his eyes on him, wondering what he was thinking. There was a long period of silence. James slowly rose to his feet. Charles pulled him down to rest.

'When I was in France, I made discreet enquiries about your father,' Mr Charles said.

'My father? I thought he was dead.'

'As far as I know he lives. He's abroad in exile. Keeps himself in seclusion, I was told. He must have his reasons. I'm sorry. I did my best to find out more.'

'I remember little of my father. I saw him last at the age of six.'

'He was a Jacobite spy. He disappeared around the time of the Haughs of Cromdale. He feared for the safety of you and your mother. He wrote to Walter Duff stating his wishes. Duff has managed your education on his behalf.'

James wondered why Duff hadn't told him where the money came from for his education. At the back of his mind he had kept a secret wish that his father was still alive. It was the longing to be part of a family. His guardians were kind, but at a distance. Maybe that was why he felt so restless, so eager to explore.

'I would like to know how he lives now; if he is in good health…'

## 39

Andrew held up the lamp. Rows of barrels lined the cellar. The vaulted ceiling was black with fungus. There was dampness in the air. The smell of wine and spices was almost overpowering.

'I need to write some letters,' he said, forcing himself to concentrate.

'We can't stay here long,' Scarlett said. 'We must keep on the move. Every corner of Leith will be searched. Every ship will be boarded for checks.'

'I know that. After an uncomfortable night in a hay loft, hiding in closets and running around, I want to stop for a bit.'

'We could have fled to Newhaven…' Scarlett began.

'And be more conspicuous? Anyway I must send dispatches. Fetch me some writing materials, and some garments. And candles.'

Scarlett stared.

'As quick as you can.'

The lock scraped as Scarlett turned the key. A steady drip from somewhere was the only sound in the cellar. Andrew set down his lamp, shifted an empty barrel and groped about, arranging a board for writing. It would be a long wait till nightfall. He sat on the floor, leaning on a barrel, knees close to his chest. The drip ticked away the time. Doing nothing and being locked in. Was this wise? The steady draught of air, welcoming at first, was now beginning to chill his bones as the day wore on.

He jumped up, his ears concentrating on the scratching of the key in the lock, and the slow creak of the door. He crouched behind a barrel, waiting.

'Quills, inkhorn, paper, sealing wax as requested,' Francis said. 'And haddock.'

'At last.' Andrew stood up. 'Did anyone follow you?'

'I don't think so.'

Andrew swapped his coat, hat and wig, and made a bundle with his other clothes. He set up the writing materials on the board.

'What about money?' Francis asked.

Andrew held up a purse, and patted the belt of his breeches.

'Scarlett is in search of a reliable boatman to take you to the Fife coast. He will fetch you under cover of darkness,' Francis said. 'I will see that your letters are delivered.'

'How long, do you think, before they find Eleanor's body?' Andrew asked.

'Awhile, I hope. They're busy searching for you.'

'I wonder when Scarlett realised his wife was a traitor.'

'Who knows?' Francis shrugged.

Andrew took up a quill, dipped it and began to write.

Davie placed a huge bowl of steaming barley broth on the table. James stirred it with his horn spoon, finding lumps of mutton. He blew on the broth and took a sip.

'Excellent,' he said.

While watching Davie's back, he withdrew the letter from his waistcoat pocket. There was no signature, but he knew it was from Robert Charles. A small package of coin, in the care of Isabella Hunter, was available for his education at Leiden. He was to use it wisely, with good wishes from his friends. He slipped the note into his pocket.

There was a knock on the door. He nodded to Davie. 'Say I'm not to be disturbed.' Setting the dining table at the window was a good idea. It was only visible once a visitor stepped into the chamber. He placed his pistol on a chair and covered it with a cloth.

Davie opened the door a fraction. 'It's Mistress Louise,' he said.

James jumped up and rushed to the door. 'Come in, come in, and dine with us.'

She stepped forward, her hands gripping a bundle of papers. He studied her face. Their eyes met.

'Are you well? Do you go out often? Clear air and sunshine are good for your health. You must eat well.'

He was fussing too much. Taking her arm, he gently ushered her to a chair at the dining table. He whipped the pistol from the seat, but not before she noticed it.

'I am very well. I thank you,' she said. 'And yes, I venture outside more. Though I don't go far. Alas, it is the foul air of the streets I breathe.'

She laid the papers down, and took a seat at the table. James offered her bowl of soup. She dipped her spoon into the broth, and took a sip. She smiled, tore off a piece of bread and dunked it in. James watched her eat. He noticed with satisfaction that she accepted a second helping of the mutton broth. When she finished, she leaned back in her chair, her eyes darting about the chamber, seeming to avoid direct contact with his. He wasn't sure how to begin. Davie, sensing the need for private conversation, softly retired to the wee chamber.

'You have something to tell me,' James said. He glanced at the bundle of papers.

Louise picked them up and selected a letter. 'I have just been with Walter Duff. This is for you. It's from Andrew.'

James broke the seal and read:

*My dear James,*

*I am safe and well. On board a ship which will leave on the tide for the Northern Isles, under escort by the Royal Navy.*

Another sheet had more details:

*I write this in haste, as I am at present in a temporary hideout. I ask you, please, to collect a key from the right side and back of my secretaire. It opens a chest in the garret. Another small key in the same compartment opens a box in the chest which contains some coin to help further your education or purchase some books. Louise has been well provided for. She will tell you herself.*

*I hope our paths will cross some day. I'm confident, too, that better times lie ahead for our country, and our nation will be free from the sorts of troubles that have beset us recently. I wish you the best of good fortune.*

There were a few other hastily scribbled notes on the back of the sheet, referring to some of his goods and furniture; and practical tips and advice.

James raised his head. Louise had been watching him closely. Was she trying to guess his feelings? He had not considered fully the consequences of a failed rising. He had known he and Andrew would part, but it was all too sudden.

'I would have liked so much to have seen him, to wish him well.'

'So would I,' Louise said.

They paused. He listened to the clock ticking.

'And you? You received a letter from Andrew?' he asked.

'I did. And he has given instructions on his affairs to Mr Duff. Andrew wishes me to take ownership of the whole tenement. In his letter he acknowledged that, in purchasing the property bit by bit from my father all those years ago, he took advantage of my father's diminishing fortunes. He regrets that deeply. He says so in this letter.' Louise's finger touched the paper. 'Owning Lawson's Land, as many like to call it, gave him some stability amid the risks of trading.'

'We both know he may never return.'

Louise nodded. 'As soon as chambers are available, I will leave Rose and Bella's room. They have been kind,' she said. 'They need use of their workshop and storage space. There's the wee chamber near the cellars I can use. You know, the one you occupied on your first night in Edinburgh. Four years ago, it was. The problem is, I can't find the key. Duff thought Andrew was using it as a storeroom for silver plate. There must be a spare key somewhere.'

Robert Charles must still be there. She must never know.

'I'm sure you'll find it. Anyway, you may wish to move into these chambers. I'll be leaving soon. I must see Archibald Pitcairne. I owe a tremendous amount to the worthy physician. His advice and wisdom, as well as his teaching and instruction.' James leaned back in his chair.

'That's good news, James,' Louise said. 'And, yes, I think these chambers will do fine for me, for now.'

'I will return to Edinburgh.'

'I know.' Louise smiled.

# HISTORICAL NOTE

In order to blend with history, the names of some real persons are retained. Events are fictional, or based on real events with some changes to suit the story.

At the beginning of the eighteenth century, Edinburgh had a population of more than thirty thousand people. Only London and Bristol had more. Built on a ridge from the castle to Holyroodhouse, and contained within its protective walls, people of different social status lived in close proximity in high buildings, separated by narrow closes.

The wide street now known as the Lawnmarket is shown as the Land Market in William Edgar's map of 1742. It was a market area for selling produce, such as woollen goods brought in from areas surrounding Edinburgh.

Some confusion may arise with terminology. A land is an apartment block, and a tenement is a narrow plot of ground it is built on. The word 'tenement' is now used to mean an apartment building. Lawson's Land is fictional.

Archibald Pitcairne was one of a small group of independent lecturers in anatomy, botany and chemistry in Edinburgh in the early part of the eighteenth century. Jacobite supporters were among his associates.

In 1705 the French considered the possibility of opening discussions with the Scottish Jacobites. The Duke of Perth, minister at James's court at St Germain-en-Laye, corresponded by secret letters with his sister, Anne, the Countess of Errol, who was in regular communication with Jacobite supporters in east and central Scotland. The French proposed to send an agent, Colonel Nathaniel Hooke, to Slains, the home of the Countess of Errol. The fictional character David Colville is based on Hooke, whose correspondence was a source of background information for the novel. Hooke was given the name David Colville in letters, and while he was travelling in Scotland under cover as a merchant.

Captain Thomas Gordon of the small Scots Navy was successful in capturing French frigates. He was also a secret Jacobite. Off the coast of Scotland he turned a blind eye to the French frigate carrying the Jacobite agent. After the Union of 1707 Gordon joined the British Navy, and was in command of the vessel that seized the French vessel, *Le Salisbury*, in 1708. In 1714 he refused to swear allegiance to King George, and fled to the Continent. He later became admiral of the Russian Navy.

James Carron was also with the Scots Navy before serving in France. He was given command of a French frigate, and took dispatches from the Jacobite court in France to loyal supporters on the east coast of Scotland. The conspirators included Charles Hay, 13th Earl of Errol, and William Keith, 9th Earl Marischal.

Robert Charles is a fictional character based on the Hon. Charles Fleming, a Jacobite agent who was given the name Robert Charles in Hooke's secret correspondence.

Lady Comiston gave shelter to Nathaniel Hooke while on his visits to Edinburgh. Her home, Comiston Castle, was near Fairmilehead, an important crossroads outside Edinburgh. Lady Largo aided Hooke's secret communications with James Douglas, 4th Duke of Hamilton.

The French chose February 1708 to begin the invasion of Scotland. They sought to take advantage of popular risings in both Scotland and Flanders, and to draw off British regiments in Flanders. A fleet of five battleships and twenty-three frigates set out from Dunkirk, and after riding out a storm sailed north to the Aberdeenshire coast, having misjudged the entrance to the Firth of Forth. The French turned and engaged with the British Navy. One French frigate was taken. The young Prince James (the King to the Jacobites) demanded to be set ashore off the Angus coast, but the admiral took the fleet north. A storm arose and the fleet dispersed, taking James back to France.

# FURTHER READING

*Playing the Scottish Card: The Franco-Jacobite Invasion of 1708* by John S. Gibson (1988, Edinburgh University Press)

*The Old Scots Navy from 1689 to 1710*, edited by James Grant (Elibron Classics Replica Edition, 2005, of unabridged facsimile of the edition published in 1914 by the Navy Records Society, London)

*Correspondence of Colonel N. Hooke, agent from the Court of France to the Scottish Jacobites in the Years 1703–1707*, edited by William Dunn Macray (printed for the Roxburgh Club, 1870–1871, London)

*Seawolves: Pirates & the Scots* by Eric J. Graham (2005, Birlinn, Edinburgh)

*A History of the Scottish People, 1560–1830* by T. C. Smout (1998, Fontana Press, London)

# GLOSSARY

**Baxter:** baker.

**Blethering:** talking too much or talking nonsense.

**Broadside:** single sheet of paper, printed on one side.

**Caddie:** messenger.

**Chap, chapping:** knock or tap (on a door, for example).

**Chapman:** itinerant dealer, pedlar; seller of broadsides and chapbooks (small paperbacks).

**Close:** a narrow passageway between houses.

**Cruisie lamp:** a boat-shaped oil lamp.

**Coup:** upset, overturn.

**Crack:** talk, gossip.

**Creel:** a deep basket for carrying fish.

**Curfew:** a brass cover for keeping the fire low at night, and ready for the morning (from the French *couvre-feu*, or fire cover).

**Dollar:** a high value silver coin.

**Fair trade:** euphemism for smuggling.

**Feart:** frightened.

**Fever:** might have been typhus or other diseases.

**Flux:** dysentery group of diseases.

**Grandgore:** syphilis.

**Greping Office:** the name of a tavern; so called because the only way to get there was by groping along a dark passage.

**Haar:** east coast fog or mist.

**Half fou:** half drunk.

**Hawkie, hawker:** itinerant dealer, pedlar.

**Hospital:** an institution for poor relief of the city. Institutions for the non-poor sick, infirmaries, were started in the early eighteenth century – in 1729 the Royal Infirmary of Edinburgh became the first in Scotland.

**Keek:** peep.

**Kist:** a chest or large box.

**Land Market:** the top part of the High Street in Edinburgh. This was an area designated for selling inland produce; cloth, yarn, stockings, etc. It is now known as the Lawnmarket.

**Letter of Marque:** a legal document given to the master of a privateer in times of war, granting him the right to seize merchant vessels of a specified enemy.

**Luckenbooth:** a shop, booth or stall in Edinburgh's High Street that was locked up after trading.

**Messages:** sometimes used to mean shopping.

**Neeps:** turnips.

**Pattens:** overshoes worn by women to protect their shoes from dirt in the street.

**Phthisis:** a disease resulting in the wasting of tissues; pulmonary tuberculosis, consumption.

**Peenie:** pinafore, apron, overall.

**Privateer:** a private vessel which had the right, by a Letter of Marque, to seize merchant vessels of a named enemy.

**Sedan chair:** a covered chair for one person, carried by two attendants.

**Sneck:** latch.

**Supercargo:** the person appointed by the owners of a cargo to trade on their behalf.

**The Cross:** meeting place for business and trading.

**Turnpike stair:** a spiral stair.

**Waiter:** a customs officer.

**Weel kent:** well known.

**Wynd:** narrow street.